Praise for

Joni M. Fisher

"A gifted storyteller, Joni Fisher writes with energy and passion that comes to life in her characters. *North of the Killing Hand* is an intricate and suspenseful read that grips the reader from start to finish."

—John Foxjohn, International, *USA Today* and *New York Times* bestselling author

"*South of Justice* is a multilayered, intricate, and suspenseful page-turner you'll want to read in one sitting."

—Diane Capri, *New York Times* and *USA Today* bestselling author of the Hunt for Jack Reacher thrillers

"Past secrets test the bonds of family loyalty and a fledgling love affair. The unwavering strength of the protagonists, their commitment to the truth and to each other will have you cheering for *South of Justice*."

—Melissa Hladik Meyer, Author of *Good Company*

"Bottom line is: *South of Justice* is a multilayered romantic book that will grasp your attention and lure you to read it in one sitting."

—SeriousReading.com

"*South of Justice* is fantastic and fun—a crisp and suspenseful story. Fisher makes a wonderful entrance as a crime fiction writer. I can't wait for *North of the Killing Hand.*"

—Timothy D. Browne, M.D., author of the Nicklaus Hart medical thrillers

"Joni M. Fisher weaves a tale of passionate love, undying loyalty and enduring friendship between strong characters bound together and tested by deep-rooted principles. Curl up in your favorite chair with a tasty snack and a refreshing beverage—you won't want to move until you've turned the last page of *South of Justice*."

—Donna Kelly, author of *Three-Ring Threat*

"A fabulous start to an intense series with a large cast of characters I couldn't help but love and cheer for. Fisher is a master weaver of intrigue and strong characters willing to go the distance to get things done while keeping their love strong."

—K.D. Fleming, author and Golden Heart winner

"Tightly written, complex characters, intriguing plot—all the ingredients for a great read! This debut book is a winner, and I am looking forward to more books in the future."

—Diane Burke, award-winning author
of inspirational romantic suspense

"I really enjoyed this book. It was well written and the twists and turns had me turning pages deep into the night."

—Vicki W. Tharp, author of *Don't Look Back*

ALSO BY JONI M. FISHER

South of Justice

North of the Killing Hand

West of Famous

Joni M. Fisher

West of Famous

Copyright © 2018 Joni M. Fisher

ISBN-13: 978-0-9972575-4-0 (Trade paperback version)
ISBN-13: 978-0-9972575-5-7 (eBook English version)

Edited by Blue Otter Editing and Boswell Professional Writing Services
Original Cover Design by Damonza
Interior Formatting by Author E.M.S.

May we be true friends and appreciate them.

ACKNOWLEDGMENTS

Deep thanks go to Paul and Caryn Frink for hosting me on their Nordic Tug, *Seeker*, for their patience answering a thousand questions, for navigating to places in this story, and for the use of their names and their boat's name in this story. They completed their first loop and earned a gold AGLCA burgee in 2018. Thanks also to America's Great Loop Cruiser's Association for their advice and for their strong community. Any errors in nautical language or boating practice are mine.

Special thanks to Blue Otter Editing and Cynthia A. Boswell of Boswell Professional Writing Services for your sharp eyes and wisdom. Special thanks to J David Ivester, Literary Publicist and Marketing Specialist of Author Guide for directing this book's path to readers and for translating terms like pitch blurb, branding, metadata, digital rights management, and SEO into plain English.

Many blessings to these authors for their blunt and specific advice on the oh-so-rough draft: Kay Beth Avery, Donna Kelly, Terri Johnson, Carol J. Post, and C. J. Sweet.

Great thanks to brave beta readers: John M. Esser, Carol Faulkner-Davis, Chuck Davis, D'Ann Jirovec, Suzanne Roustio, Carol Speyerer, and Martha Walker for taking my long journey to publication as seriously as I do.

West of Famous

. 1 .

Martina Ramos opened her eyes in hazy darkness on a cold floor that reeked of vomit and a chemical she couldn't identify. When she lifted her head, her pulse pounded her temples, so she eased back down with a groan. She believed she could feel the rotation of the earth.

Draping one hand on her belly, she felt sequins and groaned. Somehow, she'd ended up on the floor in last night's party dress and heels. She had specifically asked for nonalcoholic drinks at the club because she couldn't afford the negative publicity storm from public drunkenness. Miami during spring break meant hundreds of hormonal college coeds were watching her in person and through social media. Staggering and puking in bushes would have damaged her carefully crafted image.

Her best friend, Nefi, would have kept track of her drinks so no one could slip her alcohol or a roofie. Nefi would have protected her from this hammering in her skull. Tall, dangerous Nefi would have told those people arguing in the room upstairs to shut up. People sensed immediately that Nefi didn't threaten or bluff. Ah, but her bestie wasn't here.

Neither was her boyfriend, Oscar. She was on her own. Her friends and family didn't know where she was because she couldn't tell them.

She tenderly rubbed her head. Her hair was stiff and stuck to her forehead. Was that puke? She slowly tucked in her arms and legs and rolled onto her hands and knees. She couldn't tell if she was swaying or the room was, but it had to stop. Forcing her eyes open, she squinted in the dark.

The voices grew louder. What on earth were people arguing about this early in the morning? She expected more civilized behavior than this at a five-star resort. *Enough.* Time to complain to management.

She thumped her shoulder against something. Disoriented and fighting vertigo, she reached for the wall and touched a small ledge, like the shelf under the sink in her room. Was this the bathroom? The floor was cold. She'd been hungover before but passing out on the bathroom floor was a first. It didn't take much alcohol to knock a one-hundred-twenty-pound woman off-balance.

She had to get on her feet to clean up. Her body ached, all stiff and heavy and drained of strength. This was like the flu but worse. Maybe food poisoning? The room pitched. Her head throbbed. And the odd chemical stench invading her nostrils didn't help.

The shouting upstairs stopped. Finally, peace. She tipped sideways and rolled onto her back. As her body turned, the room seemed to amplify her movement so that even flat on her back it felt as though the room continued to roll. She shook her head to stop the sensation. Planting her hands flat at her sides, she waited for the motion to end. When it continued, she breathed slowly. In and out, in and out. What was going on?

Dehydration? That led to headaches and hangovers. Her tongue stuck to the roof of her mouth.

Water. Get water.

To reach the sink she had to stand. She reached out and grabbed the shelf under the sink. She sighed. She'd stayed in so many hotels over the last few weeks she couldn't orient herself in the room without light. Bracing for another attempt to stand, she squeezed the edge of the shelf and ordered her body to stand so she could get light and water.

A hatch in the ceiling flung open. Bright light streamed in through a rectangular hole in the ceiling.

"She's awake," a deep voice announced.

Martina squinted upward at ugly work boots connected to dirty pants topped by a loose, wrinkled sweatshirt. The man's face was obscured by a shadow. *Who is this guy? Waitaminute. Resort rooms don't have ceiling hatches. And no one said there'd be construction. This can't be right.* Believing she was stuck in that gauzy fog state between sleep and consciousness, she sighed heavily. "Wake up. Wake up." She patted her face.

A man bent forward, revealing a green mask that covered his face.

A second man wearing a black mask stepped into view. The masks didn't fit the kind she'd seen on other construction workers that covered the nose and mouth. These masks looked like knit ski masks with holes for eyes and a mouth.

Weirdest. Dream. Ever.

"Climb up."

Climb? Oh, for pity's sake. She wearied of bizarre dreams. Maybe she was hallucinating. Maybe someone put something in her drink. LSD? Rohypnol?

Too tired to resist, she decided to play along and get it over with. She glanced around. Surely enough, her hand held a step protruding from the wall. She stared at it as if it had materialized by magic at the man's command. Why was the guy wearing a mask in Miami? Light streaming in from the hatch burned her retinas and illuminated tanks, pipes, cables, and a long propeller shaft. The rocking motion suddenly made sense. That smell wasn't paint. It was diesel. What the—?

"Now!" barked the man in the ugly work boots as he leaned over the hatch. His voice was higher than the other man's and raspy like a smoker's.

She struggled to her feet as the drumbeat in her head played faster. She turned and grabbed the step and climbed out of the engine hold as carefully as possible in three-inch heels and a tight, red sequined party dress. At least this wasn't one of those naked-in-public dreams. She was, however, way overdressed for boating.

As she climbed from the hold, the men backed away. Black Mask kicked the hatch shut. The two argued in gibberish. She rubbed her eyes against sunlight glaring through windows. This dream had amazing detail. The guy in the green mask had pale arms and a bit of a beer gut. Tattoos covered Black Mask's muscled arms up to the sleeves of his black T-shirt. In one hand he held a razor. Wait. No. A Taser.

Martina's mouth dried up and her lungs overfilled. *Uh-oh. Bad dream.* Standing on the mid-deck near the chart table, she counted three exits. The men flanked her, blocking two sliding glass pilothouse doors. Green Mask stood near the helm control panel. The windows revealed water in all directions edged with green strips of land. Blazing sunlight burned through the third exit on the far side of a combination galley and salon area. Vertigo threatened to tip Martina off her heels, so she knew she couldn't run. Stupid, pretty shoes.

"I told you she'd get sick," Green Mask said.

"Shut up."

The boat rocked her off-balance, and she fell against the chart table, where a hoodie covered a stack of large navigation maps. This hideous nightmare was so detailed it frightened her. The sights and sounds felt scary real. She grabbed the table's edge, slipped off her shoes, and tugged the hem of her party dress halfway down to her knees. In psychology class, she'd learned about lucent dreaming. Creative types, like the poet who lived in her dorm, used lucent dreaming to tap into their subconsciousness. The poet had developed a test to know when she was dreaming. In dreams, she said, the laws of physics didn't matter. A dreamer could fly or walk through walls or turn back time. Martina decided to test Sir Isaac Newton's law of gravity. She dropped one shoe.

Not only did gravity work, but both men failed the gentleman test by leaving the shoe on the floor. Once on the floor, the shoe did not move, proving Newton's first law of motion. Doubt crept in Martina's mind about being in a dream state.

"Just do as you're told, and you won't get hurt."

"Says the man with the Taser." Martina blinked at the man wearing a black mask. "Where are we?"

"This is the middle of nowhere." Black Mask's voice had an Eastern European accent. Slavic? Russian?

Green Mask pointed to a dark passageway that dead-ended at the forward stateroom. "Go in there and sit down."

Fear heightened her awareness. Close to forty feet from bow to stern and thirteen feet wide, the layout and size of the boat meant this was a recreational trawler. With the engines and generator off, the silence reminded Martina of something she dreaded while sailing with her family—dead calm. Dead calm on a boat with two masked men in the middle of nowhere. She hadn't signed up for this.

Who were these creeps in ski masks?

She eased down the steps. Swaying through the narrow passageway, she passed a small stateroom on her left and the head on her right, toward the master stateroom at the bow. Dominating the space was a queen berth with narrow pathways around it. For a second, it looked inviting. She sobered at the threshold and braced her hands on the doorjambs. "Whoa. Waitaminute. Waitaminute."

Hands shoved her toward the bed. She spun around and raised one shoe and one fist into a fighting stance. Nausea and vertigo surged through her, so she took deep breaths.

"Sit on the bed. Face the camera."

A small video camera was mounted on a tripod to the left of

the doorway. Beside it, clamped to an open cabinet door, was a battery-powered lantern. Two portholes fed a little light into the otherwise dark master stateroom. A chill raced through her. Bile surged up her throat. Fear swept away hope about fighting her way out of the stateroom with a shoe. She longed for a minute to clear her head. This nightmare threatened to turn from creepy to terrifying.

Green Mask eyed her. "Think we ought to clean her up?"

"Why not?" Black Mask stepped into the head and ran water. He emerged with a damp towel and handed it to his partner, who gave it to Martina.

"You have something on your face." Green Mask half pointed, half waved toward the left side of her head.

"I'll puke again if you touch me." It wasn't an idle threat. Who knew how much was left in her stomach? Watching the men, she scrubbed her forehead and the left side of her face and hairline until it wasn't sticky. She then tossed the towel on the floor by the camera.

Green Mask handed her a paper with large type printed on it. "Read this loud and clear when I tell you to." He switched on the lantern and the camera. "Sit here."

She glanced through the message on the paper and gasped. According to the note, she had, at best, until Friday to live.

"Read it." Black Mask pointed the Taser at the paper.

No. It wasn't possible. This was a terrible mistake. It would never work. She leaned against the bed, which sat on a raised platform. Her hands dropped to her sides. Her eyes burned. Her head hurt. Everything was wrong. Wrong. So horribly wrong. The situation was surreal. She had to make it stop. She refused to believe she had only four days to live, but fear seized her.

If I die in a dream, do I die in real life?

As her heart raced, she grew alarmed she might die in her sleep from panic. Everything was wrong. This wasn't real. It couldn't be. To force herself awake, she shouted, "Nooooo."

Her mind registered two realities in rapid succession. One, Black Mask stepped toward her. Two, blinding pain exploded through her body.

. 2 .

Monday, April 19, 2010

Vincent Gunnerson entered an interview room at the Jacob Javits building, the New York City office of the FBI, where two women in business suits sat across the table from Special Agent Lenny Lorenzo. A normally gregarious guy, Lenny was so Italian through and through that people joked he couldn't talk with his hands tied. Lenny clasped his hands on the table and looked up at Vincent with uncharacteristic weariness.

Vincent shut the door and took a chair beside Lenny.

"These ladies are Mrs. Campbell and Miss Chen. They claim they have urgent information to share about a video Mrs. Campbell received this morning at ten." Lenny's tone suggested the ladies were wasting his time. "When I asked them why they waited until three in the afternoon to share this information, they said they would share it only after we met certain conditions. Ladies, this is Special Agent Vincent Gunnerson."

Their conditions? Vincent eyed Mrs. Campbell, a fortyish woman with blonde upswept hair and large clunky jewelry. She wore a white silk, low-cut blouse under a bright green jacket. Miss Chen had jet-black shoulder-length hair and looked thirty years old tops. Dressed in all black, Chen hunched over her

8

smartphone, repeatedly brushing her fingers across the screen.

Mrs. Campbell squared her shoulders and addressed Vincent, "We get crazy fan mail all the time, but this is a first. We want you to verify that this…message is a hoax. So far, we haven't found it posted on any social media, but if word gets out there, well, we want to be able to say that the FBI says it's a hoax." She nudged her companion.

"Nothing on social media so far." Miss Chen looked up at Vincent and sat up straighter. She sneaked a peek at Vincent's left hand.

Vincent did not reciprocate because he didn't care if she was single or married. He turned his attention toward Lenny instead. "Have you seen the urgent message?"

"Nope." Lenny tapped his pen on a pad of paper. The corners of his mouth twitched, signaling he had noticed Miss Chen's sudden shift of attention.

"What is it you do that generates fan mail?" Vincent asked Mrs. Campbell, who seemed to have authority over the younger woman.

"Oh, not us. Our client," Mrs. Campbell whispered as if the entire office might be eavesdropping. "We also need your word that whatever happens, our client won't be named in any way in the news."

Lenny leaned his elbows on the table. "We don't control the news."

"What's your client's name?" Vincent asked.

"They don't want to say," Lenny deadpanned. "They aren't lawyers evoking client confidentiality. In fact, they're from the Campbell Agency. They represent," he said, sliding a business card across the tabletop to Vincent, "performing artists."

Performing artists was vague enough to encompass actors, dancers, musicians, or those self-proclaimed performance artists who occasionally took their clothes off in Central Park and smeared paint on each other while shouting poetry. Vincent sighed. "So, are you going to hand over your entire client list and make us guess which one you're talking about, or do you have only one client?"

Mrs. Campbell arched an unnaturally dark eyebrow at Vincent. "Do we have your word you'll keep this out of the press?"

"No." Vincent and Lenny answered at once.

Miss Chen glared at Mrs. Campbell until the older woman squirmed. "Our client is Ruby."

"We need her full name," Lenny said with his pen poised over a legal pad.

"Oh, come on," Mrs. Campbell said. "She's had two platinum albums." She looked at Miss Chen as if for confirmation that everyone in the world recognized the name.

Miss Chen shook her head. "Wrong demographic." To Vincent, she said, "Roxanne Wharton is a pop singer. She's known as Ruby."

Lenny bristled. "All right, so you have a video fan message that you want us to prove is a hoax. Did you take it to the police?"

Mrs. Campbell leaned forward. "I thought the FBI handled kidnappings."

A chill swept the room as Vincent and Lenny inhaled sharply.

"Give us whatever information you have right now." Vincent's voice had lowered to an authoritative whisper.

Mrs. Campbell fumbled in her giant gold-studded leather purse, jingling her collection of gold bangle bracelets in the process, and pulled out a palm-sized bikini-clad figurine. She stood the doll on the table in front of Vincent.

He glared at the toy.

Mrs. Campbell pulled the figure apart at the waist, revealing a jump drive. She slapped the pieces back on the table. "It's a video."

Treating it as evidence, neither agent touched it.

"How did you get it?" Lenny asked.

"It came attached to an email. I made a copy on this Ruby drive." Mrs. Campbell waved at the tiny plastic body. "It's a promotional item from her first platinum album."

Vincent and Lenny exchanged a look, silently debating who would watch the video. While still adjusting to working together, they had fallen into the good cop and bad cop roles, with Lenny as the good cop. Overall, Lenny had excellent people-handling skills. Vincent had already forgiven him for the notable lapse in judgment when Lenny had turned a particularly deceptive suspected drug dealer into a protected informant. With plenty of guilt to share for that debacle, it was time to let it go. Lenny was his new partner, like it or not, and as the senior agent, it was Lenny's call.

"Go ahead. I'll extract more info from the ladies," Lenny said. His weary tone made Vincent wonder how much time he had already spent trying.

Since Vincent didn't have to concern himself about fingerprints, he picked up the top half of the bikini figure, stood, and strode from the room with all the dignity he could muster while holding a bikini-clad doll.

Martina stared through the porthole of a small stateroom at water and swamp. After five hours of watching for boat traffic, she had neither heard nor seen another boat. Black Mask was right. They were in the middle of nowhere.

The men had forced her to record the message. After being Tasered, she'd been too terrified to resist or ask questions. She surmised from the way her face stung and the bruise on her knee that she'd kneed herself in the face during her uncontrollable, violent thrashing from being zapped. Right after the message was done, they had moved her to the smaller stateroom and run the generator for an hour.

They probably needed power to send the message. She prayed the message would reach the right people.

Since then, she'd finished a bottle of water in sips and kept it down. Her dress smelled of urine, her damp underwear stuck to her skin, and every muscle in her body burned. Crying had left a wet spot on the fabric under the sequins. None of that mattered.

She needed to find a way to escape. First, she needed to know where she was. Second, she wanted to know how she'd gotten here.

Even nowhere existed at a specific latitude and longitude. She remembered Saturday. They'd simply had to go to the hottest club in Miami to be seen by the highest concentration of social media climbers. The club owner had given them a prime table overlooking the dance floor, where they could see and be seen. He'd comped their drinks. The last memory she could dredge up from her zapped brain was heading to the ladies' room.

Had she been moved from Miami by car or by plane before being brought onto the boat?

Swampland surrounded them. All swamps looked the same to her. Snakes, buzzards, alligators, and other deadly things lurked in the water. For all she knew, she could be in Georgia, Florida, Mississippi, Louisiana, or the Bahamas. Maybe even in Central America, or South America. The only reliable thing she could determine was an approximate time of day by reading shadows outside. In the morning, shadows pointed west, at noon they shrank, and in the afternoon and evening, they pointed east.

Judging from the shadows of mangroves on the water in the distance and the unrelenting heat and humidity, it was midafternoon. Compared to weather during her school years in England, this felt sweltering.

She eyed the screened porthole. Was it big enough to squeeze through? She touched her left pinky to the edge of the opening and spread her left hand. Her piano teacher had measured her hand's reach once at seven and one quarter inches. It took the width of three more fingers to fill the space to the opposite edge of the opening. She lowered her hands to her left hip and belly. Nine inches from her left hip came to just past her belly button. No way. Her hips were four inches too wide to fit through the porthole. The same curves that Oscar adored trapped her.

She slumped back on the bed. She longed for food, a shower, fresh clothing, her cell phone, and the shelter of her father's embrace. None of which seemed forthcoming.

She found herself reaching for her missing cell phone often. It had become an electronic appendage. She kept it within reach when she slept or showered or studied. Her calendar, contacts, a clock that adjusted to her current time zone, photos, email messages, text messages, games, books, internet access, map directions, and social media links existed on her phone. In effect, her phone connected her to the world. To be without it was to be isolated. Dad had bought the latest technological wonder phone along with an international calling plan for her twenty-first birthday. Nefi had given her the protective case that sparkled as if covered in diamonds. Her beautiful, precious lifeline was gone. The creeps had probably dropped it in the water.

She sighed. The more her mind cleared, the worse her situation looked. No one knew she was missing. The couple traveling with her on the party circuit had seemed pleasant enough, but they hadn't really liked her. They didn't pretend they wanted to get to know her either. Their attention was as empty as their air kisses. Magazine writers referred to them as "the beautiful people." The entourage consisted of trust-fund kids whose parents paid for their Ivy League educations in the expectation they would make the right connections to build their bright futures.

Instead, the beautiful ones drifted from parties and fashion shows in the spring to Mediterranean beaches in the summer, art shows in the fall, and winter skiing in Switzerland. They could differentiate a Renoir from a Monet. They kept the private numbers of celebrities on their phones. They bypassed long lines to enter dance clubs. Restaurants always had a table waiting for them. Everyone greeted them like long-lost friends, but they were the loneliest people Martina had ever met. Being with them was like living in a Mardi Gras ball where everyone kept their ornate painted leather masks firmly in place. They assumed everyone had an angle or wanted something from them. Since they didn't know whom to trust, they didn't trust anyone.

The beautiful people probably didn't even notice she was gone. If they were out of bed, they would be sunning by the pool or enjoying a massage.

Her college friends wouldn't be any help either. They didn't expect her back at Oxford until the twenty-fifth to sit exams. She had lied to them about going home to Virginia for break. Her best friend thought she was on campus studying. She had also lied to her family and to Oscar, who had begged for one week of the six-week break. "Name it. Tokyo, Maui, New York, Paris." Oscar's deep voice had caused her heart to flutter. His job paid well enough to make it happen.

If only she had spared one week for him. But no. She had committed to six full weeks of make-believe partying with strangers in Europe and America. It had sounded too good to be true. She should have read the contract more carefully. Her big brother, Ruis, had a saying: "When someone tells you a lie you want to believe, it is still a lie." She'd assumed his advice was about trusting men. She should have applied the advice more widely. No one had mentioned the possibility of getting stinking kidnapped!

Her lies taunted her. Father was right. He said, "All lies come with a price."

As much as she preferred to believe her life had enormous value, she knew no one was looking for her. She would be lying to herself to believe otherwise. How long did she have before her captors discovered her biggest lie?

Please, dear God, keep them clueless for as long as possible.

Muted voices sounded outside. She pressed her ear to the stateroom door. They spoke in gibberish again. A few words reminded her of a female Russian classmate. They might as well have been speaking in Aramaic or Elvish or Klingon. She blinked, freeing pent-up tears.

If only this ordeal were a nightmare, or a prank gone bad... She willed this mistake to end. The idea that she was on her own far from civilization because two strangers wanted money was too terrifying to accept. She prayed for this mistake to be over, for an opportunity to turn back time, just this once. As the youngest child in her family, she often called for a do-over when she was losing a game.

She really needed a do-over, a reset back to the time she had her phone and her freedom. She'd even be thankful to be back at the crowded club dancing to techno music. In the do-over, she wouldn't drink at all and she'd stay away from that shadowy corridor to the bathroom, the last place she remembered being before waking up in this nightmare.

Footfalls sounded above, shattering her fantasy do-over. Once again in isolation, fear clawed at the edges of her thoughts about the value of her life. For the sake of survival, she had to stop cowering in the comfort of fantasy. She had to accept the unblinking truth of the situation.

She was at best a bargaining chip; at worst, entertainment.

. 3 .

Plopping in his chair, Vincent scooted forward and plugged the half-doll device into his laptop. After the virus scan had cleared the device, he downloaded the only item, a video titled "Ransom Demand."

A woman in a tight, cleavage-revealing, red sequined dress stared into the camera. She had a bruised and swollen left eye. Despite the harsh floodlight, her pupils were dilated. She cleared her throat, then read from a paper visible on the bottom edge of the video.

"Today is Monday, April nineteenth, 2010. My name is Ruby."

Vincent noticed her speech was slow, and she blinked often and paused as if drugged and struggling to concentrate.

"You have until Friday, April twenty-third to deliver six million dollars in bearer bonds to Tampa, Florida. You will receive another message with the location and drop-off time. Do not contact the police or you will never see me again."

As she looked up from the paper, the image froze. Her short, edgy haircut reminded Vincent of someone. Perhaps he'd seen Ruby on television. The message didn't feel like a hoax. The black eye and the girl's stoic fear seemed genuine. He replayed the video. On the second viewing, he noticed a mark on the woman's chest that appeared to be part of a tattoo peeking from the low neckline of her dress above her heart. She wore a dangling gold earring on one side but not the other. Was this a fashion thing?

On the third viewing, the woman's voice triggered a memory. Vincent shook it off. No. No way. He unplugged the jump drive and slid it into an evidence bag. He told himself the bag was for safekeeping. In fact, he didn't want other agents to assume the device was his.

He carried the evidence bag into the interview room and stood by the table. "Does Ruby have a tattoo over her heart?"

Whispering, the women bickered.

Vincent slapped his giant hand on the table.

Both women flinched and stopped talking.

"Answer me."

Mrs. Campbell leaned back in her chair and crossed her arms over her chest. "She has a cross tattoo over her heart in honor of her late mother, but I assure you the video is a hoax."

"It looks genuine to me." Speaking to Lenny, Vincent added, "It's a ransom demand for six million in bearer bonds to be delivered to Tampa by Friday."

Miss Chen pointed to the jump drive in the evidence bag. "What she means is, *that* isn't Ruby."

"The real Ruby is out of the country," Mrs. Campbell said. "I spoke with her as soon as I saw the video."

"Is this a publicity stunt?" Lenny said.

"No," the women said in unison.

"Look, technically, it is a genuine kidnapping." Mrs. Campbell spoke as if in pain. "Here's the situation. Ruby can't just disappear, or her fans would want to know where she is. So, while she's out of the public eye in an exclusive rehab facility—which shall remain nameless—we hired a body double to travel the club circuit with her boyfriend and a couple of her most trusted friends. You know, Monte Carlo, Paris, London, New York, Miami, LA. We have a duty to maintain her active presence on social media to keep the press in the dark."

Lenny rubbed his hand across his mouth as if trying to hold

back from swearing at the woman. Vincent certainly wanted to raise his voice at her, but he feared she would probably clam up or lawyer up.

Miss Chen set her smartphone face down on the table and clasped her hands over it. Setting her wrists down, she said, "I handled the contract with the look-alike. I discovered her from an online video from a singing contest in London. It's a live version of karaoke. You've heard of karaoke, right?"

Lenny and Vincent nodded. Vincent would have been insulted, but he considered that Miss Chen was probably accustomed to explaining things to the much older Mrs. Campbell.

"She's the very image of Ruby," Miss Chen said, "once she cut her hair."

"Did this impersonator get a tattoo to match Ruby's?" Lenny asked.

Miss Chen dropped her hands to her lap. "It's just henna. You know, temporary. It lasts about a month or two."

Once she cut her hair. A chill raced up Vincent's neck. Suddenly images of his fiancée Nefi's best friend flashed into his consciousness. She'd sported that ugly haircut when she confronted him in the lobby last summer and threatened him for breaking Nefi's heart. Unbidden, her name emerged from his memory and traveled to his voice. "Martina Ramos."

Both women gasped.

"How do you know that?" Miss Chen arched an eyebrow.

Vincent's stomach clenched. He rubbed his hands over his face. He had hoped his memory was mistaken.

Mrs. Campbell leaned her forearms on the table. "Can you find her by Friday?" For the first time, the older woman looked genuinely concerned.

The deadline. Vincent felt the full weight of the crime pressing on his heart. "We will draw on every resource available to rescue her." He glanced at Lenny, who had his eyebrows stuck in the up position.

Then Lenny nodded. Lenny knew Vincent's girlfriend, Nefi, and he'd heard about Nefi's best friend, Martina, and Martina's influential family. It was understood that the mention of *resources* meant Martina's older brother—the formidable Ruis Ramos. Ruis would be alarmed by the news of his sister, but he'd be dangerously angry if he wasn't told. Vincent considered him part of the need-to-know circle.

Mrs. Campbell settled back into her chair. "Good, because she has to be at the West Palm Beach Bloomingdale's at the Garden Mall on Saturday morning for the premiere of her new perfume."

Miss Chen, Lenny, and Vincent turned to gape at her.

With a shake of his head, Lenny recovered first. "I need the names, cell phone numbers, emails, and location of the people who were with her." He shoved his pad of paper and pen toward Mrs. Campbell.

Miss Chen resumed scrolling through her cell phone. She said, "I have their schedule and travel information."

Withering under the glare of agents Lenny and Vincent, Mrs. Campbell dug into her purse. "I have phone numbers. I always carry my little black book." After dredging up items from the depths of her massive purse and piling them on the table, she held up a small leather-bound address book.

Miss Chen glanced at Mrs. Campbell's little black book, sighed, and tried to hide her eye roll by closing her eyelids. A moment later, she returned her attention to her state-of-the-art cell phone.

Lenny pinched the bridge of his nose between his thumb and pointer finger while he muttered what sounded like, "And it's only Monday."

. 4 .

From the queen-size bed of the guest room, which had once been his bedroom, Ruis Ramos watched his wife, Sofia, unpack while she told him about their cruise. Though he traveled often as a US Marshal, this would be his first vacation travel in two years. They hoped for a second honeymoon. They planned to relax and, using their two years of joyful practice, to make a baby.

The six-day stopover at his parents' house in McLean, Virginia, was Sofia's idea. Every other year, the entire Ramos clan gathered for a reunion, often held on a cruise. Traditionally, the logistics and planning to coordinate the event fell on Ruis's parents, but Sofia had volunteered to help set up this year's reunion. Fourteen nights cruising the Mediterranean sounded like heaven. Like normal couples, they could spend every night and probably a few afternoons in their cabin in marital bliss because his sisters and their families would be busy with shipboard activities. His family would have time to bond with Sofia's parents and grandparents.

"I've read that it can be cold in late April in England and Ireland." Sofia's voice muted when she stepped into the closet. "We should bring some sweaters."

He'd been packing his own suitcase since age seven, but he let Sofia sort through his clothes because she had her mind set on choosing his wardrobe for the cruise.

She emerged from the storage closet with an armload of folded clothes. Holding up a camouflage-patterned sweater, she added, "Or buy them there. How about if I buy you a genuine cable-knit fisherman's sweater?"

Ruis couldn't imagine himself in one. He preferred Armani black Merino wool sweaters. Fine. Soft. Understated. "I wouldn't wear it much."

"Please expand your wardrobe beyond black on black." Sofia folded the sweater and set it aside. Next, she held up a long-sleeve turquoise-blue shirt. Made of quick-dry fabric and vented in the back, it suited warmer weather than April in Europe. The last time he had worn the shirt he was working undercover disguised as a tourist. "People think you're my bodyguard." She tucked a handful of her shiny black hair behind her ear.

"So?" With one arm, he swept her off her feet onto his lap.

They kissed. Ruis peeked to make sure the door was closed, then he slid a hand down her rib cage to the small of her back and pulled her against him. Her body fit against his by divine design. Soap with a hint of spice perfume emanated from her warm, soft skin. His cell phone vibrated on the nightstand. Even on silent mode, it had a way of announcing itself.

Sofia grabbed the device and jammed it in his hand.

"It takes messages," he pleaded.

Her expression told him he'd missed his opportunity. She peeled her body away from his and sighed. She accepted his absences without complaint, and she said she understood the dangerous nature of his work. In respecting his work time, she expected his boss to respect family time. She strode from the room and shut the door. Her footfalls sounded softly down the hall to the stairs while the cold phone buzzed in his hand.

"Ruis here."

"I would like your opinion on a ransom video." Vincent's voice had an edge to it, making it slightly higher and faster than usual.

"Okay. Ransom videos suck."

"I'm serious. You need to see it."

"I thought you had people for that." The FBI's forensic laboratory was the largest and most comprehensive state-of-the-art facility in the world. They employed hundreds of experts.

"This is a special case."

Though annoyed at the interruption, he couldn't recall any other time when Vincent had asked for his opinion on an investigation. "Send it to my email."

"Thanks."

Ruis dragged himself to his laptop and started it up. He'd associated Vincent Gunnerson with Nefi Jenkins since their mission together in Brazil. He liked Vincent because he was a fellow Catholic and because he was a great Marine. Infused with unshakable values, Vincent was a dependable, honest man. The last time they'd talked was when Vincent announced his engagement to Nefi along with the outcome end of Blake's trial last Friday.

By the time his computer booted, the message from Vincent was delivered to his inbox. He dug earphones from his briefcase and plugged them in to prevent others from hearing the video. Anyone could walk in while he was listening, and such messages were always disturbing. He clicked on the attachment while he poked the earphones in place.

A young woman with short, choppy hair and a swollen black eye appeared on the screen. Then she spoke, and her voice compelled him to listen.

It was said that our world was one of many parallel worlds in the multiverse and that we existed in each, like two mirrors reflecting each other. The common saying went that everyone had a twin. Part of Ruis's mind clung to the hope that this was an unknown doppelgänger on the video who had an uncanny resemblance to his youngest sister. As the recording ended, he realized he was standing and he had not breathed since the video began.

He drew in a deep breath. Vincent had sent the video because this person who called herself Ruby reminded him of Martina. It was a remarkable similarity. She even sounded like Martina in some ways. The main difference between the voice on this recording and Martina's voice was the tone of panic. But this couldn't be his sister. She was in England studying for exams. Wasn't she?

An alert state of numbness settled over him like a familiar coat. This was someone's daughter. This poor girl was scared and needed help. He replayed the recording. The girl on the recording had a swollen black eye. Was she blinking so often because she was scared or because her eye hurt?

He separated from himself at the emotional level, setting emotions in a metal box in the back of his mind for later because emotions clouded judgment. *Observe. Orient. Decide. Act.* He settled himself into a state he considered mission mode. Then he watched the video again through the heightened awareness that training and experience in life-threatening situations allowed him to achieve.

The voice sounded so much like Martina's he needed to hear samples of Ruby's voice when she wasn't terrified. Switching to internet access, he searched for Ruby. Photos, videos, blogs, news articles, gossip media, all presented a party-girl pop singer. Photos lined up on the screen of Ruby singing to sold-out crowds at the Red Rocks Amphitheater in Morrison, Colorado, the Greek Theater in Berkeley, California, the Philips Arena in Atlanta, the Meredith Supernatural Amphitheatre in Australia, and Slane Castle in Ireland. Except for the rebellious haircut, she could have been Martina's twin.

He found a video interview of Ruby and clicked on it. Closing his eyes, he listened. After a minute, he stopped it. The urge to deny disturbing facts was universal. Humans used it to protect themselves from disabling panic while the disturbing facts processed through the subconscious mind. In the end, the subconscious mind pushed the truth to the surface. For most people, denial took longer to overcome. For people who were trained to act decisively in emergencies, denial fell away quicker in favor of survival.

The truth he detected was that Ruby's speech was peppered with "you know" filling every pause, and her speaking voice was higher-pitched and more nasal than Martina's. As much as he wanted to reject the idea that the recording featured Martina, he couldn't convince himself the woman on the recording was the pop star.

This is Martina.

Why would she call herself Ruby?

He took a deep breath and exhaled slowly. In that moment, his mind connected the peculiar blinking to Martina and it seemed purposeful. Was she using Morse Code?

On the third viewing, he translated the blink pattern into a chilling message.

If anyone knew where Martina was, it would be her best friend, Nefi Jenkins, who answered on the second ring. He knew better than to wait for her to say a greeting. It wasn't her style. Nor was small talk. "When was the last time you spoke with Martina?"

"Friday. I called her to tell her about how Blake's trial turned out."

Right. Nefi and Vincent had attended the trial. "Anything else?"

"I told her I was just as sad as Oscar she wasn't coming home during school break."

"And when did break start?"

"Mid-March."

"So…she's back in school."

"No. Lucky girl. She gets six weeks. Plenty of time to study for exams."

Then Ruis remembered Oxford was on a trimester system. Each term lasted eight weeks. "When are exams?"

"I think she said April twenty-fifth."

The same day the cruise was scheduled to begin. "Thanks."

His next call was to Oscar, Vincent's younger brother and Martina's boyfriend. Both brothers were tall and athletic, but while Vincent looked like a fullback, Oscar looked more like a tennis player. Their family resemblance was unmistakable, especially in the jawline. Oscar was an engineer in high demand according to Martina. The rest of the family adored him, and his deep background check had come back clean, so Ruis considered him a possible long-term prospect for Martina.

Oscar answered on the fifth ring. "Hello?" Rotor sounds hummed in the background.

"This is Ruis. Can you talk?"

"Sure. Just a second." A car door slammed. "How are you?"

"Still alive. Say, when was the last time you spoke with Martina?"

A heavy sigh whooshed in Ruis's ear. "Is she mad at me?"

"Why do you ask?"

"First, she tells me she's going to stay on campus to study all through break, then I offer to come visit her, and she says no. Now she's not answering my calls or texts or emails."

Ruis closed his laptop and walked into the corridor that connected the upstairs rooms.

"Man to man, I confess I haven't dated a lot, so I'm lost here," Oscar said. "I called Vincent for advice this morning, and he acted all weird like he didn't want to talk about her. Did I do something wrong? Maybe she confided in Nefi, but I can't ask her. Nefi intimidates me."

"That's Nefi." Ruis knew he needed to call Vincent, but he stalled as if it could hold off the horrific reality of the situation for a few more minutes. He had the top floor of the house to himself, it seemed. A riot of kid noise and clanking of pots and pans downstairs filled the house.

"I have to get back outside."

"Where are you?" Ruis paced the second-floor corridor on autopilot. With his emotions tucked away, he tended toward physical activity as a distraction. In this emergency mode, his body felt like a familiar rental car. In SEAL missions, he'd learned how to shut down emotions to think decisively and objectively in life-and-death situations. In that mindset, he could objectify the threat of damage to his body in terms of how much it would cost and how long it would take to repair it. Risk carried less fear that way.

"I'm at MacDill Air Force Base in Tampa demonstrating a drone."

"Nice. I haven't heard anything bad about you, so don't give up on her."

"Thanks." The call ended.

Ruis wandered the upstairs as he placed another call. This one to Vincent, who answered on the first ring. As if picking up Nefi's habit, Vincent didn't answer with a greeting.

"What's Martina's last known location?" Ruis demanded.

"We're working on that."

Ruis sighed. "In the video, she blinks a message in Morse Code. It repeats *two men* and *boat*."

"Could you be reading that into—"

"Dad and I taught her."

"Okay, then. That's a lead."

"Why does she call herself Ruby?"

"An agency hired her to stand in for a singer for certain social events," Vincent said. "She's a body double."

That explained the haircut. "You know I won't sit on the sidelines."

"I'll talk to the assistant director."

Ruis pocketed his phone and found himself standing in Martina's room. The walls displayed photos of Martina being tossed in the air by other cheerleaders, selfies with Nefi on beaches and at Mardi Gras, candid shots of every family member, and her awards and diplomas. One photo caught his attention. In it, he, Vincent, Blake, and fourteen-year-old Nefi stood in front of a cab in Manaus, Brazil. Nefi must have given her a copy.

Martina and Nefi had become fast friends probably because they were kindred spirits—stubborn, rebellious, and adventurous. Even before Nefi arrived, Martina sought to be set apart from others her age. During summers spent sailing, he'd thought Martina wasn't listening when he and Father tried to teach her Morse Code. She had learned the code not because she cared to or because she expected to use it. She'd learned because it mattered to Father, and she was Daddy's girl. The entire family understood Martina was the admiral's favorite, possibly because she had been such a stubborn child. Not a sugar-and-spice kind of girl, she was more spit-and-vinegar.

Her room was as she had left it. The baby of the family, she held a treasured spot in everyone's heart. Collectively, Ruis and his siblings prided themselves on their contribution to raising her. Over the years, it had become a team effort to keep her from harm. As soon as Martina could crawl, she'd stuck her damp finger in an electrical outlet. The family members shared an unspoken co-ownership in her accomplishments, and they considered their responsibility of watching over her as joyful, stressful, and terrifying all at once.

Ruis donned his poker face and headed downstairs. Since Sofia already suspected the call was job-related, he'd roll with that explanation.

It was time to tell Sofia he wouldn't be flying to Europe with her for the reunion cruise. One day, he hoped his parents would forgive him for keeping this kidnapping from them. Father, a retired Navy admiral, would understand. Besides, the family couldn't help him find Martina, and if they knew the grave danger she was in, they would activate a prayer chain so extensive that news of the crime would inevitably leak out, revealing that the kidnappers had the wrong girl.

. 5 .

The FBI's main forensics lab was at Quantico. Fearing delays because of the lab's backlog of work, Vincent hoped for quicker analysis from the New York office's tech experts. The heavyset technician's dark work area resembled a gamer's paradise of geekware from the panel of eight large monitors to the racks of hard drives, recorders, and blinking black boxes Vincent didn't recognize. A second technician wore headphones while facing two screens. On one screen, the second tech had separated layers of sounds and labeled them, "male voice A," "male voice B," "background traffic bus and cars," and "machinery hum." After a glance at Vincent, he resumed his work.

Vincent handed the bikini jump drive to the huskier technician for analysis.

He peered over the rim of his glasses at Vincent. "I thought Blake didn't work here anymore."

Vincent snorted. Blake's reputation as a prankster continued in his absence. He missed his old partner. "It's a copy of a ransom demand. The victim's talent agent recorded it on one of her client's promotional items."

The technician took the drive. "You need it analyzed immediately, of course."

Vincent nodded.

"Just when you think you've seen it all," the technician

muttered at the tiny figure as he rolled his chair over to a dedicated desktop computer kept isolated from the internet and the in-house network.

Vincent returned to the interview room, where Lenny briefed him on his progress with Mrs. Campbell and Miss Chen. The women's somber faces proved that Lenny had convinced them of the gravity of their situation as well as Martina's.

"Ruby's boyfriend, Chad, and another couple in the entourage are holed up at the St. Regis Hotel on Miami Beach. They've been searching for her since yesterday morning. This morning, they finally decided to call Mrs. Campbell to report she wasn't in her room or answering her phone."

Vincent shook his head slowly at all the lost time. The celebrities had waited a day to report Martina was missing. He glared at Mrs. Campbell for waiting five hours to take the recording to the FBI. If she could have read his thoughts, she would have run for her life.

"I contacted the Miami office to hold and interview them and search their rooms." Lenny pointed to his notes. Beside the agent's name was a phone number. "This is the special agent in charge. He's going to lead the investigation from there."

Vincent put the Miami agent's name and number in his phone.

"Why don't you notify Assistant Director Watson about this case? See what he says about your outside investigator," Lenny said, "while I finish with the ladies. The Miami agent mentioned they have a full workload."

"I don't suppose I could—"

"Be objective?" Lenny challenged.

"You're right." His conflict of interest prevented him from deeper involvement in the hands-on fieldwork. Vincent considered another person who might be available.

Lenny stood. "Ladies, if you discuss this crime or the investigation with anyone, we could have you arrested for obstruction. A woman's life is at stake, and her safety depends on keeping this secret." To Mrs. Campbell, he added, "Trust me, you don't want a death tied to your client. There would be an avalanche of bad publicity."

Mrs. Campbell stood and eyed Lenny as if assessing whether his statement was a threat. After a stare down, she blinked. "I understand."

Mrs. Campbell and Miss Chen followed Lenny in silence out of the room to the elevators. Vincent followed them partway, then he veered toward Assistant Director Watson's office. Watson's administrative assistant looked up from his desk.

"I need a minute with him."

The assistant used his phone to announce Vincent's request. "Agent Vincent Gunnerson to see you. Yes, sir." He hung up and waved toward the thick dark oak door.

Vincent entered and shut the door behind him.

Assistant Director Sam Watson shook his hand. He unbuttoned his suit jacket and sat in one of two chairs in front of his desk. A second-generation British immigrant, he was an American citizen educated at schools in England from childhood through university. Only newbies whispered jokes about Sherlock Holmes and Watson. A complete lack of response to such humor from the other agents quickly shut it down. Watson was well-respected by the entire office. "Welcome back. I'm sorry Blake didn't accept my offer to return."

"Me, too, sir." Vincent sat in the empty chair. "Special Agent Lenny and I have evidence of a celebrity kidnapping. A video ransom sent to the victim's talent agency demands six million in bearer bonds to be delivered to Tampa on Friday. Lenny contacted the Miami office to lead the investigation."

"Why Miami?"

"The singer Ruby Wharton was kidnapped in Miami. They're rounding up her boyfriend and the others who were with her. She's been missing since Saturday night."

Watson groaned. "So much lost time."

"There's more to the story. The singer's body double is the one who was actually kidnapped."

Watson sighed. "So what's your plan?"

"The Miami office said they were shorthanded. I know of an off-duty US Marshal who could help with the investigation. He's familiar with the victim and speaks Spanish fluently."

Watson bowed his head. "Is this US Marshal a team player?"

Vincent could no more lie to Watson than to his own father. "He was a SEAL, so he understands the value of teamwork. The kidnap victim is his sister. I believe he'd work with anyone who can help him."

"How does he know about the kidnapping?"

"He doesn't. But if he finds out, he'll do something with or without us."

"Would your presence prevent him from going off on his own?"

"It might, but I thought about asking Blake to help." Vincent clasped his hands in his lap. "The truth is, I have a conflict of interest. I know the victim, too."

"How?"

"She's my fiancée's best friend." He knew that whether he intended to or not, he would take extreme risks to rescue Martina, for her sake, Ruis's, and Nefi's. High emotion tended to cloud judgment.

Watson sucked in a deep breath, sat back in his chair, and exhaled through his nose. "How close is Blake to the victim?"

"They'd recognize each other, but they're not close friends in any way."

Watson swiveled his chair toward his window and stood. "Do you want me to speak to the Miami office?"

"Please, sir."

Watson turned around and dropped his hands on the back of his leather chair. "Invite Blake in as a consultant. Maybe this will bring him back into the fold."

Vincent stood.

"Could this US Marshal be the same man who went with you two to Brazil?"

Amazed that Watson made the connection between Ruis and Blake, Vincent nodded. "He led the mission. Blake describes him as a combination action figure and superhero."

Watson smiled. "Keep me updated."

"Yes, sir." Vincent left the room with his cell phone in hand. As he passed the administrative assistant, who was talking on the phone, he mouthed, "Thank you."

The assistant nodded.

It was five o'clock, Monday, April nineteenth. The first forty-eight hours—that critical window of time with a high-recovery rate after a person went missing—had already passed. If Martina was alive, every hour that ticked by reduced her chances of survival. Vincent sent up a prayer that Blake would volunteer. Ruis needed a friend along like Blake, who would encourage or restrain, argue or agree, attack or be attacked, and lead or follow as the situation demanded and consider it an honor.

. 6 .

Martina pressed her ear to the stateroom door. The absence of voices gave her hope her captors might be asleep. Waves slapped the hull in a lulling rhythm echoed by the rocking motion of the boat. She gripped the lever handle and turned it slowly. It turned easily and made a *snick* sound as the latch retracted. Surprised that the door wasn't locked, she felt stupid for not trying it earlier. Easing the lightweight door inward, she peered into the darkened passageway that dead-ended at the door to the master stateroom. Its door was closed.

She opened her door all the way and listened. No alarms. No voices. No generator. No running water. An occasional *glub blub* punctuated the rocking motion of the boat as waves nudged the hull.

Across from her door was the head and to her left was the master stateroom. The escape route was to her right, upstairs to the pilothouse. From the helm level, the pilothouse doors sat on port and starboard, or she could tiptoe through the pilothouse and down the opposite stairs to cross through the salon to the stern door. Surely, there was a lifeboat of some kind back there.

As a teenager, she had occasionally sneaked out of the house. She'd known precisely which creaky stair to avoid, which window to unlock. The stakes this time rose far above being grounded. She was also unfamiliar with the boat. Her pulse quickened as she stepped barefoot into the passageway. She turned to the right.

Green Mask blocked the top of the stairs to the salon.

Stifling a gasp, she crossed her arms. "I need to use the bathroom." Her urine-soaked dress and underwear had dried, concentrating the stink. She drew in a deep breath to become her Ruby persona. "And unless you want me to smell like this for the next few days, I need a change of clothes."

Green Mask nodded toward the unknown door.

She slipped inside the compact head and locked the door. There, she exhaled and planted her shaking hands on either side of the sink. The room offered enough space to turn around from the shower stall on her left to the sink in front and the mirror and toilet to her right. A towel rack with a hand towel and bath towel hung on the back of the door. She quietly opened the sliding door of the teakwood cabinet behind the sink to search for a weapon. Her father's voice rang in her head, reminding her that, on a ship, cabinets and closets were called lockers. Martina wasn't sure if that was Navy speak or general nautical terminology. A hairbrush, a cardboard emery board, deodorant, and a bottle of clear nail polish were the only items inside.

Great, subdue them with grooming products. Some plan.

She considered staying in this locked room, but the flimsy door wouldn't hold against a man's kick. She sighed.

Was it only weeks ago that they'd stayed at the Hotel de Paris Monte Carlo in a two-bedroom suite that had twelve hundred square feet of luxurious room overlooking the Mediterranean Sea? Twenty-four-hour room service. A spa. They had lounged in a private striped cabana by the pool amid movie stars and wealthy business owners from Europe and Japan who asked for autographs.

Bang bang bang sounded on the flimsy door.

Startled, she pressed her hand over her heart to calm the pounding.

"Room service," Black Mask said, chuckling.

After opening the door, she spotted clothes piled on the floor. She reached for them.

He grabbed a handful of her hair.

"Ow. Ow." Her scalp burned. She dropped to a knee and groped the wall for support.

"While you're in there, wash your little dress and let it dry in the shower. You're going to sing for us."

Her heart sank. Ruby's music appealed to hormonal teens through suggestive lyrics and seductive dance moves. Popular in clubs, Ruby's tunes glorified carefree sex. The type of dance Ruby performed reportedly played well in strip clubs. If given a choice between dancing like Ruby for kidnappers or getting Tased, she'd choose the Taser. "I'm dehydrated, hungry, and you electrocuted me." Speaking to his shins, she sounded far braver than she felt. "Performing takes energy I don't have."

"Deal." He released her hair. "You can have food and water."

She pulled the clothes into the small bathroom and locked the door.

"Turn on the power," he shouted.

"Okay," shouted Green Mask.

Her whole body shook as she hugged the clean clothes. She attempted to rein in her helpless frustration, which resulted in hiccups. Soon, the generator hummed to life, covering her sobs.

After peeling off the sequined designer dress, she checked the laundry label. Dry clean only. How she missed room service.

Maybe washing would ruin the dress.

She laid the clean clothes out on the countertop. A woman's polo top and elastic-waist lounge pants that belonged to someone taller than Martina. They were everything the red party dress was not—comfortable, loose, and figure concealing.

Where had the clothes come from? What had happened to the woman who owned them? Speculation crept into the realm of fear, so she shook off the thoughts. She didn't have the energy to worry about the fate of others. She couldn't even fight off hiccups.

Such a boat used a diesel-powered generator at sea and AC

when docked at marinas that offered electric hookup. It powered the water heater, appliances, and an air conditioner if the boat had one. Of course, the entire boat already felt hot in the tropical sun, but the heater would boost the shower temperature after the generator ran for fifteen minutes or so. Martina refused to wait for the warmer water. She turned on the shower.

The more she tried to hold back hiccups, the louder they sounded. Each hiccup reminded her of her helplessness. She had no control over what to wear or when she could use the toilet or the shower. This wasn't the way her life should be. This wasn't fair or reasonable or just. This was no way to treat a star! This was no way to treat a dog, for that matter.

The mirror revealed bruising on her face and Taser burn marks on her neck. She was hired to do a job, to pretend she was someone else. Never before had doing her best at something gone so wrong. She touched the Taser burns. Was it her fault the kidnappers had taken her?

No. Yes. What a dangerous mess.

The hiccups didn't matter. She decided to stop wasting time and energy on things that didn't matter. She valued her life and wanted it back under her own control.

A bar of soap and a bottle of shampoo sat in the caddy under the shower head. She stepped into the warm jets of water. Suspecting the creeps on board would peek, she closed the shower's too-small portal window and smeared soap on the glass.

After draping the dress over the shower head pipe, she lathered her hair and body until the stink of urine, sweat, and vomit washed away. Citrus-scent filled the shower.

She rubbed her sore scalp. Only one kind of male hurt women. She fantasized kicking, punching, shooting, and stabbing him. No jury in America would convict her for acting in self-defense against two masked kidnappers. They outweighed her, they outnumbered her, they had a weapon, and they alone knew the way back to civilization.

Gritting her teeth, she realized her hiccups were gone. *Those jerks don't know who they kidnapped.*

Holding the dress under the water, she watched red dye swirl down the drain like blood.

. 7 .

Stas palmed the satellite phone from the table. "I'm going to call—"

"No names," Gregorio hissed.

Stas sneered at his accomplice's green-masked face. It was irritating enough to wear the itchy disguise, but he wasn't going to be bossed around by any soft, lightweight, junior criminal any more than their agreement required. He could take worse than putting up with an idiot for a few days for a once-in-a-lifetime payoff. He huffed. "I'll be out back."

Gregorio nodded as if granting permission.

Stas stepped out the door to the back of the boat and shook his head. He threw one leg over the transom for balance and sat with his torso turned toward the life raft, which hung sideways on metal supports. After turning on the satellite phone, he placed his call.

"Hello," a sultry voice answered.

"It's me."

"I forwarded your message just like you said to."

"From the café?" He had to be sure she used the internet café and not the internet from their apartment.

"Exactly." Breathing filled the silence.

"Are you packed for our vacation?"

"I'm all ready for our little getaway. I miss you."

"Soon." This time he meant it. He had been promising a trip out of the country for so long it had become the sharp point of many arguments. This time, he could follow through on grand plans for leaving their crappy lives behind. With money, they could be anyone. They could afford passports under new names and travel anywhere to begin new lives. His woman would never have to please another man ever again.

"How's your friend behaving?"

"As expected." Stas couldn't say what he really wanted to say because Gregorio might overhear it and get his little feelings hurt. After all Stas had done to protect the kid in prison, he couldn't screw it up now, on the brink of a real fortune, the kind of score he'd dreamed of for years.

"Just remember," the voice whispered, "I'm the one you want."

He hoped the reminder came from natural jealousy because women were attracted to him. If the reminder came from insecurity, well, that was plain weakness. "There isn't anyone else."

"Good. You can hold out for a few days, right?"

Stas recoiled at the suggestion he'd be tempted. He wasn't attracted to the scrawny singer. And even in prison, he hadn't liked Gregorio. "Same for you."

He disconnected the call.

. 8 .

Thirty-one-year-old Blake Clayton and his wife, Terri, had been packing Blake's bachelor apartment items all day. He thought of it as an apartment because the building housed twelve other neighbors although it was technically a condo. The closing had gone smoothly, and the contract provided them two weeks to clear out Blake's belongings, but they wanted to make a clean break with the past and move on. The place had served Blake well while he was working at the New York City FBI office. Now, unemployed thanks to the trial, he needed his investment back. Being accused of a felony was like getting a large, ugly tattoo. It took considerable effort to remove and left a scar for life. The media had championed the prosecuting attorney. Blake's arrest, therefore, had received far greater coverage than the resolution of the trial.

Blake's cell phone blared a few bars of the movie theme song "Men in Black." Amid the stacks of boxes of books, he couldn't quite tell where the sound originated. He struggled to remember where he had set his phone.

Terri strode into the study from the kitchen. Her copper-colored hair curled at the ends, where it brushed her shoulders. "Looking for this?" She gave him a wicked grin.

After his trial ended, he'd dedicated himself to catching up on months of lost lovemaking. He returned the grin. "I suppose."

"Say hello to Vincent for me." She placed the phone in his hand.

She understood him. She understood his quirky ringtone assignments. She loved him as is, which was as good as good got. Blake sighed. He called his friend's cell phone. "Aw, you miss me, don't you?"

"I sent a video to your phone. Watch it and call me back."

It took a few seconds for Blake to realize his call with Vincent had ended. Friends since Marine boot camp, they'd attended the same college and later applied to the FBI and trained in the same group of candidates. It wasn't like Vincent to be so curt or to send a video. Must be something urgent. He took a deep breath and pressed the email message icon on his phone. He found the email and activated the attachment.

Terri bumped into his shoulder and watched the video. Afterward, they stood in shocked silence, leaning against each other.

Blake squinted at his phone. "Weird. This girl looks kind of like Martina."

"Who?" Terri asked.

"Ruis's baby sister."

"Sorry. I didn't meet everyone at his wedding."

Blake smiled. That was the day he'd met Terri and invited her to crash Ruis's wedding reception.

"Or ours, for that matter. Was she there?"

Blake shook his head. He wanted to believe she had been in school, but he suspected she just didn't want to be at his wedding even though Ruis, Vincent, Oscar, and Nefi had been. Maybe Martina was the kind of person who liked to carry a grudge.

"Why'd Vincent send you this ransom message?" Terri asked. She sat on the arm of a recliner with her hip against the stacks of books balanced on the seat cushion.

"I don't know. It's way past April Fool's Day," Blake muttered as he placed a call. Besides, Vincent would go along with a prank, but he didn't initiate them. He wasn't wired that way.

Vincent answered on the first ring. "What do you think?"

"Who's Ruby?"

"Martina." His voice carried far enough to grab Terri's attention. Blake sucked air.

"It's a bit of a story. The short version is she was kidnapped for ransom in Miami on Saturday night. Ruis is heading there now. He's off the clock." That was Vincent's way of saying Ruis was not acting under his authority as a US Marshal.

"I pity the kidnappers. How can I help?"

"Watson is asking the Miami office to let you and Ruis help with the investigation."

Blake's lungs swelled at the revelation that Watson trusted him. He hadn't talked to many people because he wasn't sure who would shun him and who would treat him as the same Blake they'd known before the trial. Maybe he wasn't the same man he'd been then. "I appreciate that. I haven't spoken to Ruis since the trial started."

"You've been busy."

Blake laughed at the understatement and headed to the bedroom to pack his carry-on suitcase. "Are you leading the investigation?"

Terri followed him.

"I acknowledged my conflict of interest. Watson assigned me to research."

Blake paused inside the bedroom. "Is Watson aware of Ruis's conflict of interest?"

"I convinced him Ruis is more valuable working with the FBI than in competition with them."

Blake nodded. "Let's hope Ruis complies with that arrangement."

"I'll send you a briefing."

"Hold up. Does Nefi know?"

"No. It's bad enough that Ruis knows."

"I agree." Blake stuck his phone in his pants pocket. The fact that Vincent had already spoken to the assistant director and had a briefing ready to email proved that he knew Blake would accept the mission.

Terri hugged him, then she moved into the closet. She emerged with a medium-size wheeled suitcase. She didn't object or question his decision. Was he that transparent to his friends and family? She hefted it onto the bed and unzipped it. Blake rushed into the bathroom and tossed items into his leather kit bag. He came back into the bedroom and set the kitbag in the suitcase beside a handful of folded black T-shirts, black underwear, and socks. When he'd worked at the New York City FBI office, he kept a to-go bag packed and ready. He hadn't expected to need one after he resigned.

Blake packed in silence with worries bombarding his mind. He rolled a pair of dress pants to tuck in the suitcase, almost placing them on top of something with black lace trim.

He held up a bra. "What should I say at the security checkpoint when Transportation Security Administration officers ask if this is mine?"

Terri dropped two pairs of her pants in the suitcase. "I'm going with you."

Blake dropped the bra. His initial impulse was to argue with her that it was too dangerous for a woman, but that would irritate her. His second argument was that she wasn't trained in law enforcement. Before he could voice his objections, she had her cell phone in her hand. She was probably calling for reservations on the next commercial flight to Miami. She had a way of anticipating his needs.

"Briefer." Terri headed off to the bathroom. Her voice carried out to the bedroom as garbled sounds. She was getting a weather briefing, something she did in preparation to fly her own plane, a six-seat single-engine Cessna.

Blake sucked in a deep breath. She spoke to a briefer when she filed a flight plan. He wanted a commercial flight to minimize his time in the air. Stuck between two terrible choices, insulting his wife by insisting on a commercial flight or enduring a longer flight in her plane, his hesitation chose for him. She had stood by him through his trial when her friends and family had urged divorce. She had sacrificed her partnership in a thriving veterinary practice to stand by him. She was a fine pilot, instrument-rated, with three thousand hours of flying experience and no accidents. She might interpret his panic as lack of respect for her flying skills. She would take it personally. It would sound so lame to attempt to explain, *It's not you, honey, it's me.*

If he balked, she would probably assume it was because of his phobia instead of his need to get to Miami as quickly as possible. Sure, he didn't like flying. And flying in a small plane meant he'd feel every bump and noise, which would torment him with fear of crashing. He trusted his wife with so many things, choosing a place to live, managing their finances, decorating the house, earning a salary greater than his, cooking, and even flying. He never worried about her when she was flying without him. He just feared he would one day die in a plane crash.

Sure, it was an irrational fear. He had never been in an aviation incident of any kind. The closest he'd come to a crash was years ago when he had begged out of an experimental military plane ride that proved fatal for the others on board. Terri did not fly experimental aircraft or military aircraft. She flew a dependable, slower-moving aircraft much smaller than the MV-22 Osprey that had crashed. Nonetheless, he would have preferred flying commercially despite being cramped from knees to back, packed in like cargo, because the flight would be faster.

Terri ended her call with a thank-you, then she returned from the bathroom. "I can help. Let me."

He exhaled in defeat. The woman had willpower to spare. She hadn't graduated at the head of her class in veterinary school by coasting. And she had played a pivotal role in the last investigation. That could not be denied. The point of argument to be made last time was that her involvement indirectly affected the outcome of the trial. Even so, she had made a difference, intentional or accidental. God had shown favor on her efforts. Who was Blake Clayton, an unemployed ex-FBI agent, to interfere with the will of God? Or Terri?

He kissed her.

Terri plucked a few polo shirts from a drawer. "Tell me Nefi isn't going."

"She doesn't know."

Terri nodded. "Got it."

"How long is the flight to Miami?" He knew she could calculate the flight time easily.

"Seven hours counting a fuel stop. You can sleep on the plane."

"Seven hours." That would give him plenty of time to sleep if he could forget he was flying. He packed a few more items. He retrieved a jacket he hadn't worn since he left the FBI. After a few attempts to fold it, he was about to ask Terri to help.

She stood, rooted in place by the suitcase, staring at him. Had she said something? Was she waiting for him to reply? Like any mammal in fear, he froze.

Terri dropped a pair of shoes in the suitcase. "Seven hours is a long time." With a faraway expression, she placed another call. "Hey, by chance do you have anyone heading to Miami tonight with room for two passengers? This is an emergency situation."

Blake found his passport and tucked it in his shirt pocket.

"Deadheading?" Terri smiled like it was a good thing.

Deadheading did not sound at all appealing. He already associated airplanes with death. Maybe deadheading meant to a pilot what it meant to a trucker, going back with an empty vehicle. That wouldn't be a bad thing. A cargo plane would be faster than the Cessna. Noisier but faster.

"Oh, please. Tell him we are on our way." Terri stuck her phone in her pocket. She lunged at Blake and wrapped her arms around him. "We got a ride in a corporate jet, a Citation Ten." Her

45

excitement rose when she emphasized the model of the plane. "The pilot is heading back to Miami with just one passenger, and he'll wait for us."

Blake did not understand her excitement over the Citation, but the word *jet* filled him with relief. It didn't matter which corporation owned it. They were about to hitchhike in first-class style. Terri jammed one last item in the suitcase and zipped it up. Then they climbed into her truck and hit the road to Teterboro Airport.

. 9 .

The drive from McLean, Virginia, on I-95 to the general aviation airport north of Newark known as KTEB typically took four hours. Ruis completed it in three to catch a direct flight. Dressed in all black, he strode through the terminal to the reception desk. He asked for the pilot by name and was directed to a waiting aircraft just outside the glass doors to the tarmac. He shouldered his duffle bag and stepped from the quiet flight base of operations building into darkness and the roar of idling jet engines. When Ruis paused at the bottom of the plane's airstairs, a man in a white shirt with black epaulets waved at him to come up.

Ruis climbed the few steps into the aircraft and set his large duffle bag on end.

"Are you Ramos?" the man asked. He eyed the ballistic nylon black duffle.

"Yes."

"I'm Pete, the copilot." He spoke softly and shook Ruis's hand. "Captain Terpilowski said to get comfortable. You can stow your case here." He opened a small bulkhead storage compartment. "Is everything properly unloaded?"

Ruis knew the protocol for flying with weapons. Nodding, he secured the bag, on end, in the closet. He stepped through the curtained separator into the dark cabin. There were eight seats, four club-style separated by the aisle, followed by two forward-facing seats on either side of the aisle. He spotted the outlines of a couple seated facing each other on the right side of the aisle. He wanted to thank them for allowing him along, but they appeared to be asleep. The woman's hair, illuminated by the wing's strobe lights, glowed like a new penny. He didn't want to stare in case she was a celebrity, so he sat across the aisle in the forward-facing club seat to stretch out and sleep. He buckled his seat belt.

The airstairs thumped into place, sealing the aircraft for high-altitude flight with a distinct pressurized hiss. After the copilot disappeared into the cockpit and shut the cockpit door, the engines spun up to a whine, and the aircraft rolled toward the taxiway. Everyone, thankfully, was in a hurry to reach Miami.

"This is Captain Terpilowski. We are cleared to Miami International." The voice sounded soothing over the intercom. "Please secure your seat belts and relax. Our expected arrival time is eleven twenty and the weather is clear."

Between the darkness and the hum of the engines, Ruis should have been relaxed. Usually, he enjoyed flying. Flying time meant downtime and downtime was for socializing or rest. Two hours' sleep sounded like the best use of this time, but he doubted he could calm his mind.

He watched the ground drop away and the lights of New York City pass by. He remembered flying home after leave at the end of his first tour in the Navy in 1997. He had been on leave visiting Israel with another officer, a friend from his class at Annapolis. They were in the Mahane Yehuda open-air market in Jerusalem when two suicide bombers blew themselves up. Ruis and his friend had rendered first aid where they could among the sixteen dead and 178 civilians wounded. Too distraught to stay in Israel, he and his friend had flown back to the States. When he'd arrived at home, he told his father what had happened.

Admiral Ramos had told him, "When I wonder if my job matters, I walk through the house and watch my children sleep."

Following his father's advice, he'd visited each of his sisters' rooms, ending in Martina's, where he sat on the floor to think. Listening to his nine-year-old baby sister lightly snoring had settled his emotions. An hour later, he'd known he was destined to do more to protect his family and his nation. His major at Annapolis was operational research. He'd decided to join the Navy SEALS to apply his knowledge and hone the skills needed to make his job matter more. The best strategic plan to stop deadly enemies, he reasoned, was to become deadly to them. He wanted to destroy terrorist groups, starting with their leaders.

As clouds obscured the city lights, Ruis closed his eyes to try to sleep.

"Who did you threaten to get on this flight?" The southern drawl came from across the aisle.

Maybe the plane was owned by a country singer. Ruis opened his eyes, ready to apologize, when the man across the aisle switched on his overhead light. He had lost weight during his trial, but Ruis recognized him. "Blake? I thought you were in North Carolina."

"I'm selling the bachelor pad in New York City. Being unemployed sucks."

"How did you end up on this airplane?"

Blake laughed. "Terri sweet-talked the pilot. He's deadheading, which sounds worse than it is."

Ruis turned toward Terri. "I believe this is the first time we've met outside a wedding."

"Happier times." Terri's smile faded quickly.

A heaviness fell on Ruis, blanketing his heart. He nodded. "Since we're together, would you like me to brief you on the situation?"

"We saw the video," Blake said.

Ruis brought them up to speed on the facts, the timeline, and how Martina was mistaken for a pop star. He kept his tone even and he stuck to the known facts.

"I'm so sorry your sister's in trouble," Terri said.

Ruis blew out a breath. "She's like the free space on the Bingo card. On the path to trouble, she'll be standing in the busiest intersection. If Vincent had told me she was on a video, I would have braced myself for one of those embarrass-yourself-for-life spring break videos. Everyone believed she was studying for her master's exams at Oxford."

"Are you going to be able to remain objective?" Blake's voice was barely a whisper.

Ruis leaned his elbows on his knees and spoke toward the floor. "I've put my life on the line to protect informants, people I wouldn't allow near my family. Human traffickers, murderers, thieves, mobsters, pedophiles, you name it. The lowest forms of human life. Granted, not all protected witnesses are criminals." He looked up at Blake. "I'm in mission mode. If you see me slipping, speak up."

Blake nodded. "The FBI will work to rescue the victim and capture the kidnappers alive."

"So," Ruis said, "if we can avoid killing the kidnappers, we should." There. Having said the appropriate thing, he covered his backside. He studied his friend's somber expression. Blake understood the gravity of his choice to help. Terri, as the only non-law-enforcement-trained participant, might need to have the situation clarified. He addressed her. "Do you have any questions?"

"How can I help?"

"That's up to the lead investigator." Ruis took a deep breath and sank back in the plush seat. "I'm not sure if you should be involved. If we rescue my sister alive but the kidnappers die, we will be investigated and possibly charged with interfering with an FBI investigation. We're outsiders, so it would be easy to make us the scapegoats if this goes sideways."

"I've been charged with worse," Blake said.

Terri leveled eye contact with Ruis. After a moment, she

withdrew a plastic identification card from her wallet and handed it to him.

He read it and raised his eyebrows. "You have a carry permit?"

"Pilots can carry since nine eleven. I brought my Glock and I'm a competitive sharpshooter with a rifle."

Ruis nodded. "I met your father at Blake's wedding. He was talking about a deer hunt, but I missed the first part of the story. Was your father the hunter?"

"Was it a twelve-point buck?"

"One shot," Ruis said. "Clean through and through to the heart."

Terri clasped her hands in her lap. "That was mine."

A pilot, a veterinarian, and a hunter—Terri became more interesting every time Ruis met her. Blake had told his groomsmen he had married out of his league. Terri had stood by him through the trial. A woman of lesser character would have bolted.

Blake's eyebrows shot up and he emitted a small cough. "How do you justify being a veterinarian and a deer hunter?"

Ruis smirked. Seemed like the big guy hadn't known this about his wife.

"Compassion. Hunting deer is a way of culling the herd from overpopulation." Terri's tone was unapologetic. "I believe it's more merciful to die by a bullet than to be maimed by a car."

"If I oversaw the investigation," Ruis said, "I'd distance Terri from the action in the field."

"I agree." Blake eased back into his chair. "Deer never shoot back."

That comment earned him a scowl from Terri.

The curtain between the entryway and the passenger section parted and a man in blue pants, roper boots, and a white shirt with striped epaulets strode into the aisle. He stopped between Ruis and Blake. His butch-cut hair and perfect posture gave him a military appearance.

Ruis unbuckled his seat belt and stood. "Tapper!"

The men exchanged a manly back-slapping hug. When they separated, Ruis introduced Tapper to Blake and Terri as a former colleague. While shaking hands with Blake, Tapper's head tilted slightly to the right.

"Blake Clayton? Now why does that name sound familiar?"

"I was recently on trial."

"Oh, yeah." Tapper faced Ruis. "So, what brings an acquitted felon, a beautiful pilot, and you to Miami and can I get in on it?"

"A kidnapping," Ruis said.

"As in about to happen or has happened?" The pilot pulled a pack of gum from his shirt pocket and tapped a piece partway out. He offered it to Terri, who declined. He offered it to Blake, who also declined. Ruis waved him off. Tapper took a piece and tucked the remainder of the pack in his pocket before he unwrapped his stick of gum.

Ruis snorted dismissively. Good old Tapper was up for the action either way, no questions asked. "Let me show you." He pulled out his phone, and after a few seconds of touching his screen, he handed it to his pilot pal.

The video played. Every time Ruis heard Martina's voice, pangs of anguish shot through him. Those animals had bullied his baby sister. The black eye meant she'd probably talked back to them. No real man would strike a girl.

After the video ended, Tapper clenched his jaw.

"The FBI is running the investigation." Ruis took back his phone and sat.

"How old is this video?" Tapper dropped his gaze to the shadowed aisle.

"She's been missing since Sunday morning." Ruis's throat constricted. He took a few deep, slow breaths through his nose. He reconnected his seat belt with steady hands.

"We're taking this bird to Miami for its annual. I was going to work on my tan, but, hey, count me in." Tapper leaned closer to Ruis and whispered, "Is this guy from your last trip to the Amazon?"

Ruis nodded.

"And after we get this girl safely back, I want to hear his side of that story." Speaking louder, Tapper said, "I should get back to the cockpit and wake up my copilot. Good to meet you, Blake and Terri. I look forward to working with you on the ground." His confidence soothed Ruis's nerves. Tapper strode back to the cockpit.

Blake leaned into the aisle and posed a question to the group. "He's kidding, right?"

"About what?" Ruis asked. Tapper had absolutely volunteered. Never mind the cavalier delivery, his friend meant what he said. He was a T-type thrill-seeker personality and adrenaline junkie. He enjoyed skydiving.

"About the copilot being asleep?"

"I guess so," Ruis said, just to torment Blake.

Blake turned toward Terri. She shrugged and muttered something about an autopilot.

"I don't want a program flying the plane. I want a real, thinking human being controlling this aircraft." Blake crossed his arms. "That is not too much to ask for."

Terri leaned into the aisle toward Ruis. "Is Tapper his first or last name?"

"Nickname." Ruis realized his error too late. People always asked how soldiers earned their nicknames. Over the years, his nickname had been shortened from Double Tap, referring to his signature kill shots to the head. "Please don't ask him about it."

Blake's wide-eyed expression caught Ruis's attention.

Addressing Terri, Ruis said, "He'd probably like you to call him Captain."

Terri grunted.

"Might as well call him autopilot," Blake grumbled.

Ruis looked away to the black starless night outside. Settling back in his chair, he decided to sleep while he could. He made a mental note to tell Tapper the girl's true identity as soon as the chance came. As the plane gently rocked and hummed, Ruis surrendered everything to God.

Please, dear Lord, save Martina or show me how.

Once they landed in Miami, Ruis struggled against his desire to go straight from the airport to the FBI office in Miami. It was nearly midnight by the time they loaded their gear into his rented silver Chrysler Aspen SUV. Everyone needed rest and downtime from the adrenaline-burning urgency of the situation. He needed time to orient himself to the situation.

"I'm heading to a hotel near the FBI office," Ruis said.

Blake and Tapper looked relieved. Terri seemed surprised but said nothing.

Ruis drove toward the Fairfield Inn & Suites. "A night's sleep will help me think clearly and give me stamina."

"I second the motion," Blake said.

"All agreed, say I," Tapper said.

"I," they said in unison.

Ruis was still prayerfully fighting the urge to go to the FBI office when they rolled their luggage into the hotel lobby. After paying for their rooms and distributing room key cards, Ruis addressed his friends at the elevator. "Thank you for answering the call for this mission. The situation will be fluid, so please pack up in the morning so we can go elsewhere if needed. I'd like to leave here at seven thirty."

Blake, Terri, and Tapper nodded. Tapper yawned. He had a small flight bag secured to the top of his carry-on wheeled suitcase. The pilot's shoes had a high-gloss shine. He seemed proud of his job as a corporate air chauffeur. The four of them rode the elevator in silence. When they separated to find their rooms, Blake followed Ruis. Key card in hand, Terri continued the opposite way down the corridor, wheeling her carry-on suitcase behind.

"You don't have to pay for my room," Blake said softly.

Ruis paused and looked his friend in the eyes. "And you don't have to volunteer. But I'm grateful you did."

"I just want to win over your sister. You know she doesn't like me."

"What makes you think that?"

"She calls me names, she didn't come to my wedding, and she didn't even call when I was in court." Blake toed his suitcase, nudging it.

"I've called you names and I didn't call during the trial."

"You emailed." Blake's green eyes stared at Ruis.

"Why does Martina's opinion matter so much?"

Blake blinked rapidly as if his mind raced to form an answer. "I guess I've come to think of my family and friends the way Nefi does. You're all part of my tribe."

"That sounds like Nefi. I like that."

Blake nodded and rolled his suitcase behind him down the corridor to Terri, who held open the door to their room.

Terri waved and Ruis waved back. As he carded open his own room, he smiled. He was going hunting with his tribe. And what a skilled, loyal tribe it was.

. 10 .

The door to Martina's small state room opened. "Come into the living area," Green Mask said.

"Give me a minute." She darted across the passageway and locked the head door. Why didn't he call it the salon or the galley? Was he dumbing down nautical vocabulary for her? Perhaps he assumed a singer wouldn't know her way around a boat. Good to know.

After relieving herself, she noticed her dress was no longer hanging in the shower. She shuddered. She wasn't ready to put on the dress or dance or sing. She yawned, caught a whiff of her breath, and recoiled at a stench that would gag a buzzard. She ran her tongue over her teeth. They felt…furry. The best she could do about it was swish and spit water from the sink. No toothpaste. Ugh. By reflex, she picked up the deodorant.

Her history teacher once said that people had lived for centuries without wearing underwear, brushing their teeth, or using deodorant. To a high school sophomore, this sounded equally amusing and unbelievable. In this moment, she understood she could live without many things. The concept of smelling better gave her pause. Setting down the deodorant, she

56

embraced her breath and sweat in all their repellent glory.

She closed the small teak locker behind the sink and then she turned toward the mirror. The image that stared back sported one purple eye and hair that resembled dark, frayed rope.

"You look like I feel," she whispered.

Steeling herself for a fight, she unlocked the door and opened it. When she stepped into the narrow passageway, the scent of toasted bread aroused her hunger. She marched up three stairs to the pilothouse, counting the steps and committing their number to memory in case she had to use the stairs in the dark. At the pilothouse level in the middle of the ship, she automatically turned toward the helm control panel and the radio. The power lights on the helm instruments and radio were off.

Where was the emergency orange flare gun? Standing on the rug that covered the hatch to the engine room, she turned toward the charts to determine the boat's location, but the large navigation charts were covered by a towel.

Though the boat could be piloted from this raised middle section of the boat, Martina could barely see out the front-facing window. She'd have to stand on a footstool to navigate the boat from the pilothouse, or wheelhouse, as her British pals called it.

"Get down here." Though his expression was hidden, Green Mask's entire body radiated impatience as he stood in the salon.

She listened for footfalls above and heard none. She padded barefoot down the steps to the salon, on the lookout for Black Mask. Three steps from staterooms to helm, she reminded herself, two from helm to the salon. The combined open galley and salon had teakwood flooring, lockers above and below the counters, and a dining table. On the starboard side sat a stove flanked by two sections of countertop. A hutch with a toaster topped a dorm-size refrigerator at one end of the galley. To the aft of the galley was a corner sink, and under the counter to the right of it, beside the door to the stern, was another counter topping a small freezer.

On the port side, an L-shaped cushioned bench angled around a table that held a plate of boiled eggs and toast. The red dress wasn't in sight. She hoped that was a good thing.

Green Mask plopped a bottle of water beside the plate. "Sit."

Her heart fluttered at the offer of food and water. Then she remembered the "deal" to sing for them and hesitated. They gave her clothes and the chance to shower in trade for singing. What did they want from her for food and water?

When Green Mask took a step toward her, she recoiled. "Sit."

She scooted between the table and bench. As if to separate herself from the heathen brute in the room, she bowed her head and put her hands together at the edge of the table. *Dear God, thank you for the food.*

Green Mask laughed. "Don't thank God. I made this meal."

And please rescue me from these horrible men. Amen. She looked up. For his minor demonstration of basic human decency for feeding her, she said, "Thank you."

His head drew back, and his chest rose as if he interpreted her thanks as sarcasm. After a moment, he grunted, climbed up the steps to the pilothouse and down to the head, and shut the door. That's when Martina climbed the steps to see if the door to the large stateroom was closed. Her captors took turns on watch. The door was closed. Black Mask was probably sleeping, especially if he had been up all night.

As quietly as she could, she sneaked back through the salon to the open stern doorway onto the boarding platform. She considered stepping over the low transom wall to the swim platform to steal the white dinghy, but it was locked to supports that held it sideways. Why lock it? Sure, it made sense to secure the thing, so it wouldn't fall off in a storm, but locks? In an emergency, unlocking it would slow down evacuation. The only other reason to lock the dinghy would be to prevent theft.

And escape.

Maybe she didn't need the dinghy. She needed to know where she was. If anchored close enough to shore, she could swim. A boat this size wouldn't have enough chain to anchor in deep water. She climbed the ladder to peek at the upper deck. On the far side of the open deck was a second two-step ladder, and beyond that sat a raised flybridge covered with a beige awning. A beige-cushioned bench wrapped around the starboard side and the back, blocking her view of the flybridge. Crouching, she hurried across the open deck and peeked.

On a hanger attached to the awning, her red dress danced in the breeze. Sunlight sparkled off sequins on the undulating fabric. She suspected Black Mask had hung it there to dry. Tempted to fling it overboard, she reminded herself she'd come topside to determine an escape route.

She scrambled onto the flybridge. A trawler or a motor yacht this size probably cruised under twenty knots per hour. Maybe they hadn't gone far from Miami. Two cushioned captain's chairs, secured to the floor, faced a panel of secondary helm controls. The instruments were dead. She turned her attention outside the boat to find landmarks, radio towers, power poles, other boats, piers, buildings, or other signs of civilization to orient herself. The boat bobbed and tugged on the anchor chain in brackish water, bordered by mangrove islands as far as she could see. She estimated it was three football fields' distance to the nearest island. Whatever land supported these mangroves lay hidden under the low canopy of branches and roots that arched into the water. A stench of wormy decay, stagnant water, mud, and snails drifted on the breeze. Ecologic detritus.

Green Mask shouted and flung open the midship transom door on the starboard side. Martina cringed and backed into the middle of the flybridge. She leaned over the control panel toward the bow. Empty. She could jump overboard, but then what? Which direction should she go?

"She's up here," a voice announced from behind.

Martina wheeled around.

Black Mask's head and shoulders appeared at the top of the ladder between decks. He laughed. "Go ahead and scream. Get it out of your system." He glanced at the dress, then back at her. One side of his mouth tugged upward.

The oppressive silence of the environment told her they were miles from towns, roads, and other boats. The only sign of civilization was a jet contrail in the stratosphere. Martina scanned the flat horizon east, west, north, and south, then she sank into a vinyl-covered seat at the dead control panel.

"I could lock her in the engine hold," Green Mask said.

Black Mask looked down. "It doesn't matter."

"What if she jumps overboard?"

"Think about it," Black Mask said. "Where is she going to go?" He disappeared from the top of the ladder.

If they were going to pick up the ransom in Tampa, like the message said, then they had to be close enough to cruise there by Friday. How could they be anywhere near Tampa without radio towers or power poles in sight? Martina balled her fists and screamed.

The swamp absorbed the sound. Below, the men laughed. Martina's face burned. For weeks she had been treated like Ruby and had become accustomed to it. Drawing on her frustration, she did what she believed the kidnappers expected of a pampered star. She stomped back and forth across the flybridge.

Though her feet stung, she climbed down to the open deck and stomped across it, too, so the men would hear it throughout the salon. Glaring over the railing, she hated the nine-foot, two-man, white fiberglass dinghy and the locks that kept her from taking it. It hung sideways with its hull facing away from the trawler. The pathetic motor reminded her of a tiny lawnmower engine. It clung to the hull by rusted bolts.

She wouldn't want to depend on it in an emergency. From her high vantage point, she assessed the cheap thing as an outdated afterthought, something tacked on to pass inspection. Daddy would have called it a disgrace to contingency planning.

A seagull flew overhead, peered at the boat, and squawked without stopping. The men's laughter echoed off the dinghy up to the open top deck.

A black circle marred the dinghy's white hull under the bow. Leaning over the ladder for a better look, she recognized the black spot as a drain plug. This kind of shallow double-hull dinghy took on water easily. If it was overloaded or used in rough water, water would rush in between the hull layers, making it ride even lower. She imagined the goons in it paddling hard and sinking fast, like cartoon characters, until they were sitting with the entire dinghy below the water line and wondering why.

She descended the ladder. Reminding herself to be a pampered star, she hopped over the transom onto the swim platform and grabbed the bow of the dinghy. She shook it hard and wailed dramatically, but the rattling locks held.

The men guffawed.

Let them laugh.

With her back to the men, she screamed in mock anguish and shook the dinghy again while she secretly popped out the drain plug and dropped it in the water. Knowing they were watching her, she drooped her head and shoulders in defeat and trudged back into the salon. She plopped onto the cushion at the table and stared at the food.

Chuckling, Green Mask plucked a boiled egg off the plate on his way to the mid-deck helm.

She sighed. "Why are you doing this?"

On the steps to the helm, he answered. "We have six million reasons."

Her appetite stalled as she stared at the meager rations.

And six million reasons to kill me when they find out I'm not Ruby.

. 11 .

Tamping down his nearly overwhelming desire to take charge, Ruis entered the Miami FBI field office on Tuesday morning with his laptop case and gratitude toward everyone who wanted to rescue Martina. Blake, Terri, and Tapper followed.

Eager to learn the status of the investigation, Ruis signed in with his group and followed an escort to a conference room filled with maps and buzzing with activity. Research, phone calls, and muted conversations continued around Ruis's group as they introduced themselves to Special Agent in Charge Jorges Espinosa.

In his forties, Espinosa stood an inch taller than Ruis, but his presence filled the room with an air of authority. His demeanor and his Armani suit exuded the message of a confident man in his domain. His only smile was directed to Terri before he offered her a chair and asked if she had ever tried Cuban coffee.

"I've heard it's like espresso on steroids," she said, taking the chair.

Espinosa gave a quick reverse nod to an agent at the back of the room and flashed four fingers. The man smiled back and disappeared through the doorway. "We have been working nonstop since the New York City office notified us of the kidnapping. This office has far-reaching resources and authority. We handle crimes in nine southern counties in Florida as well as crimes against American citizens in Mexico, the Caribbean, and Central and South America."

Ruis, Tapper, and Blake settled into chairs facing Espinosa, who stood in the corner of the room between a large map of his office's territory and a table stacked with navigation charts. Ruis set his laptop on the floor beside his chair.

"Before I assign you tasks, how many of you speak Spanish?" Espinosa's gaze fell on Terri, who sat to his left.

She shook her head.

Ruis suspected she understood Latin. Though it was a dead language, medicine and other sciences used it. He embraced two Latin mottos. *Non sibi sed patiae*, not for self but country, and *semper fortis*, always strong.

Espinosa then turned toward Blake, who said he spoke only enough Spanish to order food and get basic directions. When it was his turn, Ruis said he was proficient. It wasn't bragging if it was true. Espinosa raised an eyebrow at Tapper, who sat up straight and pulled off his Cardinals baseball cap. "And you are..."

"Gene Terpilowski, sir. Call me Tapper. I don't speak Spanish, but if you need Russian or Farsi, I'm your guy." He put his cap back on.

Espinosa paused his briefing while a dark-haired agent handed out small cups of Cuban coffee. "Thank you. This is Agent Cuervo. He recently finished interviews with Ruby's entourage." .

Blake scowled. "Excuse me, but you just now finished?"

Cuervo sighed. "They insisted on waiting until Chad's attorney arrived. The boyfriend, Chad, is a Major League Baseball player and his contract demands that he has a lawyer present whenever he speaks to law enforcement. Last year two of his teammates were convicted of steroid abuse." He shrugged one shoulder.

That scandal unfolded last year in slow motion through the news over months of investigations and denials and trials. Ruis hoped Chad wasn't a steroid user, because one side effect of performance-enhancing steroids was violent, aggressive behavior.

He made a mental note to watch for aggression if given the chance to view the recorded interviews. Chad wouldn't be in a financial bind thanks to his recent record-breaking contract, so Ruis mentally moved Chad's name to the bottom of his suspect list. Ruis sipped the rich, dark coffee. Chewing coffee beans had this much flavor. It would give him a jolt like adrenaline.

Espinosa continued, "The New York office is analyzing the ransom video. We have contacted authorities in the Bahamas to share customs activity from the US involving boats from Sunday and through the course of our investigation."

"You can eliminate boats over sixty feet long," Ruis said.

"Why is that?" Espinosa asked Ruis.

"The victim was raised in a Navy family. She would have called a larger vessel a *ship* instead of a boat."

Espinosa pointed to a whiteboard on a side wall as he spoke to Cuervo. "Add that to the known facts, please." His accent sounded more Cuban than Mexican or Puerto Rican. A large, proud Cuban population had settled in Miami as if, after escaping Castro's rule, they still longed to live close to their homeland in hope of returning. Generations of Cubans, it seemed, eagerly awaited Castro's death.

Cuervo walked along the perimeter of the room, around long tables where people labored over laptops, until he reached the whiteboard. Meanwhile, Blake, Tapper, and Terri sipped their coffee. Terri closed her eyes and smiled as if the liquid restored a missing part of her.

"Thank you for volunteering. We appreciate the extra manpower; however, I need your complete cooperation to obey our rules and methods at all times. We have established a good working relationship and reputation in the community that must be protected. If you choose to work with us, we'll refer to you as civilian consultants. You will not have the authority to arrest, detain, or in any way act as an agent. Do we understand one another?" His glance at Ruis underscored his message.

All heads nodded.

"Excellent. Agent Cuervo learned from Ruby's entourage that she was last seen at a dance club called Daddy Diego's. We have obtained a warrant for their surveillance recordings. We'll also politely request external surveillance recordings from nearby businesses and residences." Special Agent Espinosa turned to Blake and Terri. "Would you accompany Agent Cuervo to the club?"

Blake and Terri stood.

"Thank you," Espinosa said.

Cuervo led Blake and Terri out of the room. Tapper downed his coffee in two gulps. Ruis sipped his.

"Agent Vincent Gunnerson told me you have a degree in operations research from Annapolis."

Ruis nodded. He was surprised that Vincent chose this information to share with the Miami FBI since most people focused on Navy SEAL experience as a credibility builder. Perhaps Vincent wanted to downplay deadly skills in favor of academics. As long as Ruis could be on the leading edge of the investigation, he would contribute in any way.

Tapper and Espinosa exchanged eye contact.

"What, may I ask, is your association with law enforcement?" Espinosa crossed his arms as if assessing Tapper's usefulness.

"I'm a retired Navy SEAL. I served under Ruis's command. We never lost a man. Now I'm a freelance corporate jet pilot. And I'm rated in helicopters and seaplanes."

"What was your specialty in the SEALs?"

Tapper's expression brightened like a teenager offered his first chance to drive. "Electronics and explosives. I'm also proficient with a handgun."

Espinosa grunted. "Well, what I need is more people on the phones. That red circle"—he pointed to the giant wall map—"is our search area." Centered over Miami, the circle included all of Florida and the Western Bahamas and stopped short of Cuba.

"This assumes the hostage is still on a boat. We're calling the marinas within that range. With each day, the range widens. There are 980 marinas in Florida and 170 in the Bahamas."

Tapper whistled and sat up straighter. "The public image of SEALs is all about the hazardous missions, you know, elbowing through mud and sneaking around at night, but the reality is that, between missions, we do a lot of deskwork. Research, analysis, whatever we're assigned." He put his ball cap back on.

"Then you'll be working in this room." Espinosa introduced Tapper to a woman he identified as Special Agent Maggie Vega.

Ruis believed Maggie was short for Magdalena, a popular Hispanic name. Certain names popular with Catholics implied holiness and as such were tough to bear, like Jesus and Magdalena.

Tapper stood, pulled off his ball cap, and shook the woman's hand. The woman smiled up at him and their eyes locked. His smile transitioned into full charm mode as Maggie asked him to sit. She set up a workstation for him with a phone and a laptop.

Anxious to do something, Ruis stood and checked his phone. Several voicemail messages appeared from Oscar, Nefi, and Vincent. Two agents who were huddled around a laptop groaned. Espinosa's head pivoted toward them and they waved him over. Ruis decided to return the most recent call, the one from Vincent. He watched Espinosa cross the room.

"I'm at the Miami office," Ruis said. "Thanks for putting in a good word for me."

"Turn on the news. Ruby's boyfriend, Chad, is being cornered by the media outside a hotel."

Ruis watched Espinosa scowl at the laptop. Espinosa glanced up at Ruis and waved him over. "Will do." He tucked his laptop case under his arm, skirted the outside edge of the room, and stepped beside Espinosa to see the screen.

A handsome athletic man and three others were backed into a wall at the entrance of an elegant hotel by a horde of reporters pointing cameras and microphones.

"Has Ruby been arrested? Is that why she hasn't been seen since Sunday?" a female reporter demanded as she elbowed other reporters to get closer to Chad.

Espinosa's smooth voice contrasted with the strident voices of the reporters. "Ah, the St. Regis Hotel."

The doorman and three bellmen pushed through the reporters and formed a line of backs to shield their guests from reporters. Two men in dark designer suits approached from the side. One announced that the media must leave because they were trespassing on private property. When none of the reporters moved, the security man pulled out his phone.

The security man on the television pocketed his phone at the same time Espinosa put his phone away.

Bellmen streamed out the front door of the St. Regis and formed a huddle around Chad and his friends that eased along the wall step by step like a rugby team, but with less grunting and wrestling. They moved Chad and his friends through the front door while blocking the media.

Moments later, Espinosa's cell phone rang in his jacket. "I see the news. I'm so sorry." He sighed. "It's an ongoing investigation. The hotel guests are *not* the subjects of it. Yes...yes. I appreciate that. Of course. I'll brief you when we have more information."

The call lasted twenty seconds.

Espinosa pocketed his phone. "The Miami police chief."

Ruis interpreted the speed of the call with familiarity and respect between the FBI and the Miami Police Department. He raised his eyebrows to demonstrate how impressed he was.

Espinosa shrugged. "Tourism is a five-billion-dollar-a-year industry here." He hooked his hand under Ruis's upper arm and led him toward the exit of the conference room. "Let's talk in my office."

After they had settled into cushioned chairs and Espinosa offered more coffee, which Ruis declined, Espinosa interlaced his fingers and set his hands on his lap. "What do you know about south Florida crime?"

Ruis parked his laptop case against the leg of his chair. "My favorite author is Carl Hiaasen."

Espinosa laughed. "That is truly a good start. Hiaasen captures the pathos of life here. From a law-enforcement perspective, let me summarize a bit of our history. During Prohibition, smugglers made a fortune bringing Cuban rum and moonshine by boat up through the Everglades. The area called the Ten Thousand Islands is a maze of shallow channels few can navigate. The Nicaraguans trained their paramilitary forces here. At one time, the KKK had a presence. In the seventies, Colombians brought shiploads of marijuana offshore and the locals ferried the drugs through the swamp in small boats to towns like Everglades City and others along Highway 41."

"Alligator Alley?"

"Alligator Alley is State Highway 84. Another dangerous road. In fact, the west end toll plaza of Alligator Alley was dedicated in honor of a toll taker who was killed by two men on horseback for a handful of coins." Espinosa sighed. "Highway 41 is called the Tamiami Trail. It runs parallel to Alligator Alley farther south."

It sounded like a swampy version of the Wild West to Ruis.

"Highway 41 was popular with drug runners from Miami to Naples. In the eighties, smugglers used seaplanes to drop bales of marijuana offshore for boats to pick up. In the summer of '83, every major law enforcement bureau was involved in a record-breaking raid on towns along this road. Those arrested in the early eighties are now back on the streets. We also have new players—Haitians, Russians mobsters, Korean gangs, various drug cartels, grifters, and human traffickers." Espinosa paused as if to give Ruis time to absorb the information.

"That's a lot of players to consider."

"It is. One factor stands out to me. Kidnapping a celebrity for ransom doesn't fit our usual criminal behavior. None of the usual suspects would risk attracting attention with such a brazen crime.

Celebrities come here because they blend in and feel safe here."

"Wasn't there a fashion designer—"

Espinosa lowered his face. "A rare exception. Gianni Versace was murdered in 1997 by a madman, an outsider to Miami." He cleared his throat and raised his head. "Look, while my people follow leads and conduct interviews, I'd like you to step outside that arena."

"In what way?" Ruis braced for a go-home speech.

"While everyone else is thinking like law enforcement professionals, I'd like you to think like a criminal. If you were planning to kidnap a celebrity using a boat, how would you plan your escape? Where would you go? Why conduct the kidnapping in Miami and the ransom drop in Tampa? I'd like you to examine the larger picture."

Though he was not a trained profiler, Ruis understood logistics and strategy. He nodded. "May I start by watching the recorded interviews?"

"Absolutely."

Ruis picked up his laptop.

"Just so you know, I've directed my people to refer to the victim at all times as Ruby. We want to maintain the impression that we're dealing with a missing celebrity with no mention of kidnapping. We warned Ruby's people to behave as though Ruby has not been kidnapped but is simply missing. We also impressed them with the need to say nothing to anyone about her. Come with me." Espinosa led him through the building to the video analysis area. There he directed him to an empty booth with a large monitor and plain laptop.

Though the special agent in charge might have been benching Ruis to remove him from contact with potential witnesses and suspects, Ruis accepted the assignment. He reminded himself that the investigation, like a mission, was in the first stage of the OODA loop. The OODA loop, developed by military strategist John Boyd, was a decision cycle that began with *observe*. The following stages were *orient, decide*, and *act*. By applying the stages in proper order, soldiers avoided the "ready, fire, aim" scenario.

Whenever fear or doubt crept in, Ruis forcefully shoved them into that metal box in the back of his mind. His mission was to rescue Martina. For the time being, he would focus his energy toward the *observe* stage of the OODA loop to gather facts on the situation—the who, what, when, where, and how. After gaining all that information, he might have insight into the why, but in criminal activity, the criminal's motivation didn't always matter. Sometimes, like Versace's killer, criminals were crazier than rabid jackals.

. 12 .

Amid block after block of vacant warehouses painted with graffiti, Blake wished he had brought a gun.

Agent Cuervo parked the agency-issued black Escalade in front of Daddy Diego's and reminded Blake and Terri to let him do the talking. They were the only people on the street.

Blake climbed out from the back seat into eighty-five-degree heat to open Terri's door. Dressed to blend in with the FBI, he longed for a summer-weight wool suit instead of what he wore from his days working at the New York City office. The windless day promised sweat and lots of it. Already sweating over the awkwardness of being an ex-agent among agents, he wanted to avoid making a fool of himself. "I have a question."

The agent met them on the sidewalk. "Yes?"

"Did I hear that Special Agent Espinosa's first name is 'hooray' or is that a nickname?"

Terri smirked and bit her bottom lip.

What? Didn't anyone else wonder why the man had such an odd name?

Agent Cuervo blinked a few times as if to compose himself. "His name is the Cuban equivalent of George. It's pronounced *whore hay*." He rolled the *r* as any proficient Spanish-speaker would.

"Oooooh. That makes more sense." Blake suddenly understood Terri's smirk. He appreciated that Cuervo answered graciously.

"So let's not mention who we're searching for to the club owner," Cuervo said. "At this point, everyone is a suspect and we need to assume people who work in a nightclub are media savvy. We don't want this crime in the news yet."

Blake and Terri nodded.

The street-facing wall of the building featured brightly colored abstract murals. Blake attempted to discern a theme. To him, the images created dissonance and an aggressive, rebellious feeling, like the artists were trying too hard. Back in his college days, if the music was too loud for conversation and the drinks were cheap, the club became the favorite place for students. The mural seemed the painter's equivalent of loud music. He had made a happy fool of himself at trendy places like this. He'd been a different man then. Now, in his thirties, he didn't mind being out of touch with the college club crowd.

"Welcome to the Wynwood Arts District," Cuervo said. "It's a transitional neighborhood. I hear developers plan to convert the warehouses into galleries and upscale clubs."

Terri's expression practically shouted that the developers were in for a challenge.

"Looks like graffiti to me," Blake said.

"They call it street art." Agent Cuervo shrugged. He marched to the door of the club and tried to open it. It didn't budge, so he balled up a fist and banged on the door.

A voice behind the door sounded, "We open at ten p.m.!"

"We have an appointment," the agent shouted back.

The door squeaked open to reveal a slender, bearded man in his forties. "Feds?"

"I'm FBI Agent Cuervo."

Smiling, the man backed out of sight, leaving the door open. "Cuervo's always welcome here. I'm Diego."

The three entered the dark, spacious club. It smelled of beer and industrial-strength cleaner.

Diego's lanky frame angled in a curve as though the hand on

his hip pushed his middle to one side. His close-cropped hair and beard accentuated his nose and elongated his face. He wore jeans, a white T-shirt, and a dark gray cardigan. "Since when is the FBI interested in electronic dance music?"

"We came to execute a warrant."

Diego eyed Terri and Blake.

"The Claytons," Cuervo said, "are civilian consultants."

Blake was grateful Cuervo hadn't introduced him by his full name since it had been in the national news so recently. He was tired of explaining his trial and the outcome. He didn't think of himself as a criminal, but accusations had a way of forming into labels. People tended to cling to whatever judgment the media promoted before, during, and after the trial.

Diego faced Cuervo. "Is this about the final-call curfew?"

"A girl has gone missing. We hope to determine who she left with."

"A minor?"

"No."

"Well that's some good news."

Cuervo handed the warrant to Diego, who scanned it.

"Surveillance recordings...interior and exterior..." He glanced at the agent. "You know, we get about three hundred people here on a Saturday night, and we're open until five in the morning."

Cuervo nodded.

Diego huffed. "This is gonna take a minute. Have a seat at the bar if you'd like."

Blake and Terri glanced at Cuervo. He nodded and turned toward the owner, who huffed again and led Agent Cuervo out of the cavernous dance hall through a small door.

Blake lifted his face toward a mirror-tiled ball centered in the ceiling of the room. "Is that a disco ball?" The more things changed, the more they stayed the same.

Terri nodded and sat at the bar.

"I'm going to look around." He hiked upstairs to the balcony, imagining the club filled with dancers, strobe lights, and blasting music. The best view of the action came from the balcony tables overlooking the lower dance floor and the band area. This was where a celebrity could see and be seen. He checked under the tables and the entire floor. He returned to the downstairs area to check the bathrooms, both his and hers. Empty-handed, he sat by Terri.

"Why," she whispered, "were you in the women's bathroom?"

"No one mentioned finding her phone or purse. The trash cans are empty."

"I'll ask the manager about the lost-and-found."

"Good thinking."

Terri leaned back in the bar chair. "I wish I'd met you in college,"

"You wouldn't have liked that man. He drank his way through two semesters. Never missed a frat party or dorm mixer. I was that guy who livened up parties. After a few beers, I'd take almost any dare. It's a wonder I survived without permanent liver damage. I *trashed* my reputation." Hanging his head, he was grateful his generation had not been able to record and share their experiences on social media.

Terri bit her lip and turned her face away. Her shoulders shook. Had he made her cry? He pressed a hand on her shoulder to comfort her. She turned toward him and burst into laughter.

"What?" Blake dropped his hand. "Were you a drinker, too?"

Terri shook her head and waved both palms at him. "Sorry. Sorry. Never mind."

"What? You gotta tell me now."

"It just struck me as funny that you think *drinking* would have been a deal breaker for us." She waved her hand between her chest and his.

"Wouldn't it?" Blake had missed something.

She laughed into her hand and leaned in to whisper, "As compared to felony kidnapping?"

Blake shook his head. "It's too soon." Way too soon to joke about his trial and facing the death penalty.

"Sorry." She leaned on his shoulder. One last chuckle escaped. Diego and Cuervo returned.

Having shown his stupid side twice already, he hesitated to ask more questions. Reminding himself that pride was a sin, he stood. "Do you get any famous people here?"

"Sure. When you watch the tapes, you'll see Ruby and Chad. They sat up there." The manager pointed to the center table in the balcony. "I think the ball player is having a good influence on her. The bartender told me Chad tipped extra and asked for nonalcoholic drinks for Ruby. Maybe they're going to have a kid. You never know."

Diego was tossing out a theory, just a theory. Martina wasn't Ruby. Blake wanted to ask more but held back. If the club owner knew who they were searching for, he might notify the media for the publicity. If he was involved, he would notify the kidnappers. Everyone was a suspect. Diego seemed more inconvenienced than upset or scared, but Cuervo was right to withhold the identity of the missing person from the club owner.

Terri appeared at Blake's side. "May I see your lost-and-found?"

Diego turned the warrant over in his hands. He blew a puff of air from his nose and then he stepped behind the bar. He hefted a box onto the counter. "Nope, sorry. This one's from last month." Then he brought up a second, lighter box. "This is this month's stuff."

Terri nudged Blake. "Do you have that phone number?"

Blake texted Ruis for Martina's phone number. Seconds later the number appeared by text message, so Blake called it.

Terri shook the box to search for purses while Cuervo pulled latex gloves from his jacket pocket. The tangle of key chains, jewelry, lipstick, wallets, and scarves did not yield a purse. Terri pointed to the lone cell phone at the bottom of the box. Cuervo snapped on the gloves to retrieve it and turn it on. It looked like a cheap burner phone. It had only two numbers in memory.

"May I take this for examination?" Cuervo asked.

The manager waved. "Sure. If anybody asks for it, I'll give them your number."

"Where is your dumpster?" Blake asked.

Cuervo handed Diego his business card. To Blake and Terri, Cuervo said, "In the alley, but yesterday was trash collection day for the neighborhood."

Blake's heart sank. *A day late.*

Diego stuck his hands in his pants pockets. "I hope you find her."

Blake, Terri, and Cuervo left the club. Later, when they were in the car, Cuervo dropped a handful of labeled jump drives and the cell phone into evidence bags. He twisted in the driver's seat to face Blake. "He also gave us contact information on his employees in case we have questions."

"Was that in the warrant?" Blake asked.

"I mentioned that we might have more questions and we could return during business hours when the staff is gathered. He agreed it would be...disruptive."

Blake sat back smiling. *Nothing like men in suits to spoil the party mood.*

Tuesday was slipping away in sweaty hours. The boat, pushed with each wave and breeze, tugged against the anchor. Once again in the small stateroom, Martina curled under the sheet and quilt of the twin-size bed. In the damp, dark stateroom, the open porthole brought a chilly breeze; closed, it smothered. Her meager meal congealed in her stomach like cement.

I don't want to die.

Black Mask had a quick temper, and Green Mask did what he was told. It was just a matter of time before they learned they'd been fooled. A quick temper and violence were the defining traits of criminals, traits Black Mask had demonstrated. Green Mask had not demonstrated the spine to disagree with his boss. She knew the instant they discovered she wasn't Ruby, they'd kill her. Or worse.

And Black Mask expected a performance. Her dread wasn't stage fright. Her vocal range matched Ruby's. She could sing Ruby's most challenging songs, and there were a few good ones among the otherwise overly repetitive pop tunes. Ruby's hits were easy compared to the arias Martina's high school voice teacher loved. In school, Martina had earned a first-place award at state competition for her solo performance of "Habanera" from the opera *Carmen*. And her vocal power also matched Ruby's thanks to years of competitive cheerleading.

She sounded like Ruby and had earned the winnings at a pub contest once to prove it. That win had led to the stand-in job that subsequently led to being kidnapped. She sighed and pulled the bedding up to her chin. She had no one to blame but herself.

These criminals weren't Ruby's fans. They saw Ruby as a money machine, not as a human, just like Black Mask's demand for a performance wasn't about the music and lyrics. Males were visually stimulated. Black Mask's unspoken demand was to watch Ruby's dance moves.

She couldn't duplicate Ruby's gyrations skillfully. She liked to dance, but the difference between having fun in a crowded, dark dance club and performing solo on stage would be obvious. If they had ever seen the pop star in concert, they would know the real Ruby wasn't on the boat as soon as Martina danced.

To distract herself from the horror of her limited future, she wondered what was happening back in civilization. Who had received the ransom message? That cold agent Mrs. Campbell or maybe Miss Chen? Chen had a soul. She would do something.

Wouldn't she? The talent agents could dismiss the message as a prank, knowing their precious Ruby was safely tucked away in a private rehab facility in Puerto Rico. That would save them six million dollars and protect their lies.

Wiping tears with the back of her hand, Martina sighed heavily. She was on her own.

The men hadn't shown their faces. They'd been careful not to call each another by name. Maybe they just wanted the money. Maybe.

They were keeping her alive for some reason. Were they the brains of this ransom plan or just the muscle? If the talent agents—or Ruby for some reason—decided to pay the ransom, they would demand to speak to "Ruby" to verify she was alive. Certainly, no one would trust kidnappers on their word. But then, people rarely acted logically, and half of the population fell on the not-so-smart side of the IQ bell curve. Placing her fate in the hope that a pop star and her agent would pay a huge ransom *and* that the kidnappers would be honest enough to turn her over for the ransom took more hope than she could muster.

Hope had its place. It kept despair at bay. But it wouldn't save her.

However, she couldn't afford to deny the reality of her situation. Denial wouldn't protect her any more than it protected an ostrich that stuck its head in the dirt.

What would it take to stay alive?

Entertain them.

If she danced like Ruby, well, she would practically be encouraging Black Mask to act on whatever horrible impulse he felt. A shudder ran through her. Nefi and her older sisters had convinced her that being a virgin would spare her from life-long regret, social diseases, and the chance of becoming an unwed mother. They were right, of course, but facing death, Martina wished she had slept with Oscar.

Just once.

She'd been a good Catholic girl and Oscar respected her as much as he loved her. Their discussions about the future, after her graduation, suggested they would spend the rest of their lives together. Her chest pinched. As a child, she used to dream of marrying a handsome prince and living happily ever after. She ached for the life she might have lived with Oscar. He wasn't a prince, but he was handsome, kind, smart, funny, and he loved her.

And to think she'd spent most of her childhood longing to be grown up. As the youngest child in the family, she'd tried to keep up. She had wanted to belong with her older sisters' friends, but they'd dismissed her as too young to go along to the movies, too annoying to take along shopping, and too little to be on their team in whatever game or sport the neighborhood kids played. She'd wanted to be an adult. Now, she was.

Be careful what you wish for. Along with freedoms, adulthood carried with it many boring responsibilities. Like protecting yourself from dangers.

When she closed her eyes, a childhood story tiptoed into her consciousness. Like so many childhood fairy tales, this one was gruesome. She loved it because her mother used to read it to her, a chapter a night, for months. It began with a bitter man named King Shahryar, whose wife was unfaithful, so he put her to death. To prevent being betrayed again, he married a virgin each night and beheaded her in the morning. Then along came the Wazir's daughter, Shahrazad, who told the king a story every night, telling all but the ending. He allowed her to live another night to hear the ending of one story and most of the next story. One night at a time, Shahrazad told a thousand and one stories to the king.

Martina sat up in bed. Shahrazad had survived because she entertained a man who planned to kill her. Martina compared her situation to Shahrazad's. The kidnappers believed she was Ruby, a girl so starved for attention she needed an audience to feel alive. What if she embraced her role as Ruby? She could sing. She could even dance if her life depended on it.

79

As Ruby, she would agree to perform for them and ask to rehearse on the upper deck. From there she would have a better vantage point to plan her escape.

In the story, the king had fallen in love with Shahrazad. The resourceful young woman had prolonged her life and eventually won a pardon from the king. Martina had other plans in her death-defying role as Ruby, the pop singer. She didn't bother hoping for a pardon, because the kidnappers had already proven their hearts' desire by the ransom demand.

. 13 .

Ruis watched the interviews of Chad and the couple who traveled with Chad and Ruby without finding much information of value. Chad had believed Martina was bored and tired and left around midnight by cab to return to the St. Regis. Baseball fans had surrounded him, so he didn't notice her absence at first. When the other couple asked him if she'd gone back to the hotel, he'd gone downstairs to look for her. The house was packed with students on spring break, so navigating through the crowd was tough. When he didn't find her, he had left a message on her cell phone. Chad and his friends believed Martina had gone back to the hotel.

The couple had drunk and danced to maintain the charade they were partying. They'd stayed at the club until three Sunday morning, when Chad had finally dragged them into a cab. On Sunday, Chad had taken a morning workout at the hotel's gym and rented time in a batting cage to stay in shape. The couple had slept until noon, eaten, and then stopped by Ruby's room to invite her to hang out by the pool. They'd become concerned near dinnertime, when she didn't answer her cell phone or the phone in the room.

Chad apologized to FBI Agent Cuervo on the recording. "I wanted to respect her and give her space. She's a smart, funny lady. It was awkward for both of us to pretend to be a couple. You know, she's got a boyfriend, and my mind is on Ruby. Miss Ramos was helping." He shook his head.

His attorney patted him on the back.

"This doesn't feel real," Chad added. "If Ruby had been here, I would have been in the same room with her. I should have stayed closer. Who would do this?" The recording ended when he dropped his face into his hands.

That convinced Ruis he wasn't a suspect. The other couple didn't seem to have the initiative or the need to stage a kidnapping. Their substantial trust funds could keep them comfortably in luxury-vacation mode for life.

Ruis stretched his legs by going to the conference room where the rest of the investigators worked. Tapper looked up from a huddle with Cuervo and Espinosa. He beckoned Ruis with a wave of the hand.

Blake's scowl gave Ruis pause. He braced for bad news while Tapper pulled out a chair in front of a laptop.

"This is from the club."

Ruis sat to watch a segment of grainy images occasionally lit up by colored strobe lights. Two men wearing sunglasses approached a third man while they held up an unconscious girl in a snug red dress. The third man nodded and pointed to the left. The two men carried the woman with her arms draped over their shoulders toward a doorway. The third man walked close behind as if to shield her from view. The door opened, and the two men disappeared with the woman. When the man shut the door and turned around, the camera captured his face.

Blake clicked pause on the laptop.

Tamping down his emotion, Ruis took deep breaths. These men had taken Martina.

"That's the club owner we met this morning." Blake glowed red.

"Bring him in," Espinosa said to Cuervo. He pointed at Blake. "You stay."

Tapper nudged Blake aside, then he pulled up another grainy recording of an older-model beige van from the side. Taken from a high angle looking down, it showed a man wearing sunglasses, looking out the window. "We couldn't get the plates."

Espinosa planted a warm hand on Ruis's shoulder. "We're checking traffic cameras for the vehicle."

Ruis nodded. It was the only reaction he trusted at the moment.

Espinosa's cell phone vibrated in his pocket. He answered and then put the phone on speaker mode. "Go ahead, Agent Gunnerson."

"Our technician said the ransom video was taken in the stateroom of a thirty-seven-foot Nordic Tug." Vincent's voice sounded calm and clear. "It's a pleasure trawler. We're comparing boats associated with known criminals, but the top speed of this model is fourteen knots. Not exactly a great getaway boat."

This information fit Ruis's model for how he'd plan a kidnapping. "It's perfect for blending in."

"I'll send you the boat's specifications."

"Thank you," Espinosa then switched the phone off speaker mode and briefed Vincent on the local findings before ending the call. He strode toward his office.

Nearby, Terri wore a headset and speaker while she checked off another marina on her list. Blake patted Ruis on the back on his way to his workstation and list.

Tapper elbowed Ruis. "You okay?"

Ruis shrugged.

Tapper leaned in close. "So," he whispered, "your sister's a pop star?"

"She was working as a body double for a pop star."

Tapper's eyes widened. "Who's on the ransom recording?"

"Martina."

"Soooo Martina looks like Ruby."

Ruis pulled out his cell phone and accessed an online video.

Handing the phone to Tapper, he added, "She can sing like her, too. She sang this in a London pub and won a contest."

Tapper watched the recording to the end. "Wow. Your baby sister—"

"Choose your next words carefully." Ruis cracked his knuckles.

Tapper winced. "Has a great voice."

"You're ahead. Quit." Ruis pivoted and strode from the conference room. Shaking off the sound of his sister singing, he focused on gathering information about trawlers. He scrolled through his contact list for a while. Searching was a waste of precious time. Pulling himself together, he called his father, Retired Admiral Ramos. After a brief chat about recreational trawlers, his father referred him to Cousin Rosalie, who lived on one. He found her number on his phone and called.

They shared catch-up talk about the family before he asked about Nordic Tugs. Rosalie enthusiastically explained how much she loved the simple life with her husband and dog, looping the eastern states.

"Looping?"

"Yep." Her laugh reminded him of summers on the lake and learning how to sail. She was known to fall out or get sick on every outing. She used to laugh just as hard when she fell out as when she swept Ruis off the Sunfish with the boom. His cousin had the worst boating skills of the twenty-five cousins. "We're Loopers. Nine years now."

"What does that mean?"

"Every year we cruise six thousand miles around the eastern states by going up the Atlantic coast in the spring, through the Hudson River into the Great Lakes, and down through the Illinois River. We follow the inland river system and end up in Mobile, Alabama. We caravan across the Gulf of Mexico, then we cruise the coastline of Florida all winter and then do it all again. It's called the Great Loop."

"You do this every year?"

"Absolutely. We're a big, happy organization. Member boats are marked with a burgee. White for first-year loopers and gold for veterans."

He was impressed she knew the proper term for the small flag. "I've never heard of Loopers before."

"Okay, it's funny that I know something about boating you don't. Pardon me while I gloat. We have a newsletter, blogs, radio programs; you name it. Add in the harbor hosts and part-timers and I'd guess we have around five hundred members." A dog barked in the background. "Look us up under the America's Great Loop Cruisers' Association."

"Why are you living on a boat?"

She chuckled. "I know, me of all people, right? We wanted to downsize and travel. Our big house became a chore to maintain. This boat's roomy. It drafts under five feet, so we can cruise shallow waterways, and like me, it's built sturdy to weather the storms. You and Sofia are welcome to join us. We're going to be near Annapolis next month." She mentioned Annapolis in a singsong way, reminding him of childhood.

"I'll talk about it with Sofia. Thanks for the intel. I have to get back to work."

"Aye, aye, cousin!"

Ruis dashed to his laptop to read about the AGLCA. Under *Contact,* he found the name and number of the director and added it to his phone. Next, he researched the schematics for the layout of the Nordic Tug 37 in case he had to board it.

His phone vibrated in his hand. A text message from Blake invited Ruis to watch the club owner's interview, so Ruis met Blake in the hallway. Blake held two cups of Cuban coffee. He offered one to Ruis.

"This stuff should be listed as a Schedule II controlled substance," Blake said.

Ruis suspected they might become addicted to it. He accepted the cup and followed Blake into the viewing area. The owner of

Daddy Diego's Dance Club and his lawyer sat across a table from Agent Cuervo and another agent on the other side of a large one-way mirror.

"When we talked earlier," Cuervo said, "we told you we were searching for a missing woman."

Diego nodded. His lawyer rested his forearms on the table.

"We were specifically trying to determine who she left with. Could you help us identify the people in this surveillance recording?"

"If I can, sure."

Cuervo opened a laptop and pulled up the section of surveillance recording. "Here it is." He turned the laptop toward Diego and the attorney and played the recording. It showed Diego interacting with two men in sunglasses holding up an unconscious woman.

From the viewing area, Ruis watched the club owner carefully for his reaction.

After the recording segment ended, Cuervo gently closed the laptop while he stared at the club owner.

Diego backed away from the table as far as his chair allowed. "She's missing?"

Cuervo nodded.

Diego spread his hands palm out to Cuervo. It was the universal gesture for stop. He opened his mouth, but his attorney pulled down one of his raised hands as if to remind his client he was there. Diego turned to his legal counsel and whispered in his ear. After a nod from the attorney, Diego again displayed the stop gesture, and then he put his hands together. "Look, she's a celebrity, and those guys were her bodyguards. She—"

"Earlier you told us that her boyfriend tipped extra for the bartender to serve her nonalcoholic drinks, so how do you explain her unconscious appearance?"

At this, the lawyer seemed interested in the answer.

"Yeah, well, I heard a rumor from one of the staffers that

someone upstairs might have been sharing Xanax. Of course, I went up to look around, but everyone knows me, so it's not like they're going to use it in front of me."

"Were these bodyguards with her all evening?"

Diego blinked rapidly and took a deep breath. "I don't know. The club was packed. They could have been there. Ruby and her friends were upstairs. I can't see up there while I'm working the dance floor."

Cuervo folded his hands on the table. "Ruby's agent, Chad, and the couple with Chad last Saturday have confirmed there were no bodyguards assigned to them. The recording shows you helping two men carry her unconscious from your club, so naturally—"

Diego sucked in air. "They said they were her bodyguards. They looked like bodyguards. They told me they wanted to get her out, so her fans wouldn't see her like that. It seemed legit." His eyes darted from Cuervo to his lawyer. "I thought I was helping her." His voice faded.

"My client will fully cooperate in any way he can," the attorney said.

"Describe them," Cuervo said.

Diego nodded vigorously. "They were in their early thirties, a little old for the club. One was taller than me with broad shoulders like a bodybuilder; the other looked...softer, out of shape. The bodybuilder had a strong accent. Eastern European, maybe. They took the service exit to the alley. They said they had a limo waiting."

"Did you see the vehicle?"

Diego shook his head. Color drained from his face. "Poor Ruby."

"We have a sketch artist—"

"Yes! Yes. I'll be glad to..." He blew out a breath into his fist.

"I expect you to keep everything about this situation secret for the sake of the kidnap victim. If we ever had to show that video in court—"

"Of course, of course." Diego and his lawyer nodded vigorously.

In the observation room, Ruis finished his coffee and sighed.

"A limo in that neighborhood would need a bodyguard." Blake snorted and left the observation room.

Ruis nodded. Diego wouldn't be much help. Eyewitnesses were the weakest link in a case. In the dark, noisy environment with flashing lights and crowds, faces blurred together. People in crowds tended to share an expectation bias—they saw what they expected to see. This also meant they ignored things out of the ordinary.

The club owner appeared genuinely distressed by the kidnapping. Ruis couldn't discern if the man's reaction was triggered by his concern for Ruby or the potential harm her kidnapping would have on his club. Owning a small business required Diego's full dedication of his time and money and he seemed proud of his club. Ruis believed the man meant to help.

The road to hell, the saying went, was paved with good intentions. Diego's intention to help added another brick in the road.

. 14 .

Green Mask let Martina out of her room for food and bottled water. In the salon, Black Mask opened and closed storage spaces above and below the counter methodically from the stern, past the sink and the tiny stovetop, toward the center of the boat. Inside a space below the counter next to a tiny refrigerator, he pulled out a handle of vodka.

Martina sat and folded her hands on the end of the table.

Black Mask elbowed the other man out of his way to the cabinet over the stove. There he nabbed a small glass. With the bottle in one hand and glass in the other, he parked himself at the table near the open stern door. "Get me a beer."

Afraid he meant for her to do it, Martina nervously glanced at the dorm-size refrigerator and freezer that flanked the galley counter. Did he keep his beer ice-cold or refrigerator-cold?

Green Mask grunted, retrieved a can of Natural Ice beer from the one by the stairs, and plunked the can on the table beside the vodka.

Smiling, Black Mask filled his tumbler with vodka then popped open the beer.

Who drinks straight vodka with cheap beer? Martina's stomach roiled at the combination. In high school, they had nicknamed Natural Ice "Natty." It was the cheapest beer of all, therefore, the most popular with the let's-get-drunk crowd. Having tried beer once, she'd decided once was enough. It tasted like watered-down champagne and it was loaded with calories.

Green Mask searched the galley until he found three plates and a box of wheat crackers.

The fact that neither of them knew where things were kept signaled that this wasn't their boat. If rented, it must have cost a bundle, because it appeared well-maintained and stocked except for the dinghy. Borrowing a boat made more sense because a rental would leave a paper trail. Surely, one of them would have been required to provide identification to rent a boat of this value. Anyone who watched cop shows knew that.

Black Mask lined up his glass with his mask's mouth hole, downed the vodka in one gulp, and chased it with a swig of beer. Green mask set two plates of boiled eggs and crackers on the table, one in front of his vodka-chugging comrade and the other in front of Martina. It showed stunningly poor manners to serve men before women, but then, why expect civility from criminals?

When Green Mask returned to the counter for the third plate of food, Martina assumed the role of Ruby, choosing words suitable for a pop star. "I'm sorry about being difficult earlier. I've chosen a song I can perform without the band or lights or backup dancers." She gave a dramatic sigh to emphasize the inconvenience. "I'd like to rehearse on the...open area upstairs." She pointed up.

"It's called the deck," Green Mask said.

Black Mask rolled his eyes.

Martina shrugged. "Whatever. The deck is the closest thing to a stage here."

Black Mask poured himself another serving of vodka. "Good." He followed the vodka with a few gulps of beer and set the sweating can gently on the table.

Movement caught her attention, so she looked up at Green Mask, who stood at the table staring at his colleague. After a small shake of his head, he set a plate of boiled eggs and crackers and a bottle of water on the table for himself.

Suppressing her own reaction to the man's drink combo, she said, "I'm used to singing at concerts, you know, when it's dark and I can't see the audience. It helps me avoid stage fright. It gets nerve-racking to know twenty thousand people paid eighty dollars a ticket or more to see you. You can almost feel them daring you to make it worth their money, you know?"

Holding his glass, Black Mask pointed at her. "You will wear the little dress and the shoes." His eyes darkened.

Though it made her insides cringe, she said, "If that's what you want. It's your show."

Black Mask banged his glass on the table. "You hear that? It's my show." He laughed until he coughed.

Green Mask's eyelids closed. Was he trying to hide eye rolling? Perhaps he didn't appreciate that his pal claimed the performance for himself or he didn't think the situation was as laughable as Black Mask treated it. His expression was tough to read through holes in his mask.

After the quickest of prayers, she dug into her eggs and crackers. If she had to guess, she would have placed Green Mask near her own age and Black Mask older by five to ten years. Black Mask was bossy, but he didn't impress her as the planning type. Brute force suited him more than intelligence. Green Mask seemed too young and timid to set up a celebrity kidnapping. That left the possibility of a third criminal, someone elsewhere to manage everything.

How far did they have to go to reach Tampa and how long would it take at trawler speed? Tuesday was slipping away.

She twisted the top off her bottled water and set it on the table. They ran the generator twice a day, which was just enough to keep the batteries charged. Were they too low on diesel to run the air-conditioning? She wished she had paid more attention to Daddy's lessons on the AC and DC systems of the boats they rented every summer. This boat had two breaker panels, one on each side of the top of the stairs in the pilothouse. So many switches. She sighed.

Three days to go until the ransom. Just enough time to worry about being exposed as a fraud. Not enough time to be the rest of her life. *Think! Think!*

Maybe they weren't going to Tampa by Friday. What if they planned to stay here while someone else picked up the ransom? Once they had the money, they didn't have to release her. Clearly, they valued the money more than her life. Money was the only thing they seemed to value, because they didn't act as familiar as brothers would be. They didn't even act like friends. If blood money was all that tied them together, then such a tenuous connection as greed deserved to be used against them.

"What are you going to do with the money?" she said in the most casual tone she could manage.

Black Mask leaned back, tucking a throw pillow behind his neck. "Whatever I want. Money is freedom."

Martina considered pointing out the irony of his statement but thought better of it. She turned toward Green Mask. "What are you going to do with your share?"

"I'll buy a boat."

Black Mask laughed. "You might as well throw your money to the wind."

Green Mask crossed his arms. "You spend your money. I'll spend mine."

Black Mask took a swig of vodka and chased it with a gulp of beer.

She aimed to drive a wedge deeper between them. Money was the wedge. Distrust was the hammer. She sipped her water and waited for conversation to resume.

Black Mask addressed Martina. "He thinks a boat will bring him happiness. A boat!"

"If you two believe money can buy happiness, you're going to be disappointed."

"Says the rich girl," Black Mask said. "You take money for granted."

Few singers maintained as many bookings a year as Ruby. "I work for my money."

Black Mask puckered his lips through the hole in his mask to suck vodka from his glass. "Ha! We work for your money, too."

Green Mask laughed.

She had to redirect the conversation. Drawing from years of reading tabloids, she dredged up a tidbit of universal truth Ruby might say. "Once you have it, you'll understand that everyone feels entitled to take it from you."

Green Mask nodded. "Her manager stole millions from her."

Oh, great. He read the tabloids, too. She tried to hammer home the wedge. "Go ahead and say it. I was an idiot to trust a greedy man."

Black Mask shifted his weight and tugged down on his mask to take a swig of beer.

She wanted him to stew on distrust, so she stopped talking and finished her food. Fools put their trust in wealth. Green Mask and Black Mask clearly valued money more than they valued much else. Her priest, quoting 1 Timothy 6:10, compared the love of money to idol worship. Certainly, many people behaved as if winning the lottery would deliver a happily-ever-after life, shielding them from problems. Martina knew that money didn't protect people from tragedy. Nefi's uncle was a US senator and owned a huge farm in the south. Money had not protected him from his son's suicide.

Money, in fact, invited scam artists, thieves, and kidnappers into the lives of the wealthy. Like Ruby.

"And what did you learn from your mistake with your manager?" Black Mask poured more vodka in his glass.

"The love of money is the root of all kinds of evil."

Black Mask clucked his tongue. "You charge eighty dollars a ticket when you could sing for free? Ha! You love money, too."

"I earn money. I don't love it. There's a big difference."

"You tell yourself that."

Green Mask leaned back in his chair. "Why are you talking to us?"

"Who else am I supposed to talk to?" She was about to confess that she wasn't accustomed to being alone after growing up in a large family, then she remembered that Ruby was an only child. Maybe loneliness caused Ruby to surround herself with the constant entourage. Or maybe the entourage came with the job.

Black Mask grunted.

The way the men stared at her made her feel pathetic and stupid. "Fine. You don't have to talk to me. I'll go rehearse."

Ruby was used to being waited on, so she would expect others to clean up. Resisting a childhood of training, she left her plate and water bottle on the table. She headed toward the stern doorway, where Black Mask grabbed her thigh, stopping her mid-step. Her body tightened in shock.

He squeezed her thigh muscles.

Fearing he might be comparing her legs to Ruby's, she kept her leg muscles taut.

"Break a leg," he said, releasing her thigh. His laugh haunted her all the way up the ladder to the upper deck.

The white fiberglass surface warmed her feet while she visualized wiping her leg with hand sanitizer. The idea of spending more days in captivity made her shudder.

Green Mask climbed up the ladder. He carried a liter of Mountain Dew and a large bag of Cheetos under one arm.

She waited for him to climb to the flybridge, which offered the only shade outside the boat. Was he a fan of Ruby's or just bored in the middle of nowhere with no Wi-Fi, no television, and no internet? He settled into the cushioned corner of the flybridge overlooking the deck. Behind him, on a plastic hanger, the red dress flapped and undulated in the breeze.

Ignore the dress. Ignore the man in the Green Mask.

With her bare feet planted in the middle of the open deck, she started humming the Ruby tune she'd performed a year ago on a dare to win two thousand euros. The win had made her a minor celebrity at Oxford because it wasn't a lip-sync karaoke contest. Fortunately for her, the contest had been about the music, not the dancing. Drawing on memory of a concert recording, she stomped one foot to mark the tempo, then she paced through the choreography in a subdued way. She certainly wasn't about to do the hip thrusts or other vamp moves with Green Mask leering at her from the shade of the flybridge.

As she hummed, the lyrics rang through her mind. What had felt daring and fun in the company of classmates in a pub felt awkward and scary on a boat with kidnappers. With her feet and arms in motion, she scanned the swamp for the nearest island. She longed to dive off the deck and swim for her life. One problem was that the boat was anchored three football field lengths from the nearest mangrove-covered sandbar. Though she was a fast swimmer, the kidnappers could launch the dinghy to intercept her before she reached the mangroves. The murky water could contain sharks, alligators, crocodiles, barracudas, or snakes. Any of those predators could cross the distance faster than she could.

The most looming problem was location. How far away was civilization? And which direction should she go if she survived the swim?

The western sky blackened, and the wind picked up. To the southwest, through a small channel between the mangroves, sunlight illuminated high waves. Deeper water!

It could be the Gulf of Mexico if they were within cruising distance to Tampa. Or it could be the Atlantic Ocean. Whichever it was, there had to be more boat traffic out there than in this isolated cove. The island on the east side of the channel seemed to be the closest to the deep water. Rollers lifted the boat, causing her to pause to maintain footing. Sweat rolled down her back. In her excitement, she lost her place in the song and had to start over. Humming louder, she paced out her movements, concentrating on the lyrics.

A gust nudged her. She kept her balance and continued. The lyrics scrolled along through her mind as she practiced the song a second and third time.

The gusts grew stronger, so she looked upwind to the west.

A wall of rain fell from a high, charcoal-gray cloud front. Father had taught her survival knowledge about weather. He'd told her lightning could strike from five miles away. He'd also taught her a trick. Since light traveled faster than sound, she could measure her distance from a thunderstorm by the number of seconds between the flash of lightning and the sound of thunder. Every five seconds between them counted as a mile.

To the north, south, and east, it was all blue skies with sunshine. Thanks to the wind, the wall of water advanced ahead of the clouds. A full rainbow formed in the sunshine. Droplets splattered on the deck as if from a clear blue sky above her. The sun shower was a strange and beautiful sight. Had she been anywhere else, she would have pulled out her cell phone to share it on social media.

The rainbow curved from high in the western sky on her right to end at the mangrove island on the east side of the channel, the one she believed was closest to the deep water. Her friend Nefi believed in signs from God. Was this a sign?

A deafening crack of lightning lit up the sky.

Jolted from her reverie, she realized the storm was less than a mile away. Deadly close. Raindrops pelted the water so hard their impact looked like rain popped up from the surface. She dashed aft toward the ladder. Wind shoved the boat like a weathervane, turning it on the axis of the anchor chain.

Green Mask lurched from his chair and barked a word in Russian. His intonation and body language indicated he was upset. His liter of soda tipped and emptied itself onto the flybridge deck. Gripping the bag of Cheetos, he took a few steps, stopped, pivoted, and hopped back to yank the dress off the hanger. After backing down the stairs from the flybridge to the upper deck one-handed, he cowered as the rain fell. His sneakers squeaked and skidded on deck. He pushed the dress against her, effectively shoving her out of his path to the ladder.

"Rehearsal is over."

She slung the dress over her shoulder as cold drops peppered her and the deck.

When the hull bumped into something, the boat lurched, then freed itself. Peering over the side, she noticed leaves floating quickly alongside the hull. For a moment, while she held one hand on the railing, she dared herself to climb over and dive. A shaft of light bore through the murky water to reveal clam shells and seagrass in what looked like eight feet of water. If she had dived from this deck, she would have broken her neck.

Green Mask slipped from the ladder and landed with a thud.

Recognizing the singular sound of a body falling on a deck, she rushed down to help. Her reaction came from years of boating and seeing cousins and sisters get injured or fall overboard. She grabbed the railing with one hand and Green Mask's arm with the other to pull him off the slick, Cheeto-littered deck.

"Get away!" he hissed as if he didn't want Black Mask to hear.

She stepped back. Fine. Let him get himself up off the wet deck. She turned toward the door and spotted Black Mask seated at the far end of the salon bench slowly shaking his head and scowling at the man sprawled on the floor. A second beer can sat on the table beside the empty vodka glass. Small wonder Black Mask wasn't eating much since he was consuming so many calories in alcohol.

Martina marched into the salon and tossed the dress on the table.

After much grunting and sliding around, Green Mask struggled to his feet. The spattering of droplets changed into a pounding waterfall punctuated by lightning and thunder.

Green Mask limped into the salon and slammed the door against the rain. He glared at Martina as if he blamed her for his fall. Water dripped off him. A few stray Cheetos stuck to his clothes.

She glared back. She blamed gluttony for his fall and pride for refusing her help.

Green Mask slumped onto the opposite end of the bench from the other man. There, he examined his swelling ankle. His pain gave Martina a fleeting moment of joy. Sure, it was petty to enjoy another person's pain, but she felt justified to despise criminals. Was the ankle merely sprained or broken? His disability would be her tactical advantage.

"Put her in the engine room." Black Mask's words came out slowly and slurred. He rose from the bench and leaned on the counter by the sink.

"I can put her back in the—"

Black Mask slammed both fists on the counter. He turned around and braced himself against the counter. "Don't argue. I'm sick of your screw-ups." The cloth under his nose puffed when he panted. He scratched his face through his ski mask.

Martina hoped he was allergic to his mask. It looked like wool.

Green Mask eased his sore foot to the floor. Limping, he shoved Martina repeatedly across the salon, up the stairs to the helm, and against the chart table. He then bent over, grunting, and flung the rug off the hatch. Next, he pulled the handle and swung the hatch open.

Green Mask's hands curled into fists as he stood rigidly straight by the helm.

Martina hurried down the step into the engine hold. The hatch slammed. Maybe, just maybe, Green Mask was tired of being pushed around by Black Mask. She hoped for more advantages, like Green Mask's injury and Black Mask's drinking. Better they focus their frustrations at each other than at her. Let them fight. Let them question whether or not to trust one another. She had done what she could to sow discord and to drive the wedge of greed between them deeper.

With the engines and generator off, the hold smelled more like saltwater than diesel. As her eyes adjusted to the sweltering darkness, a faint line of light appeared along the edges of the hull. Upon inspection, she found light coming through air vents. Above, footfalls thumped up the stairs to the pilothouse and down the stairs toward the bow, and then a door slammed.

I should have escaped in the storm.

Retching sounds came from above. Black Mask liked vodka too much, apparently. She smirked, glad that he, too, was suffering for a change. She was sick of being scared, sick of being captive in the middle of nowhere, and sick of being a victim. Nefi would have crippled Black Mask the moment after he grabbed her leg. Ruis would never put up with this. By now, Ruis would be driving the boat with both kidnappers roped like deer to the bow railing.

Nefi and Ruis were right. The world really was a dangerous place. They accepted danger as the norm. Nefi dealt with danger by learning defensive skills, like hand-to-hand combat and using knives and guns. Ruis *was* a weapon. They had a different perspective on things because they had been through life-threatening situations. To their credit, Ruis and Nefi had tried to teach her survival thinking.

Nefi had tried. She'd even dragged her into judo and karate classes. After fracturing her wrist, Martina had bailed out of further lessons.

Ruis had tried. After a student at Northern Illinois University had shot people in a lecture hall, Ruis had a serious talk with his sisters, instructing them to think outside of their "normalcy bias" during an emergency. To survive, he'd said, you had to stop being polite and kind and modest. He talked about kicking through drywall and using furniture to barricade windows and doors and using everyday items as weapons. Everyday objects could become a weapon or a shield. A shooter couldn't shoot while dodging chairs and books.

Why didn't I escape when I had the chance?

In the silence that followed, the answer rose into her consciousness.

Because Ruis will rescue me.

From her earliest memories, her brother and sisters had protected her. They'd taken scissors from her when she ran. They'd picked her up when she fell. Between her stubbornness and her desire to keep pace with her older brother and her sisters, she'd fallen often. Ruis especially played the role of guardian angel. He was a shadow who prayed over her in her half-asleep state. His was the shadow who'd passed over her and pulled her from the deep end of the neighbor's pool after she fell in. His shadow had appeared at the back of the hall at graduation.

This time, Ruis wasn't around to save her. He had a job protecting other people.

She scanned the engine hold. It was time to think like Ruis. What would he do? She had learned a few things about boats during summer vacations with the cousins. She crawled around the equipment, assessing each piece's purpose and operation. This was a water-cooled system, so shutting the sea valves would overheat the engine. Eventually. Disabling the bilge pump could sink the boat, but this was not a smart move considering she was stuck in the hold. What could be done to strand her captors in the middle of nowhere? Then they would have to be rescued. They couldn't row the dinghy far, though she longed to witness an attempt.

Whatever she could do had to be done before nightfall. The ambient light from the air vents along the hull was fading. Exploring the hold, she braced herself on equipment while storm waves rocked the boat.

A small canvas object was stuffed between the hull and the blackwater tank. She reached through the narrow gap and pinched the edge of it. Thunder roared over the continuous rush of rain, muffling the clank of metal on metal from the bag. She pulled it into her lap. Wrenches, pliers, and screwdrivers packed the inside space. She squeezed the tool kit to her chest.

She believed it was a sign to sabotage the boat. Whether she escaped or not, her kidnappers wouldn't be driving this boat home.

She didn't want to sink the ship because they might leave her in the engine hold, so she searched for a way to disable the boat. The circuit breaker boxes were near the pilothouse for easy access. The engine was situated in the center of the hold. Its white steel casing revealed the shape of the cylinders. She considered removing the casing to pry out the sparkplugs. How many screws and bolts would it take to reach the sparkplugs? If just one screw was tightened by machine or a strong man, she might not be strong enough to loosen it. Systematically identifying the major pieces of equipment from memories of Daddy's summer boating lessons, she ruled out the engine, the propeller shaft, the AC generator, the HVAC control panel, the air conditioning compressors, and the raw water pump. Messing with the diesel tank or hoses could kill her or create a fire hazard. Of the many ways to die, she feared fire most of all.

I'm not a mechanic.

She had proven that as a fact the Christmas Nefi introduced her to Oscar. Her sister's car had failed to start, so the men gathered around to check under the hood. To be near Oscar, Martina had leaned in as well. He'd smiled and asked what she knew about engines.

She'd pointed. "It's right there."

After the men had stopped laughing, Oscar whispered in her ear, "I'll show you if you want to learn."

That moment of intimacy, with his lips so close to her ear, had felt like internal combustion. She adored him for offering. If only she had taken the time.

If only.

Disheartened, she sat on the metal platform at the base of the ladder and prayed to the only one who always knew where she was. At the end of her prayer, looking heavenward, she opened her eyes to something she had not noticed earlier.

Near the ladder, a cream-colored box was attached to the underside of the ceiling. It was the size of a lunch box, with pencil-thick white and black cables running from its side up into the ceiling toward the starboard side of the boat at midship. What did this connect to? What kind of equipment was above? She stood on the platform to see what it was.

A manufacturer's label read MicroCommander and listed its part and serial number. Below that were words that captured Martina's attention: *Power 12 or 24 volts DC 160 Watts Max.* A thin, clear plastic label declared *ignition protected.*

Oooo. Electrical. This looks important.

The hatch directly above was in the middle of the ship. By the helm! No electricity to the helm, no ignition. No ignition meant no powering up the engines. Normally, she avoided electric panels of any kind, but knowing that the DC system and the engine were off, she felt emboldened. She removed the screws that held the top of the box to the bottom cover, stuffing the screws one by one in her pants pocket. Inside, colored wires disappeared into plastic pieces that reminded her of LEGOs. Two rows of the wires and blocks framed a green circuit board. Wires from the panel fed into holes at the bottom that corresponded with thicker cables outside the box.

She pried out the bottom two LEGO-like pieces and tucked them between the walls of the box and longer gray pieces. At a glance, the disconnected pieces looked plugged in. Then she noticed a yellow wire and a red one screwed down beside the words *start interlock.*

Footfalls thumped above. She held her breath and stowed the tool kit under the platform at the bottom of the ladder. Her skin tingled as if her blood rushed to hide in her heart. A scraping noise followed. The hatch flung open. Martina froze. Something dropped past her, bounced on the floor of the engine room, and rolled to a stop. The hatch closed.

A water bottle rested near her foot. Martina exhaled.

Green Mask's muffled voice called out, "She can't get out. I'm sitting on the hatch."

After more retching sounds, the toilet flushed. Black Mask groaned. It could have been the combination of alcohol and rough waves that made him ill, because Green Mask wasn't puking his guts out.

She retrieved the tool kit. Using the narrowest Phillips head screwdriver in the kit, she unscrewed the red and yellow wire tabs and tucked them behind a row of wires that curved behind the circuit board. She reattached the panel cover.

Holding the screwdriver, she asked herself if she had the courage to stab a person with it.

I'm not Nefi.

Besides, the person she wanted to stab had a Taser. After a deep sigh, she hid the tool kit where she had found it.

Her heart rate returned to normal while she drank the water and curled up on the floor. Shadows spread until they engulfed the engine room. To comfort herself, she hummed a song Nefi had sent her, one she kept on her phone. A pang of loss struck her as the lyrics scrolled along her mind. This wasn't one of Ruby's songs. Her mental replay of the song ended, leaving her cold, alone, and once again assessing her mortality.

. 15 .

By late afternoon, Ruis fought a restlessness he couldn't reason away or suppress. His attention wavered while Espinosa stood near the large map in the conference center listening to the last of the status updates. The chief of police, a DEA representative, and a Coast Guard officer stood at the back of the room. The agent assigned to calling Bahamian authorities announced that five Nordic Tugs had passed through customs since Saturday and were searched. None of the people aboard fit the descriptions of the two men from the club or Ruby. Tapper reported on the eighty-five marinas he'd called.

The police chief announced that three torched vehicles found over the weekend did not match the make and model of the suspect's beige van. He mentioned that if the suspects used a toll pass, their movements would be tracked by the state's toll pass system, "all seven hundred and twenty miles of it." All that was needed were the suspects' names or the license numbers of any vehicles registered on the toll pass. He concluded by promising his department would continue to check abandoned vans towed by the city.

While the chief spoke, Ruis checked his phone. More messages from Nefi, Oscar, and Sofia appeared. There were none from Vincent. Hearing his name, Ruis looked up. It was his turn.

"The use of a Nordic Tug suggests the kidnappers want to blend in." Ruis projected his voice to the back of the room. "At top speed, this boat moves fourteen knots an hour. Cruising speed runs closer to eight and a half knots. Provided they kept moving, stopping only to refuel, they could have traveled five hundred to one thousand nautical miles. Trawlers tend to hug the shoreline and travel in daytime, so it would attract attention to cruise at high speed or at night. A large group of boaters known as Loopers migrate up the eastern coast in the spring to make a loop through waterways, lakes, and rivers around the eastern states back to the gulf. The group is known as the AGLCA, for America's Great Loop Cruisers' Association. Their director says they're mostly retirees. They have a reputation for being social, so someone who didn't socialize might draw attention." Ruis's phone vibrated in his hand. "I believe it would be a smart strategy for the kidnappers to find a low-traffic marina or a private dock to wait for the ransom. We have lockmasters and bridgemasters on the lookout for thirty-seven-foot Nordic Tugs just in case the boat takes an inner passage."

There was a shortcut across the state. An inner passage of canals and locks ran from Stuart to Ft. Meyers, passing through the 730-square-mile Lake Okeechobee. If the kidnappers were experienced sailors, they could blend in with pleasure boaters. The downside of using this route was that the kidnappers would be forced to communicate with the lockmasters and bridgemasters through this slow-moving shortcut. An accident or incident along this path would be logged and draw attention to them even if they were struck by a careless boater.

Sometimes little things could become big things. Like when Oklahoma State Trooper Charlie Hanger had stopped a car to ticket the driver for not having a tag and then noticed the driver's gun and arrested him. The driver was Timothy McVeigh, leaving Oklahoma City after setting off a bomb that killed 168 people, including nineteen children.

Ruis pointed to the map. "How long would it take to travel through this inner passage?"

"It would take six or seven days," answered a voice in the room.

"Then they probably wouldn't risk it." Ruis held his hand toward the wall map. "The blue dots mark low-traffic and closed marinas within the trawler's estimated travel radius. Marinas with a record of criminal activity are marked in red."

A high concentration of red dots spread through the Everglades, the Keys, and Miami, providing many places for the kidnappers to refuel or dock where no one asked questions. It was common knowledge among criminals that the coastal path from Miami to Tampa offered too many criminal sanctuaries for authorities to search.

At this point in the briefing, Espinosa took over. "The ransom drop is in Tampa on Friday, so we are coordinating with Tampa Police, Coast Guard, and harbor authorities on that end. They have undercover officers looking for Nordic Tugs."

Ruis's phone vibrated again, this time a call from Oscar.

"Any questions?" Espinosa said. "Thank you. This concludes the briefing."

Since it was nearing five o'clock, many agents shut down their laptops and cleared their workspaces of coffee cups, pizza boxes, and wadded papers. Multiple conversations ensued while Espinosa crossed the room to confer with people from the outside agencies.

Ruis strode to the corridor to return Oscar's call.

"What is going on? Tell me the truth," Oscar said.

"About what?"

"I just called Martina and a guy answered. He said he found the phone and I could have it if I paid a reward."

Ruis's heart skipped a beat. "What did you tell him?"

"I asked him where he was. I figured it was another student at Oxford, but nooooo. He was in Miami. I didn't believe him, so I asked him to describe the phone for me and he nailed it all the way to the case."

"She lost her phone." That was the truth, so Ruis wasn't lying to Oscar.

"What's it doing in Miami?"

"What did you tell the guy about the reward?"

"I told him I'd pay four hundred, then he told me to come get it."

Ruis sucked in air. "And then what?"

"I hung up."

At that point, Ruis hung up and called Martina's phone. After two rings, a man answered.

"Changed your mind?"

"Yes."

"Hey, you ain't the guy I spoke to. Who's this?"

"That was her boyfriend. I'm her brother. I'll pay you four fifty. Where are you?"

"I figured this thing belonged to a girl. Is she in trouble? Cause I don't want—"

"Look, she was supposed to be studying for exams. I want the phone so I can give it back to her before Dad finds out." Ruis meant every word he told the stranger.

Terri passed by him and froze. Ruis checked his phone to make sure the stranger was still connected. The line was open.

"I want cash. And don't go accusing me of stealing. I found this in the trash fair and square."

Ruis breathed again. "Where do I bring the money?"

"Miami."

"I'm in Miami."

"Come to the Crandon Park Marina."

Ruis dashed to the giant wall map.

"The dock manager don't like me, so don't go asking around. I'll find you. What are you wearing?"

Ruis glanced at Tapper. "A Cardinals baseball cap."

"You must like to live dangerously. This is Marlin territory."

Ruis stabbed a finger on the red dot labeled Crandon Park Marina. "I'm coming from"—he checked the map for the location of the FBI—"Highway 41 west of 821."

Cuervo materialized beside Ruis. He ran his hand from the FBI office to Crandon's red dot and held up three fingers while he mouthed "thirty minutes."

"I'll be there in thirty minutes."

"See you then." The phone call ended.

When Ruis turned around, Terri, Blake, Tapper, and Cuervo were gathered within reach.

"A guy has"—Ruis remembered to refer to the victim as Ruby—"Ruby's phone. Said he found it in the trash at the Crandon Park Marina. He wants four hundred fifty dollars for it."

Cuervo waved to an agent who had been calling the Bahamas.

Agent Maggie Vega pulled off her headset and stood. "Yes, sir?" At five feet four inches tall, she had thick, dark hair pulled back into a ponytail. Her brown eyes were aimed at Cuervo.

"We're going to Crandon Park Marina," he told her. "Change into civilian clothes."

She nodded and pulled the hairband from her hair on her way toward the door.

"Meet us downstairs in two minutes." Cuervo turned to Tapper, Blake, and Ruis, who piled cash from their wallets into Ruis's hand. "Let's take two cars."

Ruis told Tapper, "I need your hat."

Tapper handed it to him. They all headed to the elevator, where Cuervo asked Terri to stay behind.

She told Blake, "If you're taking the rental car, check the glove box."

Blake kissed her.

On the elevator ride, Cuervo raised his eyebrows at Blake.

"I told her not to bring her weapon into the FBI building."

Cuervo glanced at Ruis, who said his handgun was also in the car.

They met the female agent in the parking garage. She had changed into jeans and a red polo shirt. Cuervo assigned Agent Vega to ride with Ruis in his rented Chrysler Aspen SUV. Ruis opened the driver's door for her.

"You know the roads," he said. He spotted the slightest bulge in the back of her waistband as she climbed into the driver's seat. After handing her the keys, he climbed into the front passenger seat. There, he removed his Sig Sauer 226 and holster from the glovebox.

"Call me Maggie," she said, buckling in.

"Thank you." Ruis handed Terri's Smith & Wesson Shield and an inside-the-waistband holster to Blake through the open passenger door. "Call me Ruis."

Blake took the weapon and holster, turned, and caught up with Cuervo and Tapper. They passed a row of black Escalades and climbed into a blue Toyota 4Runner. A smart choice, the 4Runner didn't announce they were federal agents like a black Escalade would. Their demeanor, number, and athletic builds labeled them law-enforcement agents as clearly as a billboard, but there wasn't time to further disguise them.

Maggie moved the seat forward. She adjusted the mirrors, started the engine, and raced out of the parking lot.

On the ride to the marina, Ruis called Oscar. "Sorry to hang up on you."

"Is she at spring break with someone else? Just tell me."

"I called. The guy found the phone in the trash in a bad part of town. I think we can safely assume she's not there partying. Are you still in Tampa?"

"Yes."

Ruis marveled at the volume of late afternoon traffic. "What's the range on your drone?"

"I'm supposed to tell you it's classified."

"All right. Would you be able to use it, say, for a field demonstration?"

"It's not a toy. It's a multimillion-dollar prototype."

"Let me rephrase. Would you and the prototype be available to assist the FBI on a missing person's case?"

"If the person is *missing*, then where would I operate the drone?"

Ruis closed his eyes to cover an eye roll. "The person might be on a boat. If we locate the boat, we'll need a way to approach it without being seen."

"I'll ask my boss. He might like to earn bragging rights for using it in a real-life situation. I also brought a spare."

"Excellent. Feel free to use my name."

"When do you need it?"

"Between now and Friday."

"I'll ask." Oscar sighed heavily. "I'm surprised she hasn't replaced her phone by now. When you talk to Martina, let her know I've been trying to reach her."

She would have, of course, if she could have. The thought plucked a nerve that resonated through Ruis's heart. He held his phone at arm's length over the dashboard while he cleared his throat, then he placed it back against his ear. "Will do." He disconnected the call and turned his face to the passenger window. By force of will, he tucked away his emotion. *Stay in the moment. Stay in the here and now.*

They passed a small airport before turning south on Interstate 95. Ruis had driven on I-95 from Virginia to New England long ago. He knew the road ran down the East Coast to Florida and he had wondered since childhood where it ended. Now he knew. It disappeared at the junction of Highway 1 and the Rickenbacker Causeway. Just like that. Gone.

"It's a good thing I'm driving," Maggie said. "The causeway is a dangerous bridge. You have to watch for cyclists."

Maggie must have sensed his mood, because she made no more attempts to engage him in conversation. They rode in silence until Cuervo called. Maggie spoke with him briefly and set her phone in the drink holder. "The distress signal is for you to take off your hat."

"Got it."

"Crandon Park is on the other side of the next bridge."

Sure enough, it was the first turn past the bridge to the right. To call this a park was being generously imaginative. The main part of the marina was a U-shaped body of water featuring a grid of eight floating cement docks framed by Biscayne Bay, a narrow strip of coarse grass and weeds, a road, and a large parking area. The main building squatted on one corner of the marina. The sunbaked parking lot, decorated with a few struggling palms and dead grass, had the marina on one end and a fenced-in lot for trailered boats on the farthest end. Along the water's edge of the parking area sat a few small buildings. Maggie parked in front of one labeled Bait Shop.

Ruis climbed out and pulled Tapper's baseball cap snug on his head and donned sunglasses. "Our seller found the phone in the trash. He said the dock manager didn't like him."

"Probably homeless." She leaned against the silver rental car. "I don't see many places to hide."

"We don't have to."

The blue 4Runner pulled in near the main marina building a short walk from the bait shop.

Across from the docks sat a green strip of land that ended at the water with a stand of scruffy trees and bushes. "If I were homeless in this unrelenting heat, I'd set up camp in the shade. Let's walk so he can find us."

They crossed the sun-bleached cement parking lot to the docks, then skirted one side of the docks to the main building. Circling it, they continued along the docks to a narrow field. A green garbage truck labeled with a WM logo rumbled down the road and turned into the parking lot. Ruis turned toward it. He began a text message to Cuervo when Maggie placed her hand on his wrist.

"They saw it."

Cuervo stopped the truck before it reached the metal dumpster.

Ruis and Maggie resumed their stroll. Ruis reprimanded himself for not thinking about securing the trash and its potential evidence when they arrived. Between the trees and the dock rested a cement-block two-door restroom building that had an overflowing metal trashcan leaning against it. A beeping sound from the parking lot told Ruis the garbage truck was backing up.

Maggie looked back. "The dumpster is staying."

They strolled on the yellowed grass toward the restrooms. Ruis spotted a shadow moving behind the building and placed himself between her and the stranger. A thin, leathery-skinned man wearing oversized knee-length cargo shorts and a dirty green polo shirt stepped out from the shady side of the building.

"This is Marlin territory," he said.

"I live dangerously," Ruis answered.

The man relaxed. "You brought something for me?"

Ruis slowly reached into his shirt pocket and pulled out a folded stack of bills held together with a rubber band. The stranger dug the phone from his pocket and held it out with one hand while he held his other hand open, palm up. The exchange happened smoothly.

"Do you know this place well?" Ruis asked.

The man fanned the corners of the bills, smiled, and stowed the cash deep in a buttoned pocket. "You don't want to rent here." He glanced at Maggie. "This ain't the safest place to be. Not a lot of fishing going on if you know what I mean. Mostly foreigners."

Ruis pulled out his phone and held up a picture of Ruby he had downloaded from the internet. "Did my sister go out on one of these boats?"

The man shrugged.

Ruis nodded toward the marina. "Would the manager tell me if any Nordic Tugs left here last Sunday?"

"I don't know. He's a bit skittish and lazy." He squinted at the marina building, then back at Ruis.

Uh-oh. He spotted the others. Asking more questions would convince the old codger that they were law enforcement.

"I need to get out of the sun." He turned and fast-walked to the trees.

Ruis let him go. If more evidence was here, it would be in the dumpster. "Thanks for the phone."

"Don't mention it." The man waved without looking back. "To anyone."

Ruis and the agent strode to the marina building and found Blake and Cuervo talking to a bald four-hundred-pound man.

"We close at five," the man said.

Ruis handed Martina's phone to Maggie. "Where's Tapper?"

Maggie nodded at the end of the second row of slips. From that position, Tapper would have had a clear shot at the meeting spot with the homeless man. Holstering his handgun, he approached in long, easy strides.

"The floating docks are nice," Tapper said softly, "but the service is—" He stopped when he noticed the giant dockmaster. "Excuse me, but did you know there's a sunken..." His face went slack, and his mouth fell open. He spun around and ran down the dock.

Ruis silently finished Tapper's sentence. *Boat.* Then he chased Tapper. They reached the end of the dock and, panting, gaped down at a half-swamped trawler. The sunken vessel appeared to be thirty-five to forty feet long. Ruis kicked off a shoe. Adrenaline shot through his system. He had to know. He had to.

Tapper grabbed him in a bear hug. "Oh, no you don't."

Catching up, Cuervo and Maggie talked at once.

"For all we know," Tapper said in calming tones, "that might have sunk a year ago."

Reason cooled him down, so Ruis raised his hands. "Okay. Okay. You're right." Even though for six million dollars the kidnappers could afford to lose a boat, sinking it didn't cover evidence as well as burning it. Sinking it in a marina was begging for it to be found. It didn't add up.

Tapper released him. Ruis was putting his shoe on when the four-hundred-pound dockmaster lumbered down the dock and complained about the heat. Blake shadowed the large man. When the dockmaster reached the sunken trawler, he planted his hands on his ample hips.

Cuervo addressed him. "How long has this boat been underwater?"

Between breaths, the man said, "Who's asking?"

Cuervo held his credentials close to the manager's face.

"What do you care?" He swatted away Cuervo's hand. "It's not your boat."

"That," Blake said, "is assault on a federal agent while on duty."

The dockmaster sneered at Blake. "You're kidding me. I barely touched him."

Maggie ratcheted open her handcuffs. "According to Title Eighteen of the United States Code, assault doesn't require injury. A takedown of someone your size, however, that could leave a mark." She shrugged.

Raising his hands, the dockmaster took a step back from Maggie and bumped into Tapper. "It sank over the weekend. All right?"

"Who owns it?"

He pointed at Cuervo. "You need a warrant for that."

Cuervo pulled out his cell phone. The dockmaster watched as if trying to determine if Cuervo was bluffing. When Cuervo asked for a judge by name, the dockmaster spoke up.

"Hold up."

"Sorry, just a second." Cuervo held the phone by his waist.

"I don't need cop cars scaring off boaters."

Cuervo ended his call with a quick apology.

The dockmaster rubbed a hand over his bare scalp and wiped sweat on his pants. "It belongs to an old Russian guy. His nephew worked on it last week in dry dock. The kid's a certifiable idiot. I'm not surprised the boat sunk. Come in the office before I get heatstroke. I'll look up his name. I can't spell it off the top of my head." He tromped to the office complaining the whole way while Cuervo, Maggie, and Blake followed.

"Do you have security cameras here?" Maggie asked the dockmaster.

His laughter faded as Maggie, Cuervo, and Blake headed to the main building.

Tapper dropped a hand on Ruis's shoulder. "I'll stay with the boat." He had seen plenty of corpses before, burned, shot, blown up, and drowned. The merciful offer boosted Tapper another notch higher on Ruis's respect scale. Leaving him here, however, would be a waste of his skills.

"Cuervo's got this covered. Let's get the phone back for analysis." Ruis hoped it might yield something useful. After one last look in the water, he prayed Martina wasn't inside the boat. Tapper was right to stop him. If Martina's body was in there, it wasn't an image he would be able to forget.

A five-mile run had eased stress kinks out of Ruis's body and the shower afterward brought him almost back to normal. He was toweling off when banging on his hotel room door caught his attention. After securing a towel around his waist, he padded past the Tempur-Pedic king bed through the lounge area of his suite and opened the door.

Blake and Tapper entered carrying cold beer and a large white bag with grease stains. They set the food and drink on the table in front of the L-shaped sofa. Across from the sofa was a wall-mounted television and a desk. The late evening news played on the television. The desk held Ruis's laptop and papers. Blake picked up the remote and muted the television.

"We bring news," Tapper said, handing Ruis a longneck bottle. He sank into the sofa beside Blake and elbowed him. "You first."

"No, you go first."

"You can—"

"Guys." Ruis twisted open his beer.

Tapper removed his ball cap and placed it over his heart. "The sunken boat is empty. Well, it's full of water, but you know what I mean." He set his hat on his lap and tore open the bag of food. When he looked down, he revealed an area of thinning hair at the crown of his head. "Which ones are beef?"

Blake pointed to the paper-wrapped rolls marked with a check mark. "The owner—after being invited to the FBI interview room—granted permission to search the boat. Since it was cheaper to dive it than raise it, Tapper rented gear."

"The old guy was seventy and looked ninety. He practically begged us to raise it." Tapper took a swig of beer. "Said his nephew was living on it and he didn't want him back in the house because the kid played loud music all the time."

Ruis rolled the desk chair to the table and sat. He inhaled aromas of meat and spices and set his beer on the table. "Are those empanadas?"

Tapper grinned.

A diet of Cuban coffee, pizza, and vending machine snacks had left Ruis sleepless. He picked up a warm, hefty empanada and unwrapped it. When he bit through the flaky pie crust, flavors exploded in his mouth. Savory chorizo sausage, ground beef, garlic, onion, and cumin reminded him of family dinners. He moaned and chewed and silently blessed the cook.

Blake took a long swallow of beer and set his bottle on the edge of the table. "The chat with the owner went quickly. He waived his right to an attorney because he hates lawyers. And he backed up the marina manager's opinion of his nephew, Gregorio Kuznetsov, as an idiot."

"Greggy boy," Tapper said, "has a record. Started out small and ended up in juvenile detention for trying to rob the same convenience store three weekends in a row. A month after he was turned over to his uncle, he stole a truck. The police pulled him over for a traffic violation and he ran, leaving his gun and fingerprints behind. He was released from prison five weeks ago. Four weeks ago, he told his uncle he was going to make a big score."

Ruis washed down the last of his beef empanada with cold beer. Gregorio Kuznetsov demonstrated the trifecta of criminal traits—poor judgment, low impulse control, and greed. Other than finding Martina's phone at the marina, there wasn't a solid connection between her kidnapping and the sunken Nordic Tug. The big score could be a drug deal, robbery, gambling, or any number of get-rich-quick criminal endeavors. He considered mentioning this but let it slide. Tapper and Blake had volunteered their time and talent without hesitation. They were blowing off steam at the end of a long day. And they had brought him beer and empanadas. Who could ask for better friends?

Tapper devoured an empanada and reached for a second.

Ruis left the lounge area, tossed the towel onto the bathroom counter, and then put on a pair of shorts. "I thought trawlers were practically indestructible."

"Me, too," Tapper said.

Ruis returned to the lounge. Blake pushed a second beef empanada across the table to Ruis, who took it.

"While I was in the engine hold, I checked around." Tapper snorted. "The seacock was eroded and left open and the raw water intake hose had a two-inch split in it."

"Oh, man." Ruis shook his head.

"What does that mean?" Blake asked.

Tapper raised his eyebrows.

"Blake served in the Marines." Ruis bit into his second beef empanada.

"Ah." Tapper grabbed a second beer. "Nordic Tugs have reinforced hulls with very few pass-throughs, or holes. The seacock is a valve immediately above a hole where water is pumped in to cool the engine. Normally, you'd close it when the engine's off, because if the seal to the seacock is broken, water leaks into the engine hold. If the seacock valve is left open and the hose that connects it to the pump is split or rotted, well"—he twisted off the cap of his beer—"given the weight of the boat, a two-inch hole would shoot water into the hull and sink it in about four hours."

"Whoa," said Blake.

"Yeah." Tapper then elbowed Blake. "Tell him the rest."

Ruis picked up his beer.

"When Agent Cuervo requested a background check on dear old uncle, the Coast Guard called. They said his boat had been used in the eighties to fish for square grouper." Blake wiped his hands with a paper napkin.

Ruis narrowed his eyes at Blake as if he had misheard him. He shook his head and turned his free hand palm up.

"Seaplanes used to drop them offshore..."

"Oh. Got it." After a raid, the authorities always displayed seized square-shaped bales of marijuana and bricks of cocaine sealed in plastic. Maybe crime ran in the family. If the uncle was a drug pirate, why not the nephew?

"Oh, I almost forgot." Blake said. One side of his mouth tugged into a half grin. "Guess what Gregorio drives?" He drained his beer and sat back, tossing an arm over the back of the sofa.

Ruis lowered his beer. "A beige van?"

Tapper and Blake nodded like grinning bobbleheads.

"Special Agent in Charge Espinosa notified everybody to look for it." Blake pulled a paper from his pocket and handed it to

Ruis. "They're also researching known associates and prison pals."

Ruis examined enlarged color images of Gregorio's Florida driver's license and passport. Ruis imagined sunglasses on his face. It matched the grainy image of one man on the club's surveillance recording. He burned the image of the suspect in his memory. To memorize a name or other information, he relied on mnemonic devices. Whenever he held a screwdriver or ratchet, he thought of "righty-tighty, lefty-loosey." In grade school, he could name the Great Lakes from the word HOMES. Huron, Ontario, Michigan, Erie, and Superior. He easily burned the name Kuznetsov into memory because the name sounded like what Ruis wanted to do to him.

Tapper grabbed the television's remote control and turned up the sound.

Together the men watched an aerial shot of a giant plume of fire. The newscaster's voice narrated over the distinct rotor noise of a helicopter.

"...has exploded. Rescue ships are on the way. Witnesses report seeing men jump from the platform." Along the bottom of the screen, the news ticker scrolled bits of information about the Deepwater Horizon oil rig located south of Louisiana in the Gulf of Mexico...environmental disaster...fire out of control...thousands of gallons of oil flowing from the well.

Ruis's first thought about the disaster at sea was selfish. The Coast Guard would be too busy to search for a trawler.

. 16 .

After spending the night in the engine hold, Martina was awakened by her bladder. She listened for activity above and heard nothing except waves sloshing against the hull for five, then ten, then fifteen minutes. She eventually ducked alongside the AC generator with a bucket to relieve herself.

Her muscles ached from sleeping on the metal floor, so she stretched.

Suddenly the hatch banged open and Green Mask announced, "Time to come out."

Here we go. She wanted to stall by reminding him that she preferred to perform at night. Clenching her teeth, she climbed the ladder from the engine hold to the pilothouse. Once again, Green Mask and Black Mask flanked her, blocking the transom doors, and Black Mask held the Taser. The red dress she had left on the floor was spread out on the navigation charts.

"Time to make another video," Green Mask said, pointing down toward the master stateroom.

Her heart rate accelerated. Blood drained from her hands and face. "Another ransom demand?"

"A different message." Green Mask shut the hatch.

Martina trudged down the stairs to the room at the end of the passageway. The video camera and battery-powered lantern were in the same place as last time. On the shelf beside the head of the bed sat a laptop and satellite phone connected by a wire. She sat on the foot of the bed with her arms crossed.

"Are we going to have a problem this time?" Black Mask held out a paper. In his other hand, he held the Taser.

Martina took the paper. "I could use a minute to fix my hair and makeup."

Black Mask grunted. He turned toward Green Mask, who had an object tucked in the front of his waistband that pushed his shirt out. Ruis was careful to wear clothes that hid the handle of his gun and his in-the-waistband holster. Green Mask seemed to have his handgun tucked directly into his waistband. He was probably too cheap to buy a holster. Ruis once said gangs did that because they considered it cool and because they were stupid. Armed and stupid. What a terrible combination.

Green Mask stood behind the video camera fiddling with knobs and dials.

She knew she couldn't grab his gun without getting Tasered, so she read through her script. It was full of lies. *I'm still not Ruby. Today is Wednesday, not Friday. And no, I have not been treated well.* Detailed instructions followed about placing a camouflage backpack filled with bearer bonds at a certain park bench at exactly one p.m. The script ended with the usual death-to-the-girl warning about involving the police.

She realized that as soon as they recorded this, they didn't need her alive anymore. Her hands tingled, and her heartbeat thudded in her ears. *Oh, Dios mio.* Pretending to review the script, she kept her head down to stall and think. She forced herself to act like she didn't understand what it meant to record a post-dated proof-of-life message. How would Ruby react? *Think like a pop star. Be a pop star.*

"You don't have to memorize it," Black Mask said.

She pointed to the name of the park. "How do you pronounce that?"

Green Mask shrugged.

"Gads-den," said Black Mask.

Nodding, Martina tried to swallow but her tongue stuck to the roof of her mouth. It seemed peculiar that Black Mask allowed Green Mask to carry the more dangerous weapon. Perhaps it was for show. Perhaps it was another silent threat designed to keep their victim compliant. The recording script and the presence of the handgun led her to a conclusion.

They intend to kill me.

She took a deep breath. Fear crept into her heart. She decided to put that emotion to good use. Thinking like Ruby, she knew Ruby would be afraid of him. "Before I read this, I want you to know that I'll do the performance. I mean, I was ready last night, but since you weren't feeling well, you know, I can sing tonight." To sell it, she glanced at the Taser. "In the dress and shoes, like a concert."

The men exchanged a glance. Green Mask raised his eyebrows. Black Mask sighed and gazed at the floor. Green Mask busied himself with uncapping the camera. It felt as if they were avoiding eye contact with her.

She didn't want to oversell the idea, but the stakes were too high to give up. *Think like a pop star*. Unleashing her ego, she decided to launch into a Ruby-style complaint-brag. "Look, I haven't played to a crowd smaller than eight thousand in years. Between now and when you drop me off in Tampa, I won't get a chance to rehearse for my next concert." She waved the paper as she spoke. "I know you don't care, but I need to rehearse. Think of it as a command performance. Besides, I want to try out a song I haven't done before in public."

Black Mask stared at her as if seeing her for the first time. Voicing her expectation of being dropped off in Tampa could have convinced him she was too stupid to understand she had outlived her usefulness. She couldn't tell. Perhaps he was tempted to procrastinate the unpleasant, messy task of killing her. Maybe he felt powerful because she was volunteering to perform. A change registered in his eyes. He scratched his mask. "You sing at sundown."

She faced the camera. Desperately fanning a spark of hope, she said, "All right then, let's do this."

. 17 .

At the Wednesday morning briefing, Special Agent in Charge Espinosa credited the New York City office for identifying the known associates of Gregorio Kuznetsov and comparing them to the abductors in the club surveillance recording. A printout of known associates' mugshots hung on the far left of the whiteboard. Beneath it was a URL or Uniform Resource Locator, commonly known as an online link. Ruis keyed the link into his phone.

"Why is everyone copying it?" Terri whispered to Blake.

"We're downloading the photos of known associates," Blake whispered back. "When you're out in the field, you want to be able to show photos to see if people recognize one of them."

Espinosa pointed to a new photo on the whiteboard and the name printed under it. "The forensic division's facial recognition program declares Stas Petronin a ninety-one percent match. He was Gregorio's cell mate in prison."

Ruis's phone vibrated. A text message from Oscar read: *Standing by. Field demo approved.* Ruis replied with *Excellent.*

While Espinosa spoke, Agent Maggie handed out copies of the intel on Petronin that showed photos of his face and tattoos followed by a list of his arrests and convictions. Ruis immediately examined the tattoos. None of them indicated allegiance to the Russian mob. Images of snakes, skulls, and fire colored his chest and back, reminiscent of heavy-metal music album covers. Petronin had a hardened expression.

"Stas Petronin paints ships at the shipyard in Tampa. We are pursuing a warrant for his cell phone. In the meantime, Tampa Police have assigned an undercover officer to watch his apartment. Agent Cuervo will be flying to Tampa later today to coordinate a strategy for the ransom drop." Espinosa aimed his attention at Ruis. "If you want to include your people, let me know."

With the briefing over, the FBI agents returned to their duties. Blake, Tapper, and Terri huddled around Ruis at the back of the conference room. Espinosa joined them.

"Sir," Ruis began, "we have access to a state-of-the-art drone and an operator at MacDill."

Espinosa smiled and called Cuervo over. Balancing his coffee in one hand, Cuervo pulled up a chair and sat.

Ruis texted Oscar Gunnerson's name and phone number to Cuervo. "I'm sending you contact info for a drone operator at MacDill."

"Very good," Cuervo said. "When we learn the location of the drop, we'll need to stake out the perimeter and place undercover operatives in the area."

"I'll go to Tampa," Tapper said in his mission-ready voice, but he tempered his declaration by adding, "if you'd like."

Ruis, Blake, and Terri agreed to stay, so Espinosa and Cuervo arranged for Tapper to ride in the FBI's plane. Espinosa was called out of the conference room, then Cuervo stepped out to make a call, leaving Ruis and friends in their huddle.

"I need the keys to the car," Tapper said. "How do you know the drone operator?"

Ruis handed him the keys. "He's dating Martina."

"I see a problem." Tapper looked at the floor.

"He offered to help us find a missing person." Ruis's voice was barely a whisper.

Tapper removed his Cardinals cap and smoothed his hair down.

He placed it back on his head and nodded.

Cuervo returned and told Tapper to be ready to leave at ten.

"I'll get my stuff from the hotel," Tapper said a little louder than necessary and then he left.

Blake and Terri exchanged glances. They had packed their things each morning and stowed their luggage in the back of the SUV. Ruis and Tapper had taught them the importance of mobility in what they termed a *fluid mission situation*.

Blake leaned close to Ruis. "What's that about?"

"He likes to visit high-end specialty electronics stores." Ruis checked his watch. Tapper had an hour and a half before his flight. "As a civilian, he can do things the Feds can't. Things they'd need a warrant for."

"Nice." Blake grinned. "Since I'm staying, I can help the dumpster-diving techs."

"I'll keep calling marinas," Terri said.

Espinosa returned to the conference room and spoke for a minute with Maggie, who then left the room.

"Gregorio Kuznetsov's van has been located in Naples," Espinosa announced.

Applause resounded in the conference room.

"It was towed and impounded last night for parking in a towaway zone."

Hope sparked in Ruis's heart because Espinosa would have mentioned if it had been torched. "Where was it?"

"The Naples City Dock. Would you like to accompany Agent—"

"Yes, I would." Ruis phoned Tapper. "Wait in the parking lot. I'm coming down." To Espinosa, he said, "I'd like to bring Blake."

"Maggie will be in charge. Are we clear on this?" Espinosa asked. His tone demanded compliance.

"Yes, sir," Ruis and Blake said.

Blake stopped to kiss Terri while Ruis headed to the elevator. Agent Maggie, go bag in hand, waited for them. Their elevator conversation was brief.

"Normally, it's an hour and forty minutes to Naples taking I-75," Maggie said. "I can beat that time."

Ruis smiled at Maggie.

"All right then," Blake muttered.

Once in the garage, Ruis and Blake grabbed their duffle bags and guns from the rental while Tapper, in the driver's seat, kept the engine running. Maggie pulled up alongside them in a black Escalade and rolled down the passenger-side window, so Tapper rolled down his window.

"If I don't see you again, it's been good working with you," Maggie said.

"How about if I call you next time I'm in town. Buy you coffee or whatever?"

"I'd like that."

The Cuban coffee was amazing, but Ruis knew Tapper was likely more interested in the *whatever*. Blake climbed in the back of Maggie's Escalade. Ruis waited for Tapper to drive away before he buckled into the front passenger's seat. Maggie keyed in a number on her cell phone and held off activating the call until the car reached the open road. Two blocks later, she requested to speak with the dockmaster at the Naples City Dock. After a few moments on hold, she introduced herself and asked oh-so-politely if he'd be kind enough to prepare a list of all the Nordic Tugs that had passed through his fine marina since Saturday even if they'd only stopped for fuel. She mentioned she was on her way from Miami with two others assisting in an urgent investigation that she would be glad to explain to him in person, smiling and nodding through the conversation as if the dockmaster could see her. After thanking him, she ended the call.

Ruis appreciated her finesse and foresight.

"Blake," she said, "I'll drop you off at the Naples Police Department to see what their technicians find in the van since you know what to look for."

"Yes, ma'am."

"Ruis? What stuff exactly is Gene getting at the hotel?" Maggie kept her eyes on the road.

It took a moment for Ruis to recognize Tapper's first name. It took another moment of wondering why Maggie used Tapper's real name before he answered. "I couldn't say."

"Uh-huh."

Ruis had looked forward to getting out of the conference room, where the flurry of methodical, tedious activity felt more and more each hour like they were hamsters running on a wheel. The subconscious, which accepted all input as innocently and literally as a child, interpreted leaving Miami as "getting somewhere" in the investigation. They were crossing the state from the Atlantic Ocean to the Gulf of Mexico, from mega-city through swampland to a small resort town. Movement seemed like progress. And Maggie promised a high-speed drive.

According to the time stamp on the surveillance recording from the nightclub, Martina was kidnapped at midnight Saturday. Ruis checked his watch. Nine o'clock. Three days and nine hours ago, his sister was abducted. Missing for eighty-one hours. Four thousand, eight hundred and sixty minutes lost. His mind calculated the time as a distraction to prevent his heart from calculating the odds against finding her alive. Perhaps the trail of evidence would dead-end in Naples and they would have to drive back. Time would tell.

For the moment, the hamster wheel felt larger.

. 18 .

Martina ate crackers and boiled eggs and drank bottled water, then they sent her to the small stateroom for the afternoon. Prisoners on death row got a better final meal. A lifetime should last longer.

That's it, huh? All I get is twenty-two years.

The men argued in the pilothouse. Fragments of their heated conversation reached Martina.

"...hot shower. What's the problem?"

"It's not working."

"What an idiot. You can't even follow written instructions? Give them to me."

Cringing, Martina curled up on the bed while her mind and stomach churned. She couldn't remember any time in her life when she had been so alone. Growing up in a large family, she rarely had privacy long enough to be alone. Her sisters would barge in at will when she was in the tub or on the toilet so often she stopped whining about it. Because of her home environment, she'd learned how to study in chaos and noise. Today, she missed every annoying, nosey, hovering family member down to the weirdest cousin, Rosalie, whom her aunts called a hippie. For years, Martina had thought hippie meant being childless. Later she learned that Rosalie and her husband had chosen not to have children. To Martina, their life sounded lonely.

But ultimately, everyone faces death alone.

Martina sighed and climbed under the colorful quilt. Eventually, the kidnappers would connect the generator problem with leaving her in the engine hold. Even at gunpoint she wouldn't know how to undo her sabotage. She didn't remember exactly how the wiring looked before she'd pried out the connections. It was likely the men didn't know how to repair the electronic systems either.

Tears rolled over the bridge of her nose and her cheek to the soft pillow.

She would not sit exams or graduate from the Oxford master's program with her classmates in solemn black robes and mortarboards. She'd never get engaged or married or have babies to share with her sisters and brother and cousins. Oscar would not walk down the aisle with her at Vincent and Nefi's wedding. Her passport would not get stamped in Australia, New Zealand, China, Peru, Tahiti, or Sweden, or the many wondrous places she longed to discover. All the cousins and nieces and nephews would have one less person to play with, one less gift at Christmas. Mama and Father would have a hole in their hearts forever.

How long would it take for her status to change from missing to presumed dead? Without a body, would there be a funeral? Or would her family hold a memorial service like Jason Hamilton's, with a closed casket topped with flowers and a portrait? She envisioned her parents dressed in black near Senator and Mrs. Hamilton, who understood the loss of a child. Nefi would rekindle her anger at criminals for taking another person from her life. At the graveside, a handful of dirt would fall from each person's hand onto an empty casket.

She didn't deserve this surreal situation. She had loved her family, worked hard in school, and starred as the flyer on her high school's varsity competitive cheerleading squad. She felt largely responsible for civilizing Nefi, though in truth, it had taken two villages in two countries to raise that girl. Martina's treasured ribbons, trophies, awards, and diplomas would gather dust in a trunk. Her accomplishments crumbled into meaninglessness. They could not buy her another day of life.

In honest reflection, she acknowledged the decisions that had brought her here. She hadn't taken the job for the money, though the pay impressed her. At first, the job was a thrill, a lark, the result of a dare to sing in a pub contest, which captured the attention of Ruby's talent agency. When Miss Chen had told her Ruby could coordinate her six-week rehab with Oxford's spring break, pride whispered in Martina's ear that she could fool the media and fans while giving Ruby time to face down her addiction and defeat it. It would be, she reasoned, a noble thing to do.

An appearance at the opening of a new recording studio, followed by a ribbon cutting at a music store in London had offered quick, easy money. Full-fledged ego had seized control one night in Monte Carlo when Chad helped her from the limousine and they walked the red carpet into the World Music Awards gala. Martina, adorned in an elegant, full-length black Vera Wang gown, had reveled in the VIP treatment. A reporter had asked her how she felt about not being nominated in the pop/rock category and Martina had answered, "This is great. I get to spend the evening stress-free, hearing performances by the best in the world." From that moment on, she'd embraced celebrity because people treated her like someone special.

In the end, she was a fraud living a lie.

Soon I'll be dead because those who know I've been kidnapped don't care.

The kidnappers didn't care. The ransom demand didn't promise Ruby's safe return, it implied it. But even if the ransom demand had promised her safe return, people who were willing to commit a felony for money had no qualms about lying. Look at the Charles Lindbergh case. His infant son was kidnapped for fifty thousand dollars' ransom, a fortune back then, and though the ransom was paid, the baby was killed. Her kidnappers, well, Ruby's kidnappers, could get their six million dollars with or without delivering her in trade.

If Ruby was told about the ransom, would she care? She was fighting addiction. She would refuse to pay. Why risk six million dollars on the possibility of rescuing her look-alike and exposing herself as an addict? Ruby had only met Martina once with Miss Chen and Chad to arrange their schedules. Ruby might be angry or jealous about Chad partying with Martina on her expense account. Images of them together had flooded social media and the news. Chad had hammed it up for the media, often putting an arm around Martina and slowing down just enough to be photographed. Sure, Chad treated her well. Their appearance as a happy couple was an integral part of the charade to convince the media and fans that all was well in Ruby World. Chad was fun, handsome, athletic, and perfectly comfortable in the spotlight.

Martina wasn't used to it like Ruby was. A few weeks ago, Martina had met Chad after his team played an exhibition game in New York City. The intrusive media attention and the rush of screaming fans unnerved her. Chad attempted to calm her by telling her she looked beautiful. By reflex she replied, "I know." Her comment surprised him so much he laughed and pulled her against his side. That moment graced the front page of a tabloid under the words "Lovebirds Celebrate Win."

Ruby probably hated that tabloid image.

Ruby's lawyers and talent agency didn't care about Martina. Six million dollars was a fortune. By doing nothing, by keeping the ransom demand secret like the kidnappers demanded, they would preserve their client's hard-earned wealth and reputation. They could dismiss the demand as a fraud. They could leak it to the media and prove it was a fraud by having the real Ruby step in front of the cameras. Either way, they had no obligation to gamble a fortune on the possibility of rescuing a part-time employee, a virtual stranger.

The truth of her kidnapping was that those who knew didn't care, and those who cared didn't know.

She blamed herself. After all, because of her lies, those who cared about her believed she was staying at Oxford over break to study for exams. With her phone gone and the boat's radio out of reach, she couldn't call for help from anyone. Even if she could use the radio or the satellite phone, what good would that do? She didn't know where she was. Neither the radio nor the satellite phone had 911 service, did they? The Masks would laugh as she shouted on channel sixteen, "Mayday, mayday, mayday! This is a boat with no name in the middle of nowhere. Come save me!"

Did the radio broadcast a location when the emergency button was pushed? Martina sighed. She had always expected others to take care of her whenever she was boating. There was always a sister or brother or cousin or aunt or uncle around who knew how to use the navigation equipment and the radio. She was not prepared to do such things on her own and it was her own fault.

Ruby's fans wouldn't know about the kidnapping because the kidnappers demanded secrecy. When the deadline for the ransom passed and the kidnappers didn't get their money, they would disappear in search of another victim. The fans would never know a crime had occurred. Ruby would go on with her career. The world would turn without Martina Ramos.

Authorities probably didn't know anyone had been kidnapped unless someone had shared the ransom message with them. Even then, if news of a kidnapping leaked out, where would police search? The kidnappers had drugged her, so she couldn't have left a trail of clues to follow.

No matter how she thought about the situation, she came to one conclusion.

It sucks to be me.

Facing her mortality clarified her perspective in unexpected ways. She let go of her love of things. She stopped mourning the loss of her cell phone. She recognized that the things she'd worked for, the trophies and medals and high grades, meant nothing compared to memories of time spent with her family and friends.

Pride fell away. Having promised her soul to God long ago, she wanted to go straight to heaven after death and not linger in purgatory, so she prayed for forgiveness for the transgressions she could remember from childhood to the present, then she requested forgiveness for all the things she couldn't remember. It felt odd to confess directly to God instead of a priest but following centuries of Catholic tradition wasn't an option here in the swamp. With this done, she surrendered to a great and terrible emptiness that gave her peace.

In the emptiness, she claimed her true self.

I am Martina Olympias Ramos.

Staring at the white wall of the stateroom, she was afraid to sleep away her remaining precious hours of life, so, wrapped in a soft blue and green quilt, she thought about the people she would miss. Nefi, her unexpected best friend, had become her mission in high school. Nefi had needed someone to guide her through mastering English and teen culture at a prep school. Martina took pride in having groomed the wild, awkward girl into a confident, accomplished beauty. Nefi would be so angry and sad that her BFF couldn't be her maid of honor, she would kick her tombstone.

Martina missed Oscar and the life with him that might have been. He was a good man. He deserved a long, happy life. He would be a kind, loving husband and father.

Tears rolled down her numb face. Before the next sunrise, she reasoned, she'd be dead.

She prayed for her family. She asked God to forgive her for causing them sorrow. Daddy was the head of the family, but Mama was the heart of it. Remembering how they had cried when everyone thought Nefi was dead, she knew news of her death-by-kidnapping would knock the wind from their sails. But they might never know she had been kidnapped. They might never find her body.

As far as her family and friends knew, she'd vanished from Oxford during Easter break.

Southwesterly breezes nudged the anchored boat to face the wind, placing her small stateroom on the cool, shadowed side. She cocooned in the colorful quilt as she prayed for her twenty-five cousins, her uncles, her aunts, her grandparents living and dead, her sisters, and her brother. One by one, she thanked God for every member of her large, loud, loving family. She drew on memories of reunions, weddings, births, and funerals that had brought the family closer.

Hours later, one comforting thought gave her peace enough to allow the boat to rock her to sleep.

Black Mask and Green Mask were stuck here.

. 19 .

Stopping at the Naples Police Department took ten minutes of introductions and flashing of credentials so Blake would be allowed to watch the crime scene technicians process Kuznetsov's decrepit beige van. Agent Maggie said he was a civilian consultant trained by the FBI, which Ruis considered an elegant description.

The Naples police chief introduced the crime lab technicians from Ft. Myers. They explained they would process the van, but that DNA evidence would be forwarded to Tallahassee and trace evidence would go to Orlando. Having already processed the interior of the vehicle, the technicians left the doors open to search the exterior.

Ruis and Maggie continued to the Naples City Dock. On the ride there, Maggie explained that Collier County had the lowest crime rate of all metropolitan counties in Florida. Naples earned a top rank on "best of" lists for its luxurious quality of life. They drove by lush golf courses, mansions, and a fancy shopping area on the way to the marina's parking lot, where they parked between a Bentley and a Lexus.

The aromas of onion, garlic, and fried fish wafted from a nearby restaurant. After walking under the wood-carved blue and yellow Naples City Dock sign, Ruis was surprised to see fixed wooden docks. Though picturesque, fixed wooden docks required boaters to tie lines that adjusted with the tides. Seagulls wheeled over a table where early-morning fishermen cut their catch. A blue sign on the cutting table depicted a fish skeleton under the words "Don't kill pelicans with kindness."

Ruis followed Maggie down the dock past a small building for showers and laundry, past a green-roofed gazebo filled with people talking and boat watching, to the two-story building at the end, where a woman directed the fuel pumps. Inside the building, they greeted the man behind the counter.

"What can I do for you?"

By way of introduction, Maggie showed her FBI identification. "And this is a civilian consultant, Ruis Ramos."

"Are you the lady who called from Miami?" He removed his cap and leaned both hands on the countertop.

"Yes, sir. Do you have the list?"

"Well, you must have set a new land speed record." He pulled a handful of paper from the copier. "It's just the two of us manning this operation, so I didn't have time to separate out the Nordic Tugs, but the type of boat is listed in this column." He pointed.

The ten-page list included transient boats, fuel stops, charters, logging the arrival and departure of boats by time and date. Ruis appreciated the harbor master for listing the boats and their activity by date and time. He ruled out the first ten boats on the list.

"That's every boat we logged since Saturday at midnight. If this column is blank, the boat just stopped to buy fuel. Ball means they tied off to a mooring ball. And a number identifies the slip they docked in."

Maggie divided the stack and handed half to Ruis. They parked in chairs in the office and immediately took out pens to mark the lines labeled with *motor vessel*.

The harbor master handled a radio call from an incoming boater, then he asked, "What's this all about?"

"Missing person," Maggie said without looking up.

Ruis's list displayed activity from Tuesday at two a.m. to Wednesday at nine a.m. He had one Nordic Tug that stopped for fuel at five p.m. Tuesday. He waited for Maggie to finish her list.

"Missing how?"

Another radio call came in. By the time the dockmaster finished giving instructions on a boater's slip assignment, Maggie had circled five items on her papers. She pointed to a line item about a Nordic Tug 37 on a mooring ball, rented on Monday. She handed Ruis her list.

"Stay here. I'll check it out." She pointed to one of three sets of binoculars on the counter. "May I borrow one of these?"

"Sure."

Maggie shouldered open the door and fast-walked down the pier.

"I guess I can trust her to bring it back, right?"

Ruis nodded. He carried the papers to the counter. "What can you tell me about these boats and their owners?"

"How is this missing person missing?"

Ruis's heart tightened. Saying the word kidnapping pained him. Since Maggie had called it a missing person, he didn't want to say otherwise.

"We had a drug problem in the eighties, but all that's settled down." The dockmaster scowled. "If you're looking for criminals, this isn't where they go."

"I can't discuss the case, sorry."

The dockmaster huffed.

Ruis pulled out his cell phone and found the publicity photo of Ruby. "Have you seen this person?"

Sadness settled around the dockmaster's eyes. "Sorry. Pretty girl."

Ruis set the papers on the counter. "Tell me about these." He pointed to the circled line items.

"Retired couple with a cat. They're Loopers from the Outer Banks. They come by every year."

Ruis drew a line through the item.

"This one's Colonel Scott, USMC retired. Widower in his eighties. Always brings back fish."

Ruis drew a line through that item.

Maggie returned and set the binoculars back on the counter. "Family of five with small children," she said crossing off another item.

Working through the list, they eliminated all but two. The dockmaster's descriptions missed those of Kuznetsov and Petronin. Disgusted, Ruis sat and combed his fingers through his hair. Tired, frustrated, and bordering on angry, he accessed the link to the mugshots of Kuznetsov's known associates. Maggie folded the list and sighed.

"Have you seen any of these men?" Ruis showed the dockmaster how to scroll through the photos by swiping his finger across the screen.

Interrupted three times by radio calls, the dockmaster finally squinted at the last photo and handed the phone back to Ruis. "I'm glad to say none of those men look familiar."

Maggie's cell phone rang. She listened for a moment and then lowered her phone. "They found an earring in the van. Blake says it's a positive match for the earring on the ransom recording."

Ruis closed his eyes. Martina had worn only one earring in the ransom video. It's mate in the van proved she had been in Gregorio Kuznetsov's van. *Where do we go from here?*

"Anything else?" She squeezed Ruis's forearm above his watch. "Good. We'll pick you up."

Ruis opened his eyes.

Maggie thanked the dockmaster and gave him her card. "Call me if you remember anything peculiar or hear about strange activity since Sunday." She then led Ruis outside. "The techs found traces of sweat and saliva in the back seat, but no blood. They're sending the samples for DNA testing."

Ruis nodded. He longed for more than trace evidence.

Maggie found three trawlers on the list still marked as active renters. "Let's eyeball them while we're here."

They walked in silence to the first slip, where an elderly couple were seated on the open upper deck sipping wine. Maggie waved at them and kept walking to the next boat's rental slip at the end of the pier. Music played from it as couples danced in the salon and clustered on the flybridge around a cooler. Maggie pivoted and led Ruis back down to the next parallel pier. Halfway down the pier, she stopped and checked the papers.

"Think they're out for the day?" she asked Ruis as if he might know.

He had not paid attention to the weather for days. He looked up at widely scattered clouds and felt the sun cooking his skin. He shrugged.

"You missed them," a voice behind them said.

Ruis turned toward the voice, which came from a leathery-skinned man standing on the swim platform of a forty-six-foot Grand Banks trawler. He wore a yellow polo shirt, blue shorts, brown deck shoes, and classic black Ray-Ban Wayfarer sunglasses. His thick white hair curled from under his ballcap that read OLD NAVY. He appeared a weathered sixty-something-year-old sailor.

Something in the old salt's demeanor keened Ruis's attention. The older boater sounded upset. Angry? Disappointed? The dockmaster had described the Nordic Tug owners who rented the slip as recently retired Yankees, a career Navy man and a nurse. They were so far removed from the profile of Kuznetsov and his ilk that Ruis had scratched them off the list with absolute confidence.

The dark-skinned man from the Grand Banks combed his fingers through his trim beard.

"There was a Nordic Tug here?" Maggie said.

"Yep. They left."

Ruis decided the man was disappointed with the owners of the Nordic Tug, which aroused his curiosity.

"When did they leave?" Agent Maggie asked.

"Are they in trouble?" The old salt removed his sunglasses and wiped them on his shirt. The name of his gorgeous trawler was *Bottom Gun*.

Ruis pointed to the ship's name, emblazoned in three-inch letters on the stern. "Did you serve on a submarine?"

The man grinned. "Torpedo man. And you?"

Ruis smiled. "I graduated from Annapolis in operations research."

The man grunted. "Theoretical or applied operations?"

"Both," Ruis said. He kept eye contact with the stranger until the man nodded, then Ruis held up his phone to display a photo of Martina. "We're looking for a missing person."

The sailor and apparent owner of the *Bottom Gun* climbed onto the pier. He examined the photo and sighed. "Pretty girls do have a way of finding trouble." He smiled at Maggie, pulled off his hat with his left hand, and held out his right. "I'm Simon Oliver. My friends call me Skipper."

Maggie smiled and shook his hand. "I'm Maggie Vega, and this is Ruis Ramos."

Ruis shook Simon Oliver's hand.

"Sorry, I haven't seen your missing person. It's mostly retirees here."

"When did the owners of the trawler leave?" Maggie asked.

"Well, that's the thing," Skipper said, rubbing the back of his neck. "Most Loopers have headed up the East Coast by now, but this couple"—he pointed to the empty slip—"they're new Loopers. I thought for sure they rented a car two days ago to attend a wedding. Expected them back today. Maybe I misunderstood."

"What happened?" Ruis asked.

"I guess they came back early. They motored out at four in the morning on Sunday."

"In the dark?" Ruis asked.

Skipper shrugged. "It's unusual for new Loopers, but Paul's a Navy man. He's teaching his wife, Caryn, how to handle the boat. I expect them back today. They ordered a new dinghy that came in this morning. Anyway, we're planning to leave tomorrow."

A couple in their fifties pulled a loaded cart down the dock. Ruis and Maggie stepped aside to let them pass. The couple stopped at the empty slip.

"Paul?" Simon Oliver asked.

"Hey, Skipper. Who moved my boat?"

Everyone within hearing turned toward the sound.

"I thought you did," he said. "On Sunday."

Color drained from Paul's face. He glanced at his wife, who put her hand to her mouth. Paul draped an arm around her shoulders.

"Did you give permission for anyone to borrow your boat?" Ruis spoke softly to the couple.

Paul and Caryn shook their heads.

Maggie identified herself to the distraught couple and showed them her credentials. "How much fuel did you have on board?"

The husband pulled off his ball cap and rubbed his head. "Maybe fifty gallons. We were planning to fuel up today."

Maggie called the Naples Police about the missing boat and asked if the police could bring Blake to the marina.

"Do you know where my boat is?" the husband asked.

Ruis ground his teeth. "No, but I might know who took it. Did you keep a key outside?" This boat was, after all, their home, and just like homeowners, boat owners often hid a key outside in case they locked themselves out.

The man's facial expression answered the question.

"This is unreal," Caryn said to no one in particular. "We just bought it."

"Where did you buy it?" Maggie asked.

"On Key Biscayne, just outside of Miami," Paul said. He turned to his wife. "Honey, do you remember the name of the marina?"

Ruis offered an educated guess. "Crandon Park Marina?"

"That's it," Caryn said.

Ruis sighed. At last, a specific boat to search for. Granted, the boat could be anywhere in a state that had more shoreline than California and eleven thousand miles of rivers, canals, and waterways. Certainly, the fact that the boat was stolen gave the Coast Guard authority to stop and board the boat, didn't it? "What's the name of your boat?"

"*Seeker*," Caryn said.

The ransom demand video played in Ruis's mind whenever he slept. He knew the details of the stateroom as if he were standing in it, so he thought about the bedcover with its patchwork of blues and greens that created a stylized image of waves. If Kuznetsov had stolen this Nordic Tug, he probably didn't bring his own bedding. Ruis calmed the couple to ask one more question. "What does the bedspread in the master stateroom look like?"

"Our home is missing," Caryn said, "and you want to know that?"

Maggie, on hold in her call to Espinosa, watched the couple.

"Please, this is important," Ruis said.

"Okay. I sewed matching quilts for the rooms in blues and greens, the colors of the sea."

"Does the pattern look like waves?" Maggie asked.

Caryn nodded as her eyebrows rose. She whispered to her husband, "That can't be good."

Paul grimaced.

Ruis clenched his jaw. The stolen boat matched the one featured in the ransom recording.

"The police are on the way. Please wait here," Maggie told the couple. She pulled Ruis by the arm down the dock toward the entrance.

Ruis kept pace. "Are you thinking what I'm thinking?"

"That Kuznetsov panicked when he found his boat sunk," Maggie said, "so he fled and found a similar boat."

"How did he know it was here?" Ruis asked. He returned to the couple. "By any chance have you announced your travel plans on social media?"

Caryn's eyebrows rose. "I started a blog. Why?"

"I'm wondering how many people knew your boat was here," Ruis said.

"Mostly my friends and family follow my blog, but members can locate other Loopers through an app." Caryn opened an application on her smartphone and showed the phone to Ruis.

"How does it work?"

"You type in the name of a boat and its location shows up on the map."

"What if you typed in your boat's name?" Ruis asked.

"It would show the boat is here. The app is tied to my phone, not the boat." Caryn shrugged.

Ruis recalculated the range of the boat based on the new information. The kidnappers had planned to depart from the east coast of Florida. Whatever their planned destination was, they would have been forced to find a new destination or reach it through a new route if they had stolen this boat from the east coast of Florida. But where were they headed? The Bahamas became less likely from Naples. If their destination was Tampa by Friday, then leaving from Naples shaved significant time off their route. But where had they gone?

Skipper handed Ruis and Maggie his business cards. "You want to find a missing girl and I want to help find my friend's boat. Let me know what I can do to help."

Ruis accepted his card and offer. "Thank you, sir. I think our next stop is the nearest Coast Guard station."

"That'd be on Marco Island, south of here."

. 20 .

Meanwhile, in Tampa, Tapper and Cuervo met with the Tampa police chief who readily agreed to allow Tapper to do surveillance duty on Stas Petronin's apartment. The officer who had been watching the apartment spoke with Tapper on the phone.

"The girlfriend sleeps all day and works at night at a strip club. She's the only one I've seen going in or out. The apartment is on the north corner of the building facing the street on the second floor. She's there now."

"Excellent. I'm a couple minutes out in a maroon two-door rental. I'm wearing a Cardinal's cap."

"I'm sorry to hear it."

"Oh, don't tell me you're a Mets fan." Tapper had watched Saturday's game on television. The Mets had beaten his beloved Cardinals in St. Louis two to one. Losing at home left a shameful sting.

"Yep." After a chuckle, the officer added, "I'd gloat, but I appreciate you taking over surveillance."

"Save your pity for a Cubs fan."

"Roger that."

Tapper turned onto Twigg Street. He spotted a beige Ford Crown Victoria parked under an oak and parked behind it. The apartment complex backed up to the Lee Roy Selmon Expressway, named after the Pro Football Hall of Fame defensive lineman who helped define the Tampa Bay Buccaneers. Tapper thought Selmon was the finest defensive end he'd ever seen play.

The silhouette of the man in the driver's seat pivoted, then faced forward. He was holding a phone to his ear. "I'll send you what I have on the girlfriend. She drives a 2008 black Ford F-150 registered to Stas Petronin."

His phone pinged, indicating an incoming message. Images of Stas's live-in girlfriend were embedded in the message. In every photo, she wore multiple gold chains around her neck and what looked like three diamond stud earrings on each ear. Straight whitish-blonde hair hung down her back to her waist in a ponytail.

Following that was a schedule of her work nights at the Penthouse Club and one photo of her on the job. Topless.

Tapper texted the officer: TOUGH SURVEILLANCE, BUT SOMEONE HAS TO DO IT.

The officer replied: NICER STRIP CLUB THAN MOST. THEY CALL HER DIAMOND.

Tapper's phone vibrated with an incoming call. "Tapper here."

"So, she parks on the bottom floor of the parking garage and roars out of the garage exit up ahead."

"Got it. This looks like a decent apartment complex."

"The outside is the ugly part. There's a central courtyard with a pool. They have a weight room and a lounge. I looked at renting here, but it was out of my price range." The Crown Victoria started up. "Stay safe."

"Thanks. You, too." Tapper tipped his ball cap and set it on the passenger's seat. He set his cell phone in the cup holder. The shade cut most of the morning heat, so he left the car windows up. Judging by the size of the oak trees, the neighborhood was fairly new. An auto repair shop sat across from the white and gray apartment complex. The main entranceway had blue-tinted windows.

The only traffic after thirty minutes was a Grumman Long Life Vehicle, the square white boxy light transport truck designed for the US Postal Service, making its daily rounds.

The postal truck surged from mailbox to mailbox and passed Tapper's rental car. Tapper reached into the back and retrieved a box. Then his cell phone vibrated with an incoming call labeled Cuervo.

"Trapper here."

"This is Cuervo. I understand the subject sleeps most of the day, so I'd like you to come to the Tampa police department for the planning session at noon."

"I'll be there."

"Thanks." Cuervo ended the call.

Tapper pulled a tracking device from the box. The tracker was half the size of a business card. He put the device in his shirt pocket and was about to open his door when a black F-150 exited the parking garage and paused at the street before rolling out to turn right.

He watched the truck through his rearview mirror as the F-150 headed toward Ybor City, the Cuban district once known for cigar manufacturing. He followed, keeping his car two vehicles behind the truck until it turned into the parking lot of a small shopping plaza. He continued down the road for three blocks, then circled around and pulled into the parking lot, where he parked beside the black truck.

The woman wasn't in the truck. While no pedestrians were around, Tapper climbed out of his car and wiggled under the truck to place a tracker. Since he didn't work for the FBI, he wasn't technically acting under their authority, so he didn't tell Cuervo about the device. As far as Cuervo knew, Tapper was watching the apartment. Period.

Once he was on his back looking up at the undercarriage, he was about to place the tiny, matte black rectangular device when a small green light on the undercarriage keened his attention. At first glance, he froze, fearing it was a bomb. After he examined it more closely, he nearly laughed with relief. It was a bulky, cheap tracker, the kind sold on the internet to parents of teens and paranoid spouses. Even the mob and trucking companies used better equipment.

Tapper anchored his tracker behind the rear axle, where it wouldn't be noticed during a tire change or an oil change. Maybe Stas's roommate wasn't involved in the kidnapping, but given the presence of the other tracker, he was willing to waste his own tracker to find out.

He scooted out from the underside of the truck and hopped into his rental car. There, he tested the signal from the tracker to his cell phone. The signal transmitted five miles. He started up his car and drove around the block. This time, he parked across the street where he could see the entrance of the café.

Diamond was seated inside an internet cafe a table near the window with her back to the wall and a laptop open in front of her.

Tapper called Special Agent Cuervo and told him.

"Can you see her now?"

"Yes, sir. She's alone at a laptop."

"Stay with her. Let me know if she meets with anyone. If she returns to the apartment, come to the meeting."

"Yes, sir." He opened the curb-side windows an inch to let out hot air. A waitress in her forties approached Diamond. They spoke for a moment, then the waitress left. Minutes later she returned with a large cup. Diamond pried the plastic cover and blew on the drink. She stared at the laptop screen for a while, then hunched over the keyboard intently. She drank for a while and stared at the laptop screen.

Meanwhile, from the flybridge of the boat, Stas uploaded the recording to the satellite phone and transmitted it to the second email address he'd set up for his girlfriend. She had suggested setting up emails to be used one time only, one for each ransom recording. He attached the recording and sent it to the *popstarfan2* email.

A full minute after he sent the recording, he called the number of the cheap phone they had bought just for the week.

She answered on the second ring. "Got it."

Background noise reminded him of the internet café. He could almost smell the coffee and donuts. He checked his watch.

"I wish you were here," her sultry voice teased.

"Be glad you are not here."

She chuckled. "That bad?"

"No air-conditioning. No decent food. The only thing worth having on this" — he stopped himself from revealing his location in any way — "this wretched trip is the booze."

"You brought alcohol?" she hissed.

"It was already here. I couldn't let it go to waste."

"I worked last night and I'm tired. I have to go."

He checked his watch. They still had thirty seconds without risk of tracing the call. Was she getting scared? "Remember to send the message on Friday morning. See you Saturday."

"You know where to find me." The call ended with a subtle click.

He smiled. He knew exactly how to find her even if she tried to leave with the money.

After a yawn, Diamond leaned in and typed on the keyboard. She finished her drink and closed the laptop. She then pulled out a cell phone and talked.

Tapper yearned to eavesdrop, but he hadn't brought the equipment for it.

Diamond keyed something on the phone with her thumbs. Her earrings glinted. Leaving the laptop on the table, she tossed her empty cup in the trash and sashayed out of the building. Considering her side-to-side motion and her three-inch heels and the uneven pavement, it was quite a sight to witness.

On her way to the truck, she stuffed the cell phone in a public trash in front of another storefront.

Tapper waited until the truck was out of sight, then he started his car and parked where the truck had been. He tore a flap off the electronics box and bent it in half in his hand. He then climbed out of his truck and picked the phone out of the trash with the box flap. Being careful to touch only one corner of the phone to preserve Diamond's fingerprints, he climbed back into his car and set the phone in the cup holder.

A beige Crown Victoria pulled into the parking lot. The officer who had been watching Diamond that morning climbed out with a briefcase in hand, acknowledged Tapper with a glance, and entered the café.

Tapper closed his car door. He tracked the truck back to the apartment's parking garage, then he headed to the main Tampa police station. He had evidence to turn in and he was eager to meet the fellow with the drone.

. 21 .

The Marco Island Coast Guard Auxiliary, also known as Flotilla 9-5 in District 7 and Division 9, occupied a squat, cement-block structure across the street from Caxambas Park. The park's main attraction was the fishing pier and boat ramp at the end of a road that had a mowed field on one side.

Ruis had hoped Maggie's briefing would call them to action, with staff loading weapons and launching boats, but the two retirees manning the station stressed the auxiliary's non-law-enforcement and non-military roles in search and rescue. Primarily, they explained, they taught boating safety, performed vessel safety checks, and watched for polluters. They looked more physically suited to run a church bake sale than an armed rescue at sea.

Breathing deeply and slowly through his nose, Ruis waited while Maggie waded through administrative procedures and the checking of policy handbooks.

When he heard one of the retirees mention that they didn't have arrest authority, Ruis turned away to compose himself.

Blake dropped into a chair to answer text messages.

"I don't suppose you've seen the news lately," the senior officer said as he combed his fingers through his white hair, "but most of our Coast Guard vessels and planes are searching five thousand two hundred square miles of the Gulf of Mexico right now. There are men missing from the Deepwater Horizon rig explosion last night."

Ruis bowed his head. He understood the Coast Guard was duty-bound to perform the extensive grid search pattern until ordered to stand down. Timing could not have been worse to beg for help. Any boats left out of the search would be on standby to cover for local emergencies. When it became clear to Ruis that the auxiliary might not help unless Martina radioed a distress call naming her location, he excused himself to get some air.

In the blazing sun, he paced the parking lot. He felt compelled to confess the situation to his father. The admiral, as he and his siblings privately called him, forgave screw-ups faster than he forgave lies. On Monday, Ruis had kept the facts about Martina's abduction from the admiral because he had hoped to find her quickly. On Tuesday, he'd believed that the FBI's investigation would bring a cascade of leads to follow because of the manpower focused on the task. Today, the clock haunted him. How could he find one boat in a search area that widened by 160 nautical miles a day without the Coast Guard's help? Keeping Martina's kidnapping from Father felt like an unforgiveable lie.

Ruis's phone vibrated in his hand, startling him. Caller ID showed Cuervo. "Yes, sir?"

"Maggie isn't answering. Is she okay?"

"She's trying to enlist the Coast Guard auxiliary here on Marco Island for help, but they're stretched thin searching for survivors of the rig explosion."

"It's a pity we can't just ask for aerial photographs of the state, you know the kind the spy satellites take that can read a postage stamp." Cuervo sighed.

Ruis grunted. Using a spy satellite would come in handy, but that wouldn't get approved unless the president's daughter was on the boat. Ruis moved into the shade and leaned his back against the Escalade.

"Your friend Terri has been calling marinas all day. She also called the head of the Seaplane Pilots Association and asked him to spread the word about the stolen boat," Cuervo said. "She's resourceful."

"Terri's an amazing woman."

"When Maggie's available, have her call and I'll bring you three up to date on the operation in Tampa."

"Yes, sir. Thank you." Ruis stared at his phone. As he did, a call came in and the caller ID read the Admiral. He hadn't been this afraid to speak to his father since high school when he rolled his father's car. He answered as if he hadn't read the caller ID. "Ruis here."

"How's it going, son?"

Hearing his father's voice threatened to break open the Pandora's box of pent-up emotions in Ruis's head. After a deep breath, he spoke. "It's a really rough day."

"Are you hurt?"

"No, sir."

Ten seconds later, the admiral's voice returned with steel in it. "Do you want to talk about it?"

He trusted his father more than he trusted any other living soul, including his old SEAL teammates. As a Navy admiral, Father had a career of secrets locked away in his memory. Dear old Dad even held a high security clearance. But secrets had weight that bore down on a person relentlessly, disturbing rest and appetite, and sometimes they shadowed relationships, creating an invisible barrier between the secret carriers and their closest loved ones.

Ruis measured the temptation to unburden himself by confessing the whole hideous situation with his father against the emotional toll of helplessness that came along with the truth. It wouldn't lessen his own burden to share it. As much as Ruis cherished his youngest sister, Father loved her exponentially more. He couldn't tell his father that Martina had been kidnapped and was probably dead. That kind of news had to be delivered face-to-face. With a defibrillator on hand.

Out of respect, he offered what information he could. "It's a kidnapping case. A girl in her twenties." A heavy silence grew while Ruis waited for his father to respond.

After some throat clearing, the admiral responded. "What are the odds for success?"

"Statistically, over ninety-percent of missing children are found alive."

"A girl in her twenties isn't a child."

If the worst happened, his father would remember this conversation, so Ruis decided it could soften the worst news if Father faced it in theory. "She's in her early twenties. Unfortunately, law enforcement agencies don't track statistics on missing adults." He refused to utter the hopeless words that expressed his fear. He declined to voice words of false hope, so he fell silent.

"I see," his father's voice beckoned from a deep, dark distance.

Dead air filled the distance between them. Ruis loved Martina, but he could not imagine how deeply the admiral loved his youngest child. Ruis stopped himself from thinking about his mother's reaction if Martina died. Was it worth having children in such a dangerous world?

The admiral's voice cracked. "No matter what happens, I'm proud of you. I know you will do your utmost to rescue this girl as if she were one of your sisters."

Ruis's throat tightened, and his eyes stung. Droplets fell on his shirt and at his feet. For a second, he wondered if it was raining. "Thanks, Dad." He glanced at the ground nearby through a blur. The only wet spots on the ground were at his feet. "I gotta go." He disconnected the call and stuffed his phone in his pocket and his emotions back in the box in his head.

The front door of the building creaked open, then Blake and Maggie headed toward the parking lot. Their voices carried across the small front yard. Ruis ducked behind the Escalade to wipe his eyes. The door locks chirped, so Ruis moved toward the front passenger seat.

Blake eased around to Ruis's side of the vehicle.

Ruis bowed his head and opened the car door. Blake nudged his elbow, so Ruis turned to find Blake holding out a folded white monogrammed handkerchief. Ruis took it and thanked him with a nod. He climbed in and buckled his seat belt. Of course Blake the Southern Baptist gentleman carried a cloth handkerchief.

"The Coast Guard agreed to patrol the channel between here and Gullivan Bay," Maggie said. "Do you want to go with them or go to Tampa, or Miami?"

Ruis wiped the handkerchief over his eyes and he blew his nose. He found the soft cloth unexpectedly comforting against his face. "I don't know. I can't think straight anymore."

"What about you, Blake?"

"I think better on a full stomach."

"How about seafood?"

"I'd like to see food," Blake said.

Maggie headed east. "I know a place on the water."

The car rolled by neighborhoods and shopping areas and retirees walking dogs on leashes. Ruis envied these people going about their daily routines. They trusted others to protect them from dangers both foreign and domestic. They depended on the rule of law and their constitutional rights for protection and justice. Ruis thought of himself as part of that front line of defense, that wall that shielded Americans from danger. He had captured and killed men more dangerous to the world than kidnappers. Despite the blood and sacrifices he had made, despite his unique skill set for planning and executing dangerous missions, he felt inadequate because he didn't know how to rescue one of his own sisters in his own country.

Lord, show me what to do.

Goodland, Florida, a quaint tropical fishing village made up of a maze of channels and strips of land with a population of two hundred sixty-seven, boasted a handful of restaurants with docks. The Old Marco Lodge sat on the northern tip of the maze on Goodland Bay. Its restaurant spilled out from an enclosed seating area to a wide terrace separated from the docks by a handrail.

The waitress led them outside at their request. She opened a yellow umbrella over the green table bathed in sunlight. Ruis pulled a green plastic chair into the shade for Maggie. She opened her mouth as if to object, then parked herself in the chair. Ruis seated himself facing the water and the docks. The aromas of fried fish and onions wafted from the kitchen. American flags flapped atop posts along the railing of the large deck. Nearby, a charter fishing boat shut down engines as one man tied off lines and five other men spilled onto the pier in lively conversation.

Maggie fanned herself with a menu. "This is about the handiest place to fuel up if you're heading south to the Keys or into the Everglades. That channel to the north is the Marco River, the inner passage from Marco Island." She nodded east and said, "Heading that way takes you to Gullivan Bay, south into the Gulf of Mexico, and into the Ten Thousand Islands."

Ruis smiled at Maggie. Cagey lady, of course she had chosen this restaurant for a reason beyond the food. While they were here, it wouldn't hurt to ask for records of Nordic Tugs that had fueled up since Saturday. At top speed of fourteen knots, the stolen boat had five hours' worth of fuel. Traveling at eight knots, they could have gone twenty hours. It was worth asking.

They ordered, and their food arrived quickly.

After dousing his fish and chips in apple cider vinegar, Blake devoured one fish filet in three bites. Maggie added hot sauce to her fish tacos. Ruis plucked the onion off his plain cheeseburger to fend off indigestion. He ate out of habit instead of hunger. Shutting down his emotions dampened his sense of taste. Simply put, food was fuel, so he consumed proteins, fats, and carbohydrates in whatever nutritional combination he could find to keep going. Ruis chowed down his cheeseburger.

During their meal, he counted twelve boats passing through Goodland Bay. This traffic for the middle of the afternoon on a Wednesday impressed Ruis because there were so few places inhabited south and east of here. The majority of passing boats were twenty-foot-long fishing boats.

"How far is it from Marco Island to the Keys?" Ruis asked.

Maggie held up a hand as she finished her fish taco. She washed down a mouthful of taco with a gulp of ginger ale. "I'd say it's about eighty nautical miles."

It would take six hours for the trawler to travel from Marco Island to the Keys, but it couldn't go top speed through this bay or the Marco River. At eight knots, it would take thirteen hours to reach Key West. At either speed, the boat would need fuel. In the open waters of the Gulf of Mexico, the waves and currents could get rough.

Blake jabbed the last of his French fries in ketchup and popped them in his mouth. When the waitress stopped to refill their drinks, she stared at the empty plates.

"Anyone for dessert?"

They declined. Ruis asked for the check. When the waitress flipped through her order pad and handed the slip to Ruis, he handed it back with a note and a one-hundred-dollar bill, telling her to keep the change. He then asked who handled fuel at the dock.

Momentarily dumbfounded, the waitress pointed. "Louie. He's our dockmaster."

The three of them strolled from the restaurant deck toward the dock's fuel station. Maggie led the way.

"That was a generous tip," Blake said softly as he slowed his pace. When they were a few steps behind Maggie, Blake turned and pressed his open hand on Ruis's chest, stopping him mid-stride. "I saw you palm a note to her."

What was Blake thinking? "So?"

"I speak as a friend and a fellow believer. Remember your marriage vows."

"Yes, I gave her my phone number." Ruis admired Blake for speaking up. "The tip was so she'd remember me and read the note to call if she sees a trawler named *Seeker*."

Blake dropped his hand. A blush rose from his neck to his ears. "Good idea."

They caught up to Maggie. Louie, a wiry man in his seventies, eyed them from his chair in the shade. His salt-and-pepper hair curled down to his collar. From his neck scarf to his authentic brown Sperry Top-Siders, he had the weathered appearance of a lifelong boater.

Maggie took the lead, introducing herself to the manager and addressing him by name. She showed him her badge, but he didn't bother to examine it. "By any chance did a thirty-seven-foot Nordic Tug buy fuel here since Saturday night?"

The man sighed. "Why?"

"We're searching for a stolen boat." Maggie pulled up a grid of six photos on her phone. "Do you recognize any of these men?"

Four of the faces were of FBI officers dressed down to look like suspects. Their hair and general build matched the suspects'.

The dockmaster dug a pair of readers from a cloth case in his shirt pocket and slid them on. He scowled. "Maybe that one." He pointed to Gregorio's face. "I'm better at remembering boats."

"This one is called *Seeker*," Ruis said. He didn't care about the boat except that Martina might be on it. Perhaps Maggie presented the stolen boat as the reason for her inquiry to downplay the danger associated with a known criminal like Gregorio Kuznetsov or a kidnapping. People tended to avoid getting involved with the investigation of violent crimes. Some feared being identified as witnesses or possible targets of revenge. Some feared being wrong and causing harm to innocent people. A stolen boat sounded far less dangerous than a kidnapping. Asking for information to locate a stolen boat also appealed to the dockmaster's identity as a mariner.

The dockmaster turned away and disappeared into a hut.

Fishermen from the charter boat tossed scraps of food into the water, attracting two pelicans and a seagull. The captain of the charter boat stopped them. Moments later, the waitress rushed out to talk to them. The men apologized while the waitress shooed the birds away. Tourists tended to enjoy feeding wildlife without considering the nuisance they were creating for the people who came after them. Feeding birds in the water inevitably attracted fish and alligators as well. Ruis remembered reading a news story about a trucker who fed an alligator in a pond near a truck stop in Florida. After months of being fed by previous truckers, the alligator learned to associate people with food. Thus, when a trucker fell into the pond, the alligator killed him.

"I once saw a pelican try to swallow a beer can," Blake said, leaning on the railing. "The other pelicans attacked him to take it from him. It's not the strangest thing I've ever seen, but it ranks high on my list."

Maggie nodded. "We turn them into scavengers, dependent on us."

"Kinda like government handouts to illegals, eh?" Blake said.

Ruis snorted. "You realize you said that to two Hispanics."

Blake's face turned a sunburned red and his eyes widened. It seemed he had stopped breathing until Maggie's laugh broke the tension. Blake gripped the railing and shook his head slowly. Ruis hadn't laughed in days and it felt wonderful. He slapped Blake on the back.

"Relax, *amigo*. No blood, no foul."

"I agree with you," Maggie said, elbowing Blake.

In truth, Ruis bristled at the way illegals received better benefits and protections than his grandparents had when they applied legally for US citizenship, complete with two years of mandatory language classes and lessons on the Constitution. His grandparents had arrived poor and worked hard to support their children through college. Too proud to accept welfare, they'd embraced the American way of life as much as they cherished their heritage and passed along their values to their children.

The dockmaster emerged from his hut with a receipt. "Sunday morning, these foreigners were first in line for fuel when I opened up. Worst sailors I've seen in years. I can't even describe how they tied off their boat." He shuddered.

"If you can't tie a knot, tie a lot," Ruis said.

"Exactly!" The dockmaster tapped a bony hand on Ruis's chest. He handed the receipt to Maggie.

Ruis read over Maggie's shoulder. One handwritten word caught his attention. *Seeker*. He closed his eyes. *Thank you, God, for the lead. They were here.*

"May we keep this?" Maggie held the original.

"Let me make a copy." The dockmaster took the paper into the restaurant.

While he was gone, Ruis texted the new information to Vincent, and Maggie called her boss to tell him. A spark of hope ignited in the dark pit of Ruis's despair. He needed to believe they had not run out of time to save Martina.

The dockmaster returned. Maggie pulled a clear plastic evidence bag from her pocket and held it open for the man, who slid the original receipt into the bag.

"Which way did they go?" Ruis asked.

"Coon Key Pass," the dockmaster said, pointing an arthritic finger to the east. "I knew that boat was too good for them."

Maggie thanked him. Blake and Ruis shook his hand.

In the parking lot, Agent Maggie stowed the evidence in the glove box and locked it.

Ruis and Blake stood by the open doors of the vehicle. Heat radiated from the car like an oven. Ruis grabbed his laptop bag and go bag from the back of the SUV and headed toward the office of the Old Marco Lodge.

"Ruis," Agent Maggie called.

Ruis turned around. "The Coast Guard is going to patrol from Marco Island to Gullivan Bay. We need to search from there to the south and east."

Blake pulled his go bag from the SUV.

"How?" Agent Maggie planted a hand on the side of the SUV and immediately lifted it off.

Ruis credited her with toughness for not crying out. A black vehicle absorbed heat in the Florida sun like a cast-iron pan. "Let's figure it out."

Maggie closed the driver's door and then headed to the back of the vehicle. Blake lifted out her small carry-on roller suitcase and carried it and his own across the sandy, uneven faded blacktop of the parking area as if it were expected of him as a consultant. Consultant or not, he was a gentleman raised in the south.

Inside the lodge, Ruis asked for three rooms and bought NOAA navigation charts thirty-nine and forty-one. Agent Maggie paid for her room on her expense account.

They agreed to stow their belongings and meet in the Riff Raff Bar to plan. Ruis set his bag in his room. He then carried his laptop and the charts downstairs to the far end of the bar near a tinted window that offered light and privacy. Most of the tourists ate outside on the deck overlooking the water. The locals watched sports on the television at the bar. He pushed two tables together. After connecting his laptop to the Wi-Fi, he opened the navigation charts on the tables.

Coon Key Pass aimed south, where it emptied into Gullivan Bay and the Gulf of Mexico. From Gullivan Bay, Gregorio could have navigated west to a bird sanctuary or back up the west coast of Florida in open water, or he could have gone southeast into the wilds of the Everglades or the Florida Keys. Ruis found his attention drawn to the Ten Thousand Islands on the western half of the Everglades. The jigsaw puzzle of disconnected islands offered ten thousand places to hide a boat. Ruis examined the map for depth markers. The *Seeker* drafted four feet five inches, which meant it had hundreds of places to hide.

Ruis's phone vibrated in his shirt, so he pulled it out. A plain phone number without a name appeared on the screen. He answered it.

"Ruis? Where are you right this minute?"

The threatening tone of the caller amused Ruis. "And who is this?"

"Oscar Gunnerson."

A second call interrupted. The screen read *Tapper*.

"Hold please." Ruis took Tapper's call. "Ruis here."

"Sorry, man. Oscar sat in on the ransom briefing and saw the video. He's in a van headed south on I-75 and he thinks you're in Miami."

Ruis had first met him at Blake's wedding and he remembered thinking that Oscar was a thinner, better-looking version of Vincent. Oscar was the only boyfriend Martina had ever brought to a family Christmas gathering. The whole family and even Martina's best friend, Nefi, approved of him, and Nefi was a shrewd judge of character. Ruis hoped Oscar would measure up to the task of setting aside his emotions to be useful in the search. "Does he have the drone?"

"I think so. There's a Japanese guy here with another one. He volunteered to assist the authorities. I believe he's Oscar's boss."

"Thanks. Oscar's on the other line."

"Cuervo, Oscar, and I are the only ones here who know who's who."

As agreed, Tapper did not use the names Ruby or Martina. If anyone leaked the name of the kidnap victim to the media, it had to be Ruby's name. Even the Tampa police were not fully informed of the victim's identity for the sake of Martina's safety.

"Got it." Ruis disconnected the call from Tapper. "Oscar, are you there?"

"Why didn't you tell me?"

"What would happen if the kidnappers discovered what you know?"

Oscar sounded as if his lungs were deflating.

Blake and Maggie crossed the bar and took seats at the table near Ruis. Maggie tapped her finger on their current location. Blake eyed the size of their search area, aptly labeled the Ten Thousand Islands, in open-mouthed awe.

"Do you have the drone?" Ruis asked Oscar.

"Yes."

"What's the range on it?"

"In miles or minutes?"

"We need to search the Everglades for a specific boat."

Oscar expelled a long breath. "With FAA approval, I could fly it over three-hundred feet AGL for aerial surveillance."

Drones were aircraft, so, of course, Oscar used aviation terminology to specify which of the five types of altitude he meant. Vincent's brother, Oscar, and Terri had broken into a lively discussion on the different types of altitude at Blake and Terri's wedding reception after a few glasses of champagne. Ruis remembered their discussion because it was so uniquely academic, and because they had to raise their voices to be heard over the live band. Above ground level, or AGL, was the expression used for *absolute altitude,* which measured the distance between the aircraft and the terrain below by timing how long it took for radio waves to bounce back. The other types of altitude were indicated altitude, density altitude, pressure altitude, and true altitude. Ruis knew about altitude measurements from his jump training, but he'd viewed their discussion as a form of geek bonding between Terri and her new brother-in-law, Oscar.

"That'll work. Bring the drone. Drive to Old Marco Lodge in Goodland. See you soon." Ruis tucked his phone in his pocket. "Oscar's coming, and he has a drone. Sounds like his associate is staying in Tampa to operate a second one."

Blake scowled. "How many people know—"

A waitress approached and took their order for coffees.

Blake ordered a piece of pecan pie with no whipped cream. He resumed talking after the waitress moved out of earshot. "How many people know who she really is?"

"The Tampa team is calling her Ruby," Ruis said, "but Oscar recognized her." He understood Blake's concern, because as more people learned about the investigation, the chances of a leak to the press or to social media multiplied. Secrets were challenging to keep. Some liked to brag, to get recognition of the dangers and importance of their jobs. Some liked to spread secrets, like arsonists set fires, to watch the consequences unfold. They had two days to prepare for the ransom drop in Tampa, which meant Martina's life expectancy was rapidly disappearing. A leak that the kidnappers had the wrong girl could be fatal. Ruis prayed for the secret to hold.

"Since we can't get a Coast Guard boat," Blake said, "are we going to rent one?"

Ruis retrieved a business card from his wallet. "I know a guy with a boat."

. 22 .

Martina awoke to the sound of breathing. A dark figure stood next to her bed. She froze. High heels dangled from his fist. In his other hand, a red dress sparkled.

She sat up slowly. "Time for the command performance?"

"It is." Black Mask's tone chilled her. He stunk of vodka and sweat when he dropped the high-heeled shoes and dress on the bed.

Moving purposefully to hide her shaking, she flipped back the covers and swung her feet to the floor. "Okay, then." She collected the dress and shoes in her arms and shouldered past him to the head, where she closed the door. After a deep breath, she exhaled slowly.

She changed out of the loose sweatpants and sweatshirt into Ruby's snug dress, high heels, and identity. A glance in the mirror reminded her of violence. Swelling had gone down on the purplish bruise covering her eye. Then she noticed her hair. Nine months earlier, when she had stormed into the lobby of the New York City FBI to tell off Vincent for breaking Nefi's heart, Blake had been there. He had labeled her changed hairstyle "a chainsaw haircut."

Blake was right. Swamp humidity had frizzed it, too.

Out of stubbornness or pride, she finger-combed her unruly hair and shaped it with a dab of liquid hand soap into Ruby's signature style. Though she wore a stranger's clothes to sing another woman's song, Martina was herself. The youngest child of a nurse and a Navy admiral, she held an Oxford undergraduate degree. She wasn't dangerous like her best friend, Nefi, or her brother, Ruis, but she was competitive-cheerleader tough. Deep down, she feared and loved God. If it was her time to die, so be it, but she'd fight to the end and leave marks on her killers. All those self-defense classes with Nefi had to pay off now or never. Speed, she told herself, could trump size.

She whispered to her mirror image, "I'm tough. I'm loved. I don't live by the world's standards. I live and die a child of the Almighty God."

Her hands stopped shaking and she raised her chin. She strode from the head to the top of the stairs at the helm and looked down into the salon.

The masked men turned to face her. Black Mask took a long swig from a handle of vodka.

Judging it was best to keep them off-balance by being unpredictable, Martina assumed her Ruby role by planting her hands on her hips. "Are you planning to film my performance?"

The men exchanged a glance. Black Mask shook his head. Green Mask bowed his.

"No? Good, because I don't look my best. You're already getting six million from this deal, so I suppose you aren't interested in selling an exclusive to the media." She descended the steps into the salon and continued past the men to the stern door. Climbing a ladder in heels was no small feat, but she rushed and stepped onto the upper deck before either man exited the salon and looked up.

On the open deck, two cloth and metal folding chairs sat along the stern railing, so Martina positioned herself in the center of the deck facing them. Night fell under a waxing crescent moon and thousands of stars. It was a beautiful night to die.

After engaging in a discussion conducted in harsh hushed

tones, the men followed her to the upper deck. Black Mask slid his chair to the corner with his back to the stern, then he sat and draped his right arm over the starboard railing. With his left hand resting in his lap, he held the Taser. Black Mask was strong enough to kill with his bare hands, so the Taser seemed like an odd accessory.

Green Mask complained with each step up the ladder. He limped to his chair and sat with his back to the stern and both hands in his lap. The handle of a black pistol stuck up from the front of his waistband. Clearly, he wanted easy, quick access to the weapon. His pudgy hands and clumsy movements didn't suit a killer. A gun, it seemed, served as compensation for his unintimidating appearance.

The gun confirmed their intent to kill her. She suspected Green Mask was stupid enough to believe carrying a gun made him tough enough to use it. She also suspected Black Mask was smart enough to keep his own fingerprints off a murder weapon. She didn't dare ask if the gun was loaded. Realizing she was staring at a man's lap, she aimed her attention to Black Mask's eyes.

"Does the gun scare you?"

She knew he was sneering under that mask. Rather than take the bait, she shrugged. "Did he lose the holster?"

Green Mask patted the gun. "I don't need one."

Black Mask nodded as if agreeing that holsters were things for lesser criminals.

Fine. Whatever. Idiots.

A six-knot breeze from the southwest occasionally gusted, gently rocking the boat. In the background, the dark water lapped mangrove roots that looked like pale arms arching into the water. As calmness settled over her, she considered the future. With the proof-of-life video recording done, the masked creeps didn't need her alive anymore, so if they were smart—and that was a big if— they would kill her and dispose of the body here in the swamp and go collect six million in bearer bonds. If they planned to kill her anyway, they would have no hesitation to do whatever they wanted to her first. That thought raised bile in her throat.

She doubted they would trade her for the ransom, but if that was their plan, they would eventually need to start the engine. Having sabotaged the starter, she suspected they would figure out that the engine had worked fine before they locked her down there. Even fools didn't believe in coincidence that much. Whether they planned to kill her or trade her, the situation would soon turn dangerous.

Black Mask tapped his foot on the deck.

"I haven't done this first song in public before, but it's one of my favorites. It was written by Britt Nicole. It's perfect for tonight."

Green Mask scratched his neck through his mask.

"The title is 'The Lost Get Found.'"

Black Mask grunted. Green Mask rolled his eyes.

Martina stepped side to side to set the beat in time with the music in her mind. She clapped on the downbeat through the instrumental stanzas, then she sang in a clear, strong voice. As she reached the chorus, she powered up to send the words to God's ears. "Don't let your lights go down. Don't let your fire burn out. 'Cause somewhere, somebody needs a reason to believe…"

The song empowered her to imagine having a future. Her future on the boat meant violence and death. She did not want these two greedy, violent men to burn out her light. Singing, she spun with her arms outstretched. All her reasons to live flashed through her mind, each face and name calling for her to survive. Her voice embodied the song's message of hope until she sensed her beloved family and friends with her on the deck. She knew what she had to do. At the end of the chorus, halfway through the song, she drew in a deep breath and turned her back on the men.

In two strides, she reached the railing and vaulted feet-first over it. A gunshot sounded as she hit the water.

Shouting was muted by rushing water bubbling around her as her high heels impaled the muddy bottom. She pried her feet from the imbedded shoes and swam toward the hull. The hard, smooth hull curved in as she followed it toward the bow below the waterline. Staying close to the boat would make it harder for her kidnappers to shoot at her. The shallow water prevented her from swimming under the boat, so she continued to the bow. Between the bow and the anchor, she bobbed to the surface for a gulp of air.

Adrenaline roared through her system, narrowing her vision and accelerating her breathing. Her heart thumped so hard she thought the kidnappers might hear it.

Above came shouting and screaming. A spotlight danced across the surface of the water off the port side where she had jumped in. Her wake rippled outward, forming concentric circles from her landing point. She seized the opportunity to swim in the opposite direction. Taking another deep, deep breath, she dipped under the surface and swam a modified breaststroke eastward until her lungs burned. She rolled face up and waited for the air in her lungs to lift her nose out of the water. As she rose, she watched for the searchlight. When her face emerged into the night air, her skin cooled with the breeze. A wormy stench of decay filled her nose.

This time the shouting and screaming sounded distant. Being careful not to disturb the water, she dared angle her face, exposing her forehead, to peek at the boat. Green Mask cursed and shouted. She couldn't see him. Black Mask paced the flybridge and aimed his flashlight off the far side of the boat.

Floating at an angle, so that only her face broke the surface, she turned gently to see how far she had to swim. She had covered one-third of the distance from the boat to a mangrove island. After three deep breaths, she eased down into the water and then swam hard below the surface toward the trees. It took three more underwater swims before her hand bumped into slimy roots. By the time she came up for air, Black Mask had widened the search area to the front of the boat. His flashlight painted the dark water with wide, frantic yellow streaks.

Panic urged her to scramble over the tree roots but climbing up the roots in a red sequined dress would announce her position.

Just breathe.

After a few minutes, her heart rate slowed from full-out panic to shock at being alive. To avoid detection, she kept her arms and body under the surface of the water, pulling herself along from one submerged root to the next, scraping her legs on shells in the shallows, until the mangrove-covered sandbar curved out of sight of the boat.

Hidden, Martina held a slimy mangrove root to take in her environment. Moonlight illuminated an archway formed from mangrove branches. A current moved under the archway suggesting a channel between sandbars, between the two groupings of mangroves whose branches overlapped. As her eyes adjusted to the moonlight, she spotted a strip of sand on the other side of the archway. She swam with her head above water toward the sand. Her knees and elbows struck shells, forcing her to crawl onto the narrow, shell-covered beach. Shells shifted and broke under her weight, causing her to freeze to prevent a cascade of tumbling shells. Small crabs scurried away.

Gradually, she crept over layers of shells into the shadows of a thick copse of mangrove trees. Her dress reflected tiny shafts of moonlight.

I might as well be wearing a disco ball.

She wiggled out of the tight, wet dress and wrung out as much water as she could, then she tugged the dress on inside out. Thousands of sequins scraped her skin in the process of putting it on. Saltwater stung each tiny abrasion. The taupe lining blended like camouflage with the sand and shadows around her.

Cold, wet, hungry, and sitting alone in the dark, she thanked God she was alive. She had no food, no shelter, no fresh water, and no plan for what to do next. Exhausted, she assessed that she wasn't safe from hypothermia, alligators, snakes, bugs, or starvation. Everyone she loved was too far away to help her even if they somehow discovered she was missing. Nonetheless, she had never before felt so alive.

She could accept death as a free person.

Eventually, she shivered herself to sleep.

. 23 .

Stas had spent the night wiping down the boat from the front to the back with towels soaked in bleach and water while arguing with himself. If he burned the boat, he'd destroy all fingerprints and DNA and other evidence, but the smoke would attract the Coast Guard and other boaters to the site.

If he knew how, he could sink the boat. Would saltwater destroy fingerprints and DNA? He had to be sure no one could tie him to the kidnapping or death or this boat. What a stupid, stupid mess! Leave it to Gregorio to ruin a simple plan.

For all Stas knew, the girl's body could be floating out to sea, where anybody could find it. He had to clean up Gregorio's mess or lose the whole perfect plan and six million dollars.

At four in the morning, using one foot to prop open the bathroom door, he dumped the towels in the shower on top of his bleach-soaked mask. Done with cleaning at last, he stomped into the narrow passageway, then up and down the stairs to the long, cushioned bench behind the table and stretched out to sleep. The chemical stench dissipated into the breeze that ran through the open windows and doors.

He wished he could start up the generator for air-conditioning one more time, but he didn't know how, and Gregorio was, as always, useless. Stas's attempts had failed. He wanted to use the satellite phone, but he needed to stick to the plan, or what was left of it.

As soon as he reached land, he would shave off the itchy beard. After all, he had to look like his passport photo.

He fell asleep smiling, with one word on his mind.

Soon.

Ruis paced the dock at the Old Marco Lodge, waiting for Skipper to arrive with his Grand Banks trawler, *Bottom Gun*. The waterway served as a choke point for boat traffic traveling to and from the Ten Thousand Islands area and a popular place to stop for food and fuel. Under the blazing noontime sun, he spoke into his cell phone to Blake. "How's it going there?"

"Agent Maggie lit a fire under the Coasties. She's perched on the bow with the fanciest binoculars I've ever seen. We're in Caxambas Bay, west of Gullivan Bay. We just passed the strangest cement house built on stilts. They call it the Cape Romano Dome House and it looks like giant white mushrooms rising out of the water." Blake's voice rose over the background engine noise.

Ruis sighed because it had taken the retirees manning the Marco Island Auxiliary Coast Guard station all morning to fuel up and travel through a small section of their search area. Basically, they were at the beginning of the Ten Thousand Islands.

"Our Coast Guard hosts suggested the structure as a possible hideout, so Maggie and I took a dinghy to it. No signs of recent activity there. Just old beer cans and birds' nests. We're on our way around Cape Romano and Grassy Bay before we go to Gullivan Bay."

"What kind of boat are you on?"

"Uh, it's about thirty feet long and it has a shallow hull. I've rented larger boats for fishing."

A Grand Banks trawler approached from the west. Other similar-size boats followed in its wake like a midday rush hour. Fishing was better early in the morning than in the afternoon, but Ruis hadn't been deep-sea fishing. Maybe afternoon conditions favored fishing in the Gulf of Mexico and the Everglades. Ruis turned to check on Oscar, who paced the dock from the restaurant to his pile of gear.

"Stay sharp," Ruis told Blake.

"You betcha, boss," Blake replied. "Godspeed."

"Godspeed." Ruis tucked his phone in a pocket. Pointing to the trawler, he addressed Oscar. "I think our ride is here."

Oscar stopped by his gear.

Flanking the bow of the boat were two figures holding lines. A woman on the port side and a tall man on starboard. Skipper, a retired Navy man, had brought along the owners of *Seeker*. The *Bottom Gun* eased up to the closest dock, where Ruis stood to catch the line. The engines kept running as a man stepped off the boat.

Ruis tied off the line and stood. "Paul?"

Paul turned toward Ruis and smiled as if pleased Ruis remembered his name. "Yes. Caryn and I asked to come along. We want to help."

Ruis shook his hand. "Excellent."

Oscar wheeled his drone case down the dock behind Ruis. He had a black duffle bag slung over his shoulder.

Ruis took the line Caryn handed him and tied it off to the dock.

"This is Oscar Gunnerson," Ruis told Paul. He then turned to Oscar and said, "Meet the owners of *Seeker*, Paul and Caryn. The man piloting this fine Grand Banks pleasure motorboat is Captain Simon Oliver."

Oscar shook hands with Paul and Caryn. Ruis, Oscar, and Paul quickly loaded Oscar's gear onto the boat. Skipper waved for Ruis to come up to the flybridge.

While Oscar and Paul moved the gear into the salon, Ruis continued to the pilothouse. "Thank you, Captain Oliver. The Coast Guard is stretched thin since the explosion in the Gulf."

"Please call me Skipper. I recruited some friends to widen the search grid," Skipper said with a wave to a passing fishing boat. When he raised his arm, a holstered 1911 peeked from under his shirt. "Not all Navy. But solid sailors."

The captain of the fishing boat waved his hat.

Ruis returned his attention to Skipper's face.

Skipper tugged his shirt hem over his weapon. "We met last night to divide up the map. They understand the need for radio silence, so if they find *Seeker*, they call your satellite phone, and you can notify the Coast Guard or anybody else you see fit to tell."

Two more boats passed, their captains raising hats and coffee mugs in salute.

A lump of hope formed in Ruis's throat. "How many friends did you recruit?"

"Eleven boats. Half headed north. How many did the Coast Guard send?"

"One. It's an auxiliary station made up of *retirees*." Ruis sighed heavily.

"Retirees you say?"

Ruis flinched. Explaining what he meant would not help. He bowed his head in apology.

Skipper snorted and lightly swatted Ruis on the back.

Oscar and Caryn gathered behind Ruis and Skipper. Paul untied the spring lines and stepped back on board. After he spooled the line and tied it to the rail, he entered the cabin.

"Caryn, would you show our guests our search area?" Skipper motored into Goodland Bay heading southeast at the end of a parade of search boats.

Caryn pointed to markings east of Gullivan Bay on the NOAA chart. "We divided up the Ten Thousand Islands area from Marco Island to Everglades City into sections. We start at White Horse Key, searching as far inland as possible in every passage and back out to West Pass."

Ruis had identified this range of islands as the most likely hiding spot for the kidnappers because of its proximity to Tampa and its remoteness. By now, all the marinas in Florida and the Bahamas had been notified to watch for *Seeker* with instructions to report its location to the Miami FBI or Bahamian authorities because it was stolen property. The instructions, no doubt, included a warning not to approach the boat or those on it because they were considered armed and dangerous. That kind of wording discouraged civilians from doing anything beyond placing an anonymous call. With no mention of reward, the incentive was to follow the Golden Rule, to treat others the way you wanted to be treated. Ruis believed boaters valued their boats the way men in the Old West valued their horses. In the Old West, horse stealing was a crime so unthinkable it warranted the death penalty.

Oscar turned away. "I'll set up the drone."

Ruis and Paul followed him to the piles of gear. Ruis didn't know much about drones, and being eager to learn, he launched the first question.

"How much area can this drone cover?"

Oscar removed a lightweight helmet from one of the hard cases stacked in the salon. "Do you want a precise explanation with the calculations or do you want the top-brass version?"

"The top-brass version," Ruis and Paul answered in unison.

Oscar gave them a half grin. "At fifty feet above sea level, the line of sight horizon extends twenty miles. Take it one hundred feet higher, add forty miles."

"By line of sight do you mean visual only?" Paul asked.

Oscar shook his head as he opened a larger case revealing the drone. "I programmed it last night to scan for shapes that match the dimensions of a thirty-seven-foot Nordic Tug."

The drone was smaller and more fragile-looking than Ruis expected. In fact, it resembled a sky-blue plastic toy from the thin metal rotors to the highly polished surface.

"What kind of heat signature would your boat have at anchor?" Oscar asked Paul.

"They have to run the generator twice a day," Paul said. "When that's off, the grill and people would give off heat. I'm curious. Are you in special operations?"

"I work for a civilian contractor. This is a prototype, so I'd appreciate it if you didn't discuss this drone with anyone. It might be best if you forgot I was here, too." Oscar looked at Paul as if waiting for a promise.

"I understand a girl is missing." Paul sat on the bench seat by the salon's dining table.

Ruis and Oscar shared a grim expression.

Ruis sighed. "She was kidnapped."

In the salon, everyone could hear the conversation, including Caryn in the galley and Skipper at the helm. Ruis held his breath in anticipation that they might back out of the search.

Paul nodded. "Skipper and I suspected as much."

"And you still came."

Paul nodded and looked at Caryn, who was preparing food at the counter. "We want our boat back. We also have a daughter."

Ruis nodded. His heart swelled. *Thank you, God, for good people.*

"I read that certain metropolitan police departments use drones and robots to go into places too risky for officers," Paul said. "Is flying the drone like playing a video game?"

Oscar smiled. "In some ways, yeah."

Ruis found Paul's enthusiasm for technology like Oscar's. "Paul, what did you do in the Navy?"

"I kept the power plant on the sub running."

"You were a nuclear engineer?" Ruis suddenly felt like the dumbest man in the room.

Paul nodded. His easygoing demeanor disarmed Ruis. Soon Paul and Oscar were swapping stories about electronics.

Ruis watched mangroves along Coon Key Pass through the window of the salon. He cherished the moment, surrounded by good people who were putting themselves at risk to save a boat and a stranger. It gave him hope that the world was not falling apart at the seams. While many whined that "someone should do something" about evil and injustice, others quietly took action. Such everyday heroes drove police cars, manned fire stations and military posts, labored in hospitals on holidays, arrived first on the scene of accidents, and served in hospice care. Today's everyday heroes, in Ruis's view, piloted boats in search of a missing girl and a missing boat in April. Yes, some were retirees. He deeply regretted his earlier assessment of retirees. He hoped he would have the same courage at age seventy that he possessed in his thirties.

Caryn set a tray of fresh fruit and cheese on the table. "Who wants coffee?"

All hands raised.

"So how high can this drone fly?" Paul asked.

"I can't discuss the service ceiling. Today, however, she's topping out at four thousand feet MSL," Oscar said. He opened a laptop and set it on the dining table.

"So you'll get a seventy-seven-mile line of sight horizon?" Paul asked.

Oscar's head snapped up from his laptop. "Exactly."

Feeling dumber by the minute, Ruis climbed back up to the helm. There, Skipper handed him a pair of binoculars, so Ruis slipped outside to scan for boats tucked into hideaways as they cruised toward White Horse Key. The surf in Gullivan Bay was calm with an occasional low, rolling wake from a long-departed boat or a larger ship at sea. In the distance, the other search boats appeared as dots on an expanse of water framed by the Everglades and the islands of the keys.

While it was wonderful to have a torpedo man, a programmer, an engineer, and a nurse on the mission, Ruis knew that the deciding factor in success wasn't always based on brain power. And it certainly wasn't luck or coincidence, which unbelievers credited. His mother had drawn from a long career in nursing when she told Ruis one evening that doctors and nurses used tools, skills, technology, and every asset at their disposal to save patients, and yet, she'd witnessed the unlikely survival of dying patients and the shocking deaths of apparently healthy ones. She had concluded that God's will ultimately superseded human efforts.

Mother had intended to comfort him with the reminder that a human life is like the blink of an eye in the long view of eternity. That all suffering, no matter how painful, passed, losing its significance and horror in the great expanse of time.

Ruis understood the fleeting nature of life. But he still fought for it. Today, he had volunteers, tools, technology, and weapons to assist him in the battle for his sister's life.

May it all be enough and in time.

Stas awoke to what sounded like footfalls above him. He grabbed the Taser and peered through the window. He had to kill anyone who saw him here. After sneaking from window to window, he couldn't see another boat.

Could the girl be alive?

Vowing to fix that problem, he crept to the stern door and climbed the ladder to the deck. Strange scratching sounds aroused his curiosity. Peeking over the ladder, he saw large birds gathering on the deck. He slapped his hand on the deck and the birds scattered.

"Time to go," he said. He didn't expect nor did he receive a reply.

He eased back down the ladder and collected the video camera, his duffle bag, the last bottle of water, and the last beer and went to the back of the boat. He passed through the cockpit, through the transom's swinging door to the swim platform in front of the dinghy, where he piled the items.

"Where did you leave the key?" he muttered. "Useless."

He tromped through the boat, searching each room, each drawer and cabinet and cubbyhole. In the kitchen area, he even crawled on his hands and knees to look under the table and smacked the back of his head. Shouting and cursing in Russian, he rolled away, holding the sore spot with both hands until it stopped stinging. There, on his side, he spotted a rack of keys by the back door over the window.

He grabbed them all and took them to try on the lock that held the dinghy to the rack attached to the end of the boat. One by one he dropped the non-working key rings over the transom, littering the boarding platform.

Sweaty, hungry, and irritated, he reminded himself to be calm like a multimillionaire. Soon, he'd be so rich he'd forget all about this miserable week. He'd be so rich he'd never have to ride in a small boat again for the rest of his life.

Key by key, he worked through the choices, until one key released the lock with a satisfying *click*. This working key had two other keys on the ring. One of them should start the dinghy. The other, a wide U-shaped piece of metal, didn't look like a key at all. He jammed the keyring in his pocket and lowered the dinghy into the water.

He tied a rope to prevent the dinghy from floating away. After he loaded his things into the little craft, he returned to the shower for the bleach-soaked cloths. On his way out of the boat, he wiped whatever he remembered touching that morning, then he dropped the cloth into the water.

. 24 .

Tap. Tap. Tap. Tap. Tap.

Aware of something touching her face, Martina opened her eyes.

Tap. Tap.

Martina reached for her temple but there was nothing on her skin but water. Dew had settled on the leaves and shells around her. Fresh water! She squirmed under the mangrove branch to catch dew in her mouth until the dripping stopped. It tasted salty. She understood that saltwater would dehydrate her, but she was too thirsty to spit it out.

Shadows passed over her, causing her to freeze in fear.

Have they found me?

Above the mangroves, two black birds with wide wingspans circled. At a glance, they looked like turkeys. They had red heads or were those waddles? She shook her head. Turkeys didn't fly that high. Did they? She sighed. From her damp scalp to her sand-encrusted toes, she ached from falling asleep on a bed of sun-bleached, broken shells and hard-packed, coarse sand.

She crawled over and under mangrove roots toward sunlight to spy on the boat. Every sequin that scraped and dug into her skin under her arms and along her belly as she moved reminded her that her dress was inside out. From the safety of the shadows, she spotted a large, muscular figure emerging from the stern door. Black Mask. His shouting carried across the water.

Guessing he couldn't start the boat's engines, Martina smiled. He disappeared into the salon and returned to dump an armload of things on the swim platform near the dinghy.

Uh-oh.

After his third armload, he lowered the dinghy. He wasn't wearing his mask. The beginnings of a beard covered the bottom half of his face. He had thick, dark wavy hair framing a prominent brow and dark eyes. At a glance, he could have been mistaken for handsome. Blackbeard.

His combination of attractive features and sociopathic personality sent a chill through Martina. He must have assumed she was dead to forgo his mask. Did Green Mask share his barefaced confidence that they had rid themselves of their victim?

She watched the hulking figure load the camera equipment, a handheld radio, and other items into the dinghy. She longed for the men to leave the boat, so she could swim back to it for shelter and fresh water and scraps of food left behind. Wouldn't it be wonderful to find a second radio or a flare gun to use to call for help? And then what? How would she identify her position?

Her ankle tickled as a walnut-size fiddler crab crawled over her skin. She gritted her teeth until the creature fell off the side and continued toward her other leg. She bent her leg at the knee to clear the way for the crab to go on his way. The sputter of the dinghy's motor drew her attention back to the boat. Black Beard released the line and shoved the dinghy from the back of the boat, revealing large black letters on the stern. *SEEKER.*

In her mind, the name *Seeker* became seek her. For some reason it struck her as funny and she laughed, then she covered her mouth with her hand. Sitting beside the tiny motor, he couldn't have heard her, but her fear remained that she would be recaptured.

Her plans for returning to the boat unraveled. Green Mask was still on the boat. She scooted deeper into the shadows as Blackbeard steered the lifeboat toward her. She clutched a sharp broken shell in fear he would land on the shell-covered strip of beach nearby. The only reason to land would be to search for her. Did he have the gun or the Taser?

The boat puttered closer and closer until she saw the open drain hole at the front of the dinghy just below the rubber-edged gunnel. His weight kept the drain hole above the waterline. The vessel sat low in the water, but not low enough to swamp the back. He wasn't wearing a life vest, as if he hadn't intended to go far from the *Seeker*.

Martina held her breath in the shadows of the mangrove. Weathered broken shells dug into her forearms and knees. Gnats buzzed at her eyes and ears.

Blackbeard kept his gaze aimed off the front of the dinghy. The puny motor chugged on through the calm cove heading south according to Martina's interpretation of the morning shadows. Was he headed to this mangrove island? She decided that if the motor stopped, she would scramble into the channel under the mangrove archway to the copse of mangroves she'd swum to last night. She was smaller and could crawl through tighter places than he could follow. He was lazy, so he'd probably just shoot.

The engine sound continued.

The dinghy's white hull reflected through gaps in the mangrove roots and branches. He stood, letting the boat drift, as he scanned the mangroves. The dinghy rocked, so he crouched and grabbed the gunnel.

Tensing to flee, Martina watched him sit and rev the motor. The sound of the small laboring engine faded gradually as the lifeboat continued toward deeper water. Drawing in a breath, Martina rose to her hands and knees and picked her way around and over plants, shells, and scurrying crabs to follow the path of the dinghy as it cruised low in the water through mild waves in the cove. As the small craft entered open water, the engine revved and turned westerly. After it shrank into a tiny white speck in the distance, Martina relaxed.

Reasoning that Blackbeard was headed toward Tampa to collect the ransom, she guessed that she was in the Everglades, that vast swamp at the bottom of the map of Florida. Given the size and range of the dinghy, the kidnapper was either confident he could reach a marina or desperate enough to search for another boat.

If only she could get to the trawler and see the navigation charts, she would know the distance to boat traffic or civilization. But she couldn't return to the boat, not with Green Mask still there. He'd probably kept the gun. The Taser hurt like being struck by lightning, but it wasn't lethal.

She climbed back to the hidden beach and the archway of branches in search of a large shell she could use to collect dew. Without water, she knew she wouldn't last long. If she could last three days, the kidnappers would have their ransom and leave. Black Mask would have the money to rent a boat to come back for Green Mask. Neither man seemed comfortably at home on the boat, so they'd abandon it, or repair it and leave. Either way, she needed to stay hidden and stay alive until they were both gone. Then, and only then, would she feel safe to signal a ship for help.

Stepping gently on the rounded shells and black, dried strings of seaweed, she searched for a large shell. The exoskeleton of a horseshoe crab looked promising until she noticed the crack that ran the length of it. Sunlight glinted off a piece of glass. When she stooped closer to inspect it, she recognized the label of a handle of vodka. Unweathered, this had to be the empty bottle Blackbeard had thrown overboard days ago. It would hold enough water to last for days. She was thirsty and hungry. Even if she could catch a fish, she couldn't risk starting a fire to cook it, and she wasn't hungry enough yet to consider eating it raw. Sushi didn't appeal to her even when she could drown it in fancy sauces.

She sighed. She couldn't start a fire without matches or a lighter. No doubt, Ruis and Nefi knew how to start a fire by rubbing sticks together. They were resourceful. They could survive anywhere. Martina realized she'd never even started a grill. She had grown up depending on others to do things.

The sun dried her clothes and warmed her skin during the hour she searched for useful items among the broken shells. A handful of filament netting, driftwood, bits of plastic, and an empty beer can all sat in a pile at her feet, waiting for her imagination to find uses for them. A beer can could reflect sunlight to signal a boat, provided the positions of the boat and the sun cooperated. She scooped out a place to sit and examine her collection.

Shadows moved across the shells. Above, five large birds circled.

"Are those herons or storks?"

The voice startled her. It came from the direction of the mangrove archway between the sandbars. She scrambled over the shells and dove into the shadows of the nearest mangroves. Her heart banged in her chest like a wild bird in a cage. A kayak floated under the archway and in it sat a man and a woman in their fifties wearing orange life vests over their shirts. Their kayak was headed into the cove where *Seeker* lay at anchor.

Martina burst from the shadows and dashed over shells to stop them.

The man seated in the back of the kayak gasped and recoiled.

"Please stop! You're in danger," Martina whispered intensely as she held out her palms, her fingers spread wide at the couple.

The woman gave a small squeak.

Moving to the water's edge, Martina pressed a finger to her lips. "Stop. Stop. Stop."

The man backpaddled, causing an orange kayak behind him to veer toward the beach to avoid the kayak.

A second two-person kayak pulled up alongside. It held a man and a cooler. The man in it took charge of the others by directing them to stop. He wore an orange vest over a long-sleeve tan shirt. His baggy knee-length shorts had a camouflage pattern. The eco-tourists all started talking at once.

Martina waved her arms. "Please don't make noise. There's a boat anchored nearby. The man on it has a gun. He thinks I'm dead."

Whether it was her inside-out dress, her bare feet, or her terrified behavior that convinced them to be quiet, she didn't know. But she knew the guide took her seriously after he dug a radio out of his waterproof bag. She leaped into the water to grab his hands.

"He has a radio, too. If he finds out I'm alive, he'll kill everyone." She cried against her will. It was one thing to die, but worse to be responsible for the deaths of others. Of course, she looked and sounded like a madwoman. Her pals at Oxford would have called her barking mad if they were here. She didn't care what anyone thought of her so long as they understood the immediate danger.

The guide lowered the radio back into the bag and sealed it. He climbed out of his kayak, removed his orange vest, his hat, and his Wayfarer sunglasses. Standing waist deep in water, he dug into his bag and found binoculars. "Everyone, stay here. Bill, give this woman a bottle of water. I'm going to take a look."

Martina shivered in the warm water. How far could Green Mask shoot accurately with a handgun? She watched the tour guide walk in a crouch, then a crawl, then lie on his front. He eased the binoculars up and held them up for a full minute before he crawled backwards. Shells crunched and slid under him. Someone handed a sweating plastic bottle of water to Martina. She gulped water while she stared at the guide.

He returned, tucking the binoculars into the bag. His eyebrows bunched over his nose and his mouth formed a firm, tight line. He grabbed the edge of the first kayak and towed it back toward his kayak. "How many people are on the boat?"

"One. The other took the dinghy west." Instead of hugging the stranger for believing her, she wiped her eyes. Hope ballooned in her that she might survive after all.

His hazel eyes energized her. "What's your name?"

Muscles in her chest squeezed. Telling them one name would create a media circus and ruin the ransom drop. Telling them the truth would mean her family would be notified. "I can't tell you."

His eyebrows rose, and his mouth fell open. It took him a moment to recover and close his mouth.

She leaned close enough to talk to him and him alone. "I need to talk to the FBI."

Coconut suntan lotion and aftershave wafted from him as he pulled off his shirt and handed it to her. The mother and daughter tourists smiled at his bare sculpted chest and stomach. He plucked a T-shirt from his bag and tugged it on.

Martina put his large long-sleeve shirt on over her inside-out dress. It covered her dress and the cuffs dangled past her fingertips. It smelled like coconuts.

He handed her his ball cap embroidered with the words Everglades Area Tours, so she donned the cap and fastened it snug in the back. The older woman in the double kayak held out her giant dark sunglasses.

Martina waded to her and took the glasses. "Thank you," she whispered.

"People, we're going to backtrack to the main boat at a steady pace." The guide spoke in hushed tones. "This is now a rescue mission. Our change of course will cut one hour from the tour."

No one complained.

The eco-tourists drank water and relayed granola bars and fruit from kayak to kayak to their guide. He lifted the cooler and directed Martina to sit in the front of his kayak. After she was situated, he set the cooler on her lap and gave her the food others had donated. The tourists, a family of four, quietly turned their vessels around and paddled back under the mangrove archway with their guide following.

. 25 .

From the open flybridge, Ruis had a clear view of the swamp and wildlife as the boat idled. They had traveled as far as shallow water would allow. Skipper expertly executed a 180-degree turn in a sixty-foot-long boat without bumping a shoal.

Ruis's satellite phone rang twice before he answered it.

"Hey, Ruis, we got a distress call from a fisherman near Turtle Key," Blake said. "The Coast Guard has to drop out of the search. There's no telling how long this will take."

Ruis ran his finger over his navigation chart and found Turtle Key. It was within the Coast Guard's search area in Gullivan Bay. The rest of the volunteers were searching farther southeast, so he figured others could check the area the Coast Guard missed on the way back to Naples.

"I understand."

Skipper eased the *Bottom Gun* between Hog Key and Panther Key. He and Paul were below at the helm. Their voices carried through the open doors as they consulted the depth finder and the navigation charts to avoid running aground.

Ruis pocketed his phone. Below in the salon, Oscar operated the drone through a combination of a heads-up navigation helmet, voice commands, and a complicated laptop. Oscar had said his drone's authorized flight ceiling was four thousand feet today.

The more he learned about Oscar, the more he could accept

him as potential family. The young man had managed to talk his boss into allowing him to operate a multimillion-dollar prototype over the Everglades. Oscar had volunteered before he knew who the missing person was, which impressed Ruis.

Ruis picked up motion in the sky to the southeast and raised his binoculars toward it. At first, it appeared to be a bird floating on a current of air, then on closer inspection, the shape revealed it as a drone. Why was it descending? At about one thousand feet above sea level, it hovered in place, staying there for a full minute.

Ruis climbed down to the boarding platform and stepped into the salon to ask Oscar about it.

Paul, Skipper, and Caryn were staring at Oscar.

"What did he say?" Skipper asked Paul.

"Sounded like bingo."

"I thought he said hold." Caryn set her binoculars on the chart table.

Oscar removed his helmet and set it beside his laptop. "I have a positive ID on *Seeker*." He then dashed out the stern door and puked over the gunwale.

Martina boarded the twin-engine Everglades Area Tours boat anchored near the mouth of Indian Key Pass. The guide escorted her into the small cabin and wrapped a blanket around her. She flinched violently, causing the blanket to fall off.

"I'm sorry. I didn't mean to—"

"I'm just jumpy." She removed the sunglasses and handed them to the guide. "Please thank the lady for me."

He held the sunglasses and backed toward the steps up to the helm. "You're safe."

"Please don't close the door," she begged. "And don't let anyone call on the radio about me."

"You can take that up with my boss." The guide returned to his guests.

Outside, the others used a lever arm to lift the kayaks onto the deck. They spoke in hushed tones as if trying to discover the exciting secret about the strange girl they'd rescued from the middle of nowhere. After some conversation, everyone settled in for the ride to the tour base.

A balding man in his forties, wearing a company logo polo shirt, stepped into the cabin just inside the door. "I am obligated to report finding you to authorities. We need to get medical care for you, too."

Martina stood as tall as she could and took two steps toward him. She had not survived captivity to waste the opportunity to catch the kidnappers now. She dug deep for her mother's most serious tone of voice, the low-throated whisper that stopped children and grandchildren in their tracks. "If you announce on the radio that you found a woman, one of the likely consequences will be my death. Do you understand?"

"You sound awfully dramatic making demands like that." His glance sized her up.

"When we get to land, I'll call the FBI, or you can call them, but please, don't mention finding me over the radio." She wanted to be convincing, to speak with authority, but emotion rose in her, overflowing through her eyes. With her left hand, she wiped a tear off her nose in a quick gesture as if her body betrayed her spirit.

"I tell you what. If you stay in here and don't make trouble with my tour guests, we have a deal."

Martina stuck out her hand and shook his.

Nodding, the guide backed out of the cabin. Soon afterward, the engines rumbled to life and the anchor chain rattled up into its locker.

The younger guide stuck his head in the cabin. "We'll be in Chokoloskee in an hour."

Martina didn't care where Chokoloskee was except that it was away from the men who wanted to kill her. She was alive. She wouldn't feel entirely safe until she knew Black Mask and Green Mask were in custody. She dreaded calling Ruis. First, she'd have to convince him that she was in Florida and not in England studying for exams. Then she would have to explain how she had ended up getting kidnapped. It was going to sound insane no matter how she said it. Would he believe any of it?

No.

She couldn't call Nefi or Oscar because they would be angry she had lied to them. Where had the kidnappers sent the ransom video? Who had access to Ruby's money? Ruby's agent. The woman had probably written off the video as a prank since she knew full well Ruby was safely tucked away in a posh rehab center in Puerto Rico. Besides, she didn't know the agent's phone number because it was in her lost phone. If the tour company had a computer, she could search online for the agency's number.

The boat bobbed gently over waves while Martina pulled the blanket around her shoulders. She settled onto a cushioned bench seat. Who wouldn't be too angry to help?

The local FBI.

The people to trust to do something were FBI agents in the nearest field office. If she could reach the FBI before the ransom drop-off, they could catch Black Mask. She was eager to tell them where to pick up Green Mask. During the rest of the ride to Chokoloskee, she planned what she would say to the FBI so they would believe her.

. 26 .

Ruis steeled his nerves and strode to the laptop to see what had caused Oscar to puke. The screen showed two panels. One displayed dials that looked like those in a cockpit. Altitude, attitude compared to the horizon, speed, distance, and remaining fuel in minutes. The speed held at zero. The second panel displayed a grid of camera images, and in the center image, a body lay face up on the white open deck. A reddish-black stain spread from the body outward.

By the size and shape, it was a man. A handgun sat beside him. A chill climbed up Ruis's back.

Paul stood beside Ruis and pointed to the screen. "Is that—"

Ruis nodded.

Caryn pulled a ginger drink from the small refrigerator in Skipper's galley.

"Oscar!" Ruis called.

Oscar braced himself in the doorway at the stern for a moment before crossing the room to the laptop. "Sorry." He cleared his throat and sat.

Caryn handed him the drink. "This helps with nausea."

"Thank you." Oscar took a long draw from the can.

Paul led his wife by the elbow up to the pilothouse. "Let's give him some room."

"Can you fly inside? Does this have a sound feed?" Ruis said softly.

"You can't tell anyone about this thing I'm about to do, okay?" Oscar's lips formed a tight straight line.

"You aren't going to contaminate evidence, are you?"

Oscar shook his head. He glanced at the pilothouse, where Skipper, Caryn, and Paul stood, then he keyed in a command code. The central image on the screen zoomed down to the body. The other images on the grid remained as they were, unmoved.

The central image enlarged, showing the chest of the man, and then it revealed his bloated, scratched face and empty eye sockets.

Oscar cleared his throat. "When I lowered the drone," he whispered, "it scared vultures away."

"How can you zoom in like that?" Ruis redirected Oscar's attention from the corpse to the operation of the drone. He didn't want Oscar to get ill again. He needed him to check the rest of the boat for Martina.

"The drone contains smaller drones that can fly independently." Oscar's voice was low and soft, barely above a whisper. He keyed in another command and leaned back from the screen.

The smaller drone rose and moved forward to show the flybridge, where the camera performed a quick spin and then flew over the body and down to the stern's cockpit. From there it zipped through the open doorway into the salon and spun again before it flew up to the empty pilothouse. The tiny device dove from the helm into the dark passageway that held three doors. Checking in the smaller stateroom, it found an unmade bed.

Ruis breathed slowly and fully and prayerfully. Chill bumps rose up his spine. He had to know if Martina was dead or alive, though a part of him wanted to delay bad news as long as possible.

Oscar directed the drone from the small stateroom to the master stateroom. Beer and vodka bottles littered the floor and the shelves. A camera tripod sat in the corner. The unmade bed had no human-size lumps, so Ruis breathed easier.

The drone returned to the passageway and stopped by the closed door to the head.

"I've checked all around the outside already," Oscar said. He sighed and rubbed his hands over his face. His eyes dimmed like a man standing on a ledge, peering off into the depth of despair.

Ruis gripped Oscar's forearm. He, too, stood on the ledge. "This is good news."

Oscar gaped at him. "What did you see that I didn't?"

"It's what I didn't see." Ruis used his free hand to point to the small image of the boat's stern. "No dinghy."

Oscar's mouth fell open. When Oscar smiled, Ruis let go of his arm. Oscar was back among the hopeful.

"How long can the drone stay over the boat?"

"Three hours."

Ruis pointed to numbers at the bottom of the screen. "Are those the latitude and longitude coordinates of the *Seeker*?"

Oscar nodded. "I'll show you how close we are." He keyed in a command that returned the small drone to the bottom of the larger drone, then the drone rose straight up.

The image of the boat shrank. A wave of vertigo led Ruis to close his eyes.

"Sorry," Oscar said. "That takes some getting used to. Open your eyes."

Ruis looked where Oscar pointed. One boat moved south toward Gomez point, the southern tip of Panther Key, according to the chart overlay on the screen. On the opposite side of the island to the east, a red dot pulsed over an anchored boat.

"That's us," Oscar said pointing to the moving boat.

Ruis dashed up the stairs to the helm, startling Skipper and Paul. "Oscar found *Seeker*. Here." He showed them on the chart. "And the dinghy's missing."

Skipper eased the throttle and squinted at the chart. "How close do you want to get to her?"

"I should approach by dinghy," Ruis said, bounding down the stairs to the salon. As he dug his Kevlar vest from his duffle bag, he said, "Oscar can keep watch from the drone." After he secured his vest, he called Maggie on his satellite phone. He gave the coordinates of *Seeker*, then he reported the body and his plan to board the ship alone.

"Please wait for backup," Maggie said. She had to follow FBI protocols.

Ruis had no intention to wait hours for the Coast Guard or the FBI to show up. He secured his holster to his right thigh. "The dinghy from the *Seeker* is missing."

"The dinghy's missing? Okay. What kind is it?"

In the background, Blake's voice sounded, but the words were unclear. This was followed by a rustling sound like something muffling the phone.

"What did Blake say?" Ruis loaded a full magazine in his Sig Sauer 226 and chambered a round. He then removed the magazine, thumbed in another round and shoved the magazine back into the base of the handle.

"Nothing." The nothing sounded like something Maggie didn't want to share.

Ruis asked Paul, "What kind of dinghy was on your boat?"

Paul stepped down into the salon. "A cheap white double-hull fiberglass one with a two-cylinder gas engine." He shrugged as if ashamed of it.

Ruis relayed the information to Maggie.

"Got it. Thanks," Maggie said.

Ruis waited. He knew how uncomfortable silence could be and how it could coax a person into filling that void. Maybe the FBI agent wanted to be on site for first contact. Maybe she was concerned Ruis might overreact or disturb evidence. If she didn't know him better than that by now, there was nothing he could do about it. Blake's voice sounded in the background. Maybe Blake was vouching for him.

"Be careful, Ruis," Maggie said. She disconnected the call.

Ruis placed quick calls to the volunteers, thanking them for their help and giving them an update.

Oscar and Paul volunteered to go with him. It was no small thing to head into a potentially dangerous situation. While he inwardly applauded their courage, outwardly, he had to dissuade them and at the same time preserve their honor. "The dinghy's missing and there's a dead man on the deck."

Skipper let the boat idle. Paul and Caryn exchanged glances. Oscar sat on a cushioned bench and held his face in his hands with his elbows resting on his legs.

Paul stepped out of the salon and came back holding up a large life vest. "Think this will protect me from a bullet?" His lopsided grin suggested he knew the answer.

Ruis shook his head.

"Then you can go first." Paul strapped on the life vest. "Skipper, permission to launch your dinghy?"

Skipper motioned for Paul to come to the helm. There, Skipper removed his belt and handed it to Paul with a .45 caliber Les Baer 1911 pistol and holster. Skipper racked the slide to put a bullet in the chamber and he slid the safety on with his thumb as Paul watched. "Cocked and locked."

Paul nodded and strapped on the belt and holster.

Skipper then handed Paul the lifeboat key attached to a floating key ring.

Ruis waited while Paul and Caryn hugged. To her credit, Caryn maintained a calm demeanor. Ruis's mother had taught him that nurses learned how to school their emotions. When Paul turned away to walk toward the dinghy, Caryn closed her eyes in a long blink. Ruis didn't want to see her next expression, so he turned his attention to Oscar.

"Record what happens on the boat," Ruis told Oscar.

Oscar nodded and wiped his eyes on his wrists. His mouth formed a tight line and his jaw muscles bulged.

Paul and Ruis were soon in the dinghy headed around Gomez Point toward *Seeker*. Ruis sat in front wearing a life vest over his Kevlar vest. Paul piloted the craft from the back seat. Neither spoke on the ride. Both were fully aware that the sound of the lifeboat's motor announced their approach, so they watched *Seeker*.

Though Ruis saw no shadows in the windows or movement on the Nordic Tug, he expected armed resistance when he boarded the boat. The drone circled, then hovered low behind the stern. A lens aimed at Ruis, so he signaled that he would board the boat at the stern and enter the salon.

The drone dipped and raised its front.

"If I run back out," Ruis whispered to Paul, "shoot any man who follows."

"Okay." Paul eased the small vessel alongside the swim platform.

Gun in hand, Ruis stepped onto the platform. He then rushed into the salon, then up to the helm and down the stairs to the smaller stateroom. Empty. Next, he opened the door to the head, checking left to right and into the shower stall. Clear. Then, dashing into the master stateroom, he checked every locker space large enough for Martina to hide.

He returned to the helm and yanked a small rug from the hatch to the engine hold. He flipped open the hatch and ducked. Grabbing a small flashlight from his Kevlar vest, he shined light into the hold.

A tiny whirring sound made him look up. The smaller drone, about the size of a hummingbird, hovered above him. Ruis pointed down and the drone zipped down into the hold and illuminated it with brilliant lights. After a minute, the drone rose from the hold and turned left, right, left.

"No one there?" Ruis asked.

The drone turned left, right, left again.

Ruis slouched. He then climbed down the step into the hold.

An acrid smell filled the space. Urine. He aimed his flashlight at the fluid sloshing around the propeller shaft. It had a distinct yellow tinge. After checking the engine hold, he entered the tank hold.

Why had they abandoned the boat?

He climbed back to the helm, through the salon, and then up the ladder to the upper deck. Lines of brown dried blood traced down the deck to the drain holes.

On the upper deck he found a fat, pale body. It somewhat resembled the photo of Gregorio Kutznetsov that was handed around at the Miami FBI office. Ruis holstered his weapon and pulled out his cell phone. He took photos of the body from various angles and sent them to Maggie with a note—Gregorio?

Ruis felt cheated that Gregorio was dead. He wanted to rescue his sister. None of his hoped-for scenario had materialized.

The gun lying beside the corpse was a Lorcin P25 pistol, a cheap handgun, the kind often found at crime scenes with the serial numbers filed off. Two holes, surrounded by dried blood, marked where a bullet passed through Gregorio's pants. One hole above his crotch lined up with a second hole in his thigh at the femoral artery. By the blood pattern, the man had dropped after a step or two and bled out.

Two folding chairs sat by the railing. Why would they sit out in the sun instead of up in the shade of the flybridge? Or below in the living quarters?

He took close-up photos of the eyeless face, blue hands, and bullet holes. Even without seeing the purple waxy skin and large spread of dried blood, Ruis knew by the smell that Gregorio had been dead longer than twelve hours. Avoiding the dried blood pool, Ruis reached down and stuck his hand under one shoulder and lifted it off the deck. The whole body tilted like a wooden carving. Full rigor.

He walked around the outside of the boat shining his flashlight into the water, praying nothing Martina-shaped reflected back. When he reached the stern boarding platform, he turned off his flashlight. "Except for the body on the upper deck, the boat's empty."

Paul holstered his weapon and tied the dinghy to *Seeker*. "Is it okay if I come aboard?"

Ruis held out his hand and Paul passed him a line.

A few minutes later, Ruis's cell phone rang.

"I didn't want to tell you this until it was confirmed. The Coast Guard has recovered the body of a male that has tattoos matching those of Stas Petronin," Agent Maggie said in a weary tone. "We found a submerged dinghy nearby. No sign of anyone else."

The world dimmed for a moment and Ruis leaned against the stern wall. Key rings were strewn on the floor.

"Are you there?" Maggie's voice emerged from the cell phone.

Ruis drew in a deep breath. "The body on the open deck is in full rigor and starting to stink. What do you want me to do?"

"Secure the crime scene. Take more photos of as much as you can and see if the boat is operational. I'll call in to see what the boss wants." Maggie sounded detached, as if she needed to follow protocol to handle the situation and her own disappointment. "I'm so sorry."

Ruis nodded. He was sorry, too.

"The dinghy we found is a nine-foot West Marine hard-shell tri-hull. When you see the owners of *Seeker*, would you confirm this was theirs?"

Ruis cleared his tightening throat. He wrestled his emotions back into the box in his mind. "The owner's here with me." He handed the cell phone to Paul.

Paul introduced himself and then listened. "Yes. Yes." He handed the phone back to Ruis.

"I hate to ask, but since it's so late..." Maggie said.

He wanted to leave on Skipper's beautiful boat. There was easily enough daylight to motor back to Old Marco Lodge.

Nonetheless, he knew Agent Maggie wanted him to secure the crime scene and she trusted him to do so. No doubt she had a paper storm of reports and forms to complete from finding Petronin. He glanced skyward. "We can secure it down until tomorrow."

"I'll be there at first light."

"See you tomorrow." Ruis disconnected the call. It would be a long night and the weight of disappointment hung on him like a lead cape. "We're supposed to secure the crime scene and see if the boat is operational." He heard his own flat-toned voice and the hopelessness in it. After placing his cell phone in his pocket, he braced his hands on the railing of the *Seeker*. Shallow currents nudged the boat as it bobbed in between uninhabited islands.

Paul sighed. "I'm surprised the dinghy worked. It was an old, cheap model. Skipper recommended a replacement, so we bought one. It's waiting for us back in Naples."

"It sunk, and they found a man's body nearby."

Paul cringed. "What about the girl?"

"No sign of her."

"Is that good or bad?"

"I don't know." Ruis pointed to the key rings. "Are these yours?"

"Yes." Paul peered into the salon and rubbed his beard stubble. "Do you want me to turn on the generator or start the engines?"

"Test the all systems. The kidnappers were here for days, so there are plenty of places to get fingerprints besides the helm."

"Okay then." Paul gathered the keys and stepped to the drain in the cockpit and stared down at it. "Is that...?"

"Dried DNA evidence. The body is on the deck." Ruis pointed up.

Paul entered the salon while Ruis called Skipper and asked him to anchor as close as he could to *Seeker*.

Paul returned to the cockpit and handed a plain white bedsheet to Ruis. "Would you drape this over the body?"

Ruis wasn't sure if Paul wanted to preserve evidence or protect the others from the sight of a bloated dead man and the dried pool of blood. Why preserve the crime scene if both kidnappers were dead? Procedures and policies. Who was left to prosecute? Ruis carried the sheet upstairs. He stared at the body. With the kidnappers dead, who was left to pick up the ransom? Was Petronin headed to Tampa? Had he double-crossed Gregorio Kuznetsov?

The chairs could prevent the sheet from blowing away but moving the chairs would disturb the immediate crime scene. He searched the flybridge and found a long, coiled yellow shore power cable stored under the cushions of the L-shaped bench seat. He pulled the coil up his arm and over his shoulder in order to back down the short ladder to the open deck and the body. He flung the sheet over the body. After anchoring the sheet with the uncoiled yellow cord, he then climbed back up to the flybridge to see as far as he could. Swamp in all directions.

If Petronin had taken Martina in the dinghy, then where was she? In his heart, Ruis longed to believe his sister had escaped. She had become a strong swimmer after a few scares as a toddler. The water was warm. She might be alive. *Please, God.* He softly sang the song he, Blake, and Vincent had used to call out to another missing girl. Nefi had been in the heart of the Amazon rainforest on her own after her parents had been murdered. Blake had suggested they sing a hymn she might know to differentiate them from the criminals. The song also brought them comfort at a time when they were low on hope of finding Nefi alive.

On the chorus, the words caught in his throat and changed into a low moan. He hoped the engine noise of the Grand Banks trawler covered his sound of despair. In time, he pulled himself together and climbed down to the salon.

Past the salon in the pilothouse, Paul read his pre-start checklist aloud. He tried the starter. Muttering to himself, he tried the starter again, but the engines didn't respond. He checked the

AC and DC panels at the top of the stairs between the salon and the helm.

As the *Bottom Gun* approached, Ruis stood outside on the boarding platform. The ship's rocking motion reminded him of instability. Exhaustion and despair threatened to pull him into the dark theater of the mind that played an endless reel of worst-case scenarios.

Be in the moment. Be in the here and now.

A short while later, Caryn was tossing lines to Ruis as Skipper maneuvered his larger boat alongside *Seeker*. Fenders kept the boats from banging together. Lines secured the boats together and anchors kept them centered over the deepest part of the cove, which was nine feet.

Paul emerged from the engine hold. "Can Skipper come aboard? I'm having trouble starting the engines and he's got more experience with these engines."

"Of course. Just don't clean anything." Ruis followed Paul through the stern door to the swim platform. "Let's brief him."

Paul followed Ruis onto the sixty-foot Grand Banks trawler. Skipper, Oscar, and Caryn stared at Ruis.

"The girl isn't on the *Seeker*," Ruis stated flatly. "I spoke with the FBI. They found the *Seeker*'s lifeboat and a man's body. They can't get here until morning." Ruis stared back at three blank faces.

The drone sat in a large case in the middle of the salon floor. Oscar looked as drained as Ruis felt.

In the silence, Caryn handed out bottles of cool water. She planted one hand on a hip. Her assessing look reminded Ruis of his mother, who was also a nurse. Her tone and body language showed a unique mastery of compassion and implied threat that nurses used to manage patients. "Good thing for you guys that I cook when I'm stressed." She eyed the gun her husband wore, then she pivoted toward the galley.

"I've been operating on caffeine and adrenaline all day," Oscar said.

"Me, too." Ruis considered it a good sign that he had not completely shut down his senses—he recognized the scent of beef stew. He wasn't hungry, but he had to eat to keep going. Running on autopilot with his emotions shut down made food taste like texture without flavor. He sat beside Oscar.

Paul handed the belt and the holstered Les Baer 1911 to Skipper, who strapped it on himself. Skipper carted a tool kit as he followed Paul off the Grand Banks trawler to *Seeker*.

Oscar sighed heavily as he slouched over his laptop. "I suppose I should tell my boss that this real-world field test was successful."

Ruis patted Oscar's back. "I'm impressed."

Oscar nodded. "Thanks. I wish success was enough."

"We do our best and leave the rest up to God." Ruis sat back with his hands on his knees. He and Oscar shared two important things, their love of Martina and their faith. Both were being tested to the limits.

"I'm going to report in and see what's happening in Tampa," Oscar said. He keyed an encrypted message from his laptop, which was equipped with a satellite uplink.

Both men deflected the untouchable topic. Rather than discuss Martina directly, Ruis withdrew into his mind to retrace his steps, to see if he'd missed something critical that could have led to a better outcome. He and the FBI had followed the evidence. They had interviewed those associated with the evidence. Maggie and Blake had discovered the body and dinghy from *Seeker*. He and Skipper, Paul, Oscar, and Caryn had located and secured *Seeker* and found the body of the other kidnapper. All that was missing was Martina.

Ruis had never failed in a mission as a Navy SEAL or as a US Marshal. Throughout adulthood, he'd been attacked by violent people with guns, knives, rocks, cars, and rocket launchers yet none of these obstacles had prevented his team from achieving their mission goal. Shutting down emotionally protected him from facing the fact that his sister was missing and probably dead. He wasn't denying the bare truth of the situation, because logic wouldn't allow it. Survival depended on situational awareness. Training had ingrained that lesson in his mind.

For the moment, he denied the situation to his heart. He refused to release his grip on hope until he saw her body. Until then, he would lock down his feelings and trust that Martina's time on earth continued. It wasn't his place to question God's plans any more than it was his place to question his commanding officers. He would only challenge a superior if he believed an order violated the law. He wouldn't challenge Almighty God because God could not do evil. Through free will, God allowed evil, so Ruis blamed the evildoers, like Petronin and Kuznetsov. If they'd killed Martina, they'd answer to God.

Ruis bowed his head.

Please, Father God, show me what to do. I'm tapped out.

. 27 .

Martina and her rescuers reached the Chokoloskee Everglades Area Tours Office at dusk. The tour guide ushered her into his office.

"You said you want to talk to the FBI." He closed the door. "I'll stay here with you." He was staring at her as if he expected an objection.

Martina stared back. "I think the nearest FBI office is in Miami." She handed him his ball cap.

He tossed the cap on his desk. "It is."

"Let's call them."

The guide wrestled with the curled white pages of an outdated Miami phone book before he dialed a long number on an ancient black push-button phone. Martina's grandmother had a phone just like it. The rest of the family used to tease her that it belonged in the Alexander Graham Bell museum.

"Hello, I'm a tour guide with the Everglades Area Tours office in Chokoloskee and I found a young woman on a mangrove sandbar near Panther Key," he said, watching Martina. "What? Yes, I'll hold."

Fluorescent lights buzzed, and the window air-conditioner unit whirred.

He placed his hand over the mouthpiece and said, "They probably think I'm crazy."

"Join the club," Martina said.

A male voice sounded through the earpiece.

"Hello? Yes, sir." His eyebrows rose, and he nodded. "No visible injuries. Hispanic, short, and big attitude."

"Hey!" Martina scowled at him.

"I will. She refused to give me her name, so I—" He sighed. "They want to talk to you." He handed the phone to Martina and left the room, closing the door on his way out.

Martina held the heavy, clunky antique receiver to her ear and absently stepped away from the desk, dragging the phone toward the edge. Tethered, she quickly moved back. "Hello?"

"This is Special Agent in Charge Jorges Espinosa. What's your name?"

The simple question gave her pause. Which name were they expecting? She could no longer pretend to be Ruby. Ruby hadn't been drugged and held on a boat in the middle of the Florida swampland. Ruby wasn't the person who'd escaped kidnappers and spent the night sleeping on broken shells. She squared her shoulders. "I am Martina Olympias Ramos."

Cheering blasted her ear, disorienting her. Her skin tingled hot and cold.

"We have been searching for you, Miss Ramos."

What? She gasped, and soon hot tears flowed. How was it possible?

"Stay where you are. I'm sending a female agent and a consultant to bring you to the Miami office. Please don't talk to anyone, because this is an ongoing investigation."

"There's a man on the boat near where the tour guide found me."

"We have secured the boat. You're safe now."

"What about the *man* on the boat?"

"Secured."

Amen! "But there's another…"

"We know, Miss Ramos. Please don't say anything. This is an ongoing investigation."

There was no mistaking his shut-up-now tone, so Martina complied. "Yes, sir." Joy bubbled up in her. Whatever the FBI was doing, they were on top of it. They knew her real name. They had captured *Seeker* and Green Mask. Maybe they were tracking Black Mask to the ransom drop. But how did they know?

"We will debrief you in Miami. Do you need medical attention?"

She interpreted what he was really asking, and no she didn't need a rape kit. She just wanted a hot meal, a long shower, and a safe place to sleep. "No, sir. I have just a few cuts and scrapes."

"Excellent. So sit tight."

Wiping her eyes with her free hand, she sniffled. "Yes, sir. I'll wait here."

"I look forward to meeting you."

"How many people know?"

"Very few and we'd like to keep it that way. I've asked the tour guide to keep you isolated."

"Okay. Thank you, Mr. Espinosa." The call ended. "I mean Special Agent Espinosa." She hoped he wasn't insulted that she'd remembered his title too late. Ugh.

He'd said to sit tight. She'd been tight with anxiety and fear for days on end. The adrenaline coursing through her veins had depleted her energy. She wanted nothing more than to fall apart and unravel into a heap of gratitude for being alive. For the first time in long days and nights, she could relax, so she curled up on a musty old mustard-colored leather sofa and listened to the hum of the air conditioner.

Muted voices entered Martina's dream, but the voices didn't fit in at the family reunion. The admiral stood at the grill, while the rest of the family played in the backyard. Momma stepped in front of Martina and said, "Wake up."

Martina sat up to find a shapely, dark-haired woman standing by the sofa. She had clothing tucked under her arm and a large paper bag in her hand.

"Martina Ramos?"

Martina ran her hands over her hair to revive the Ruby-style cut. Satisfied that was the best she could do with her appearance, she stood, tugged down the hem of Ruby's dress and the guide's shirt, and nodded.

"I'm FBI Special Agent Magdalena Vega," the woman said, showing her identification badge and card. "Please call me Maggie. I'm here to take you to the Miami office."

"Okay."

"Please change into these things and place what you're wearing in this bag." Maggie set fresh clothes on the sofa. "All of it."

Eager to get out of her captivity clothes and the tour guide's long-sleeved shirt, she pulled the shirt over her head and stuffed it in the paper bag. She tugged the snug dress over her head as hundreds of sequins scraped her skin one last time.

"I'll step out if you want," the agent said.

"I'm from a large family." Naked, Martina jammed her gritty strapless bra and thong into the paper bag and turned toward the FBI agent.

The agent chuckled, pulled price tags off panties and a bra, and handed them to Martina.

Holding the new bra and panties, Martina glanced around for a bathroom big enough to contain a shower.

"I already asked, and they don't have a shower," Maggie said. "You can clean up in Miami."

Martina put on the fresh underwear. Though her skin was coated with a layer of dirt and sand, and the thousands of sequin cuts stung, she climbed into a soft light blue sweatshirt and sweatpants, white socks, and white tennis shoes. "Wow. The FBI knows my underwear size. I don't know whether to be happy or creeped out."

The corner of the left side of the agent's mouth tugged into a half smile. She folded over the top of the bag, taped it shut, and wrote the date, time, place, and Martina's full name on it. Under that, she signed her name. She tucked the bag under her arm and opened the office door. "Let's go."

Martina marched into the compact lobby, where the tour guide turned to face her. He had loaned her the shirt off his back and rescued her at an unnamed mangrove-covered sandbar. She should have asked for his name. Since she had already refused to tell him her name, it would have been awkward to ask for his. While she tried to form the right words to thank him, Maggie spoke and held out her hand to the guide.

"Thank you for your help, Mister..."

"Tom Guidry," he said, shaking her hand.

Martina held out her hand. "Thank you for rescuing me, Mr. Guidry. I'm sorry about the tour group."

"We don't usually do a mystery tour." Tom gently shook Martina's hand. "Are you going to tell me your name?"

Martina shook her head.

He sighed. "Are you going to be all right?"

She nodded.

Maggie opened the door to the outside and held it open. Martina padded out of the cement-block building to a crushed-shell parking lot. The cool night air carried the flinty scent of sand and concrete. Parked nearby, a black Escalade reflected street lights, and beside it, a tall, broad-shouldered man held open the rear passenger door. For a second, she felt like a VIP again, the celebrity who never touched a door or picked up the check or looked the help in the eyes.

Martina looked the man in the face and froze. Certainly, many men transitioned from the Marines into the service of the FBI, but the resemblance of this red-haired man to another agent she knew was uncanny. She squinted in the dark at him. "Blake Clayton?"

"On the recording you looked like you'd been shot from a cannon. Tonight, I'd say you look better than expected."

"I know, right?"

"Aaaaand she's back," he said, smiling.

The fact that someone knew her comforted her more than she could put into words. She was alive. And a person she knew by name had been looking for her. She didn't understand how he knew, but here he was—all two hundred thirty pounds of him. Ruis and Vincent called him a friend. He'd just been through the nightmare of a trial and he was here. She felt redeemed and valuable as herself. She missed her big, happy family. She missed Oscar and Nefi, and she desperately needed a hug. Before she could think about it, she crashed against him and wrapped her arms around his waist, surprising them both.

"Ooof." He draped his arms around her and patted her back. "It's good to see you, too."

Blake was real, a flesh-and-blood human she knew. He was one of the good guys. Happily married, a believer in God, and he was here instead of home with his family to take her back to civilization. In that moment, she understood the love it took for people like him, like Vincent, Ruis, and Nefi, to risk their lives for others. It was a high calling. Despite the way she'd treated him, Blake would take a bullet to protect her. She clung to him like a lifeline. She had never felt so exhausted. In that moment, she realized she was crying and couldn't stop. She'd been mean to him since the day she confronted Vincent at the New York FBI office, as if he'd somehow been to blame when Vincent broke Nefi's heart. It had been a strange, horrible misunderstanding. Blake had not been at fault. She regretted every time she'd laughed when Oscar referred to him as Vincent's redneck friend. She regretted snubbing his wedding invitation.

Blake held her until Maggie cleared her throat behind him. He then swept Martina up in his arms like her daddy used to do. He placed her on the seat, buckled her in, and draped his jacket over her. Although he shut the door, his voice carried.

"Whatever you do," Blake said to the woman agent, "don't tell Ruis I made his sister cry."

Martina smiled that Blake feared big brother Ruis. She rubbed her eyes to look at the squat cement-block building painted robin's-egg blue. Two trailers parked nearby carried yellow polyethylene kayaks. The residential neighborhood consisted of trailers and single-story cement-block homes with dirt yards, palm trees, and scrubby bushes.

The vehicle dipped a little when Blake climbed into the front passenger seat.

Exhaustion pulled Martina into darkness. Images and sounds faded away with the steady rumble of the engine and the hiss of the air vents. She fought to keep her eyes open.

The vehicle bounced hard, jolting her awake. Most of the day had felt hyper-real, as if she'd consumed far too much caffeine. Seeing Blake, however, seemed surreal. The last time she had spoken to Nefi, Blake was in Asheville, North Carolina, and no longer working for the FBI. "Blake, what are you doing here?"

"Vincent asked me to help. Apparently, I'm the finder of lost girls. First Nefi—"

"Vincent? Oh, no. Who else knows?"

Blake pulled a cell phone from his shirt pocket and held it out between the front seats. "I believe Ruis would appreciate a call from you."

Martina groaned and took the phone. Her brother's name and phone number glowed from the screen. Confessing her dangerous stupidity to Ruis was going to cripple her pride. She sniffled. A moment later, a box of tissues appeared between the seats. "Thanks," she said, taking it. Sometimes when you peeled off a bandage, the wound opened.

Blake stared at her from the front passenger's seat. Martina's eyes welled as she pressed the call symbol. Blake turned away. In the confines of the Escalade, this was as much privacy as she could get. The phone rang twice.

"Ruis here." His flat tone told her how stressed he was. Surely, he didn't always answer a call from Blake like that.

"Hey, Ruis. You won't believe where I am—"

His gasp cut her off. Muffled sounds followed. Martina glanced at the phone to see if the call had been dropped.

There was more scuffling. "Blake? What happened? What is it?" a deeper masculine voice demanded through the phone.

What on earth? "Oscar?"

"Oh, my God." His voice rose higher with each word as if his throat tightened. It carried throughout the car.

"Nope, just me."

Oscar cleared his throat. "Where are you?"

"I'm with an FBI agent named Maggie and Blake, of all people."

Oscar chuckled. "Let it go."

Blake peered through the gap between the front seats.

Martina waved at him dismissively. Long ago, she had confided in Oscar that she once called Blake a man whore to his face and that Blake had danced with Nefi at Ruis's wedding right in front of Vincent. Until recently, she'd considered Blake a player. "We're headed to the Miami FBI office. Where are you?"

"I'm on a boat tied to *Seeker*."

"What? Oh, no. Please, tell me Nefi's not there."

"Of course not. Why would she be here?"

Who wasn't involved? She tossed up her free hand. "I don't know. I didn't expect you or Blake or Ruis to be involved, but you are. Ruis is mad at me, isn't he? Why won't he speak to me?"

"He's on his knees." Oscar's voice dropped to a whisper. "I think he's praying."

This news struck her like a slap on the face. Her dangerous, tough-as-nails brother was on his knees, because of her. She had lied to everyone who loved her about where she was over school break. She had refused to go on vacation with Oscar. They had to be so angry and disappointed in her. "I'm so sorry." Her eyes burned, and her throat threatened to squeeze shut.

"She's alive!" Oscar said.

Cheering sounded from the phone.

"So, um, sweetheart" — Oscar's voice sounded nearly normal — "by any chance do you know if the kidnappers disabled the boat?"

"That was me."

"Ha! Good for you," Oscar nearly shouted. Voices in the background grew louder. "Yeah, okay. Okay. We're trying to figure out how to get the boat going again. Can you tell me precisely what you did?"

It took about ten minutes of questions and answers while Oscar relayed information from her to someone in the engine hold to undo her minor sabotage. She waited on the line until Oscar said the boat was fixed.

More shuffling sounded.

"You did well," Ruis said.

Under normal circumstances, she would joke about being praised, but since this was as gushy as Ruis got, Martina owned it. She had survived a deadly criminal situation. Sure, her big brother had been through worse lots of times. He didn't flinch when guns fired. He dealt with smarter, tougher, better-armed bad guys daily. She still had every right to be proud. She didn't have his training or teammates to back her up. She had been alone. She choked out, "Thanks."

"I'll see you in Miami," Ruis said.

She disconnected the call and handed the phone to Blake. Blake, Vincent, Ruis, Oscar, the FBI, and untold other people had been searching for her the whole time she feared she was forgotten. If only she hadn't taken that stinking job. She then used up the rest of the box of tissues on happy tears.

"We'll be in Miami within an hour." Maggie's voice carried throughout the car. "I have a hotel room for you. Tomorrow's going to be a long day and you need rest. And I'm betting you want a shower."

"I want to be pressure washed." Gazing out the window into black nothingness, Martina searched for streetlights, headlights, or other signs of civilization. She was on land, but still far from civilization. Above the moss-bearded trees, the stars flickered. Mr. Magnuson, her sixth-grade science teacher, had once explained that some stars were so far away that their light reached us long after the stars burned out.

Like fame. An illusion of substance. Martina sighed heavily.

Dumb as a moth, she had played in the bright-burning flame of stardom and survived.

By the time Ruis got up from his knees, Paul and Skipper were standing on the deck with their arms crossed.

Oscar handed Ruis his satellite phone.

Ruis tucked it in his pocket.

"We have a trickle charge going to the battery," Skipper said. "It'll be a few hours before we can start *Seeker*. How's about we spend that time on my boat so you can explain what's really going on?"

"Now, that she's safe," Ruis said, "I can tell you everything."

Skipper uncrossed his arms. The men were careful about stepping around the blood trails on their way to the ladder and Skipper's boat. No one spoke until they were all settled in seats in Skipper's salon. Caryn, who had stayed on the Grand Banks trawler, apparently noticed their collective mood, so she took a seat at the end of the cushioned bench.

"I heard shouting," she said.

Ruis smiled. "The missing girl, the kidnap victim, is safe."

Caryn slapped her hands on her legs. "That's wonderful!"

Ruis bowed his head as emotions roared through him again. His eyes welled. "I'm going to tell you everything I couldn't tell you before. But before I do, I have to thank you for your help. I don't know what I would have done without you. I also have to ask another huge favor."

Skipper raised his eyebrows. Caryn and Paul exchanged a quizzical look.

"I have to ask you to keep what I'm about to tell you a secret. You'll understand why after you hear the whole story." Ruis took a deep breath.

"I believe you can trust us," Skipper said.

Caryn and Paul nodded.

Ruis then told them everything starting with the phone call from Vincent on Monday.

. 28 .

Early Friday morning, Maggie badged into the FBI employee entrance in the parking garage and held the door open for Martina and Blake. In that order, they passed through security and rode the elevator.

Maggie steered her by the elbow down a narrow corridor and stopped at a door. "You will probably be asked to repeat everything that happened to you over and over again. Before your interview, they might read you your rights. Remain calm."

"When will Ruis get here?"

"I don't know."

What if the ransom money was taken? Would Ruby or her agent lay any blame on the victim?

Maggie opened the door to a small room, revealing a plain table secured to the floor. Two chairs sat on either side of the table.

Having watched far too many crime procedurals on television, Martina grew uneasy. "Can Blake stay?"

"I'll ask. Please have a seat."

Martina chose the seat to her right. She flinched when the door clicked shut. It didn't sound like it locked, yet the noise seemed unnaturally loud. The room did not have a giant one-way mirror like the crime shows had. After she'd spent a minute of listening to the air conditioner hum and staring at bare walls, the door opened, and she flinched again.

A well-dressed man approached with his hand out. He wore an Italian-made designer suit and an air of confidence that reminded her of Ruis. His warm hand gently enveloped hers and then released. "Miss Ramos, thank you for coming in. I'm Special Agent in Charge Jorges Espinosa." He placed a legal pad, a file folder, and pen on the table. "Do you want water, coffee, soda, tea?"

She shook her head.

The door opened again, and Blake carried in a chair that he parked beside her. When he sat on it, the chair creaked in protest. He had lost weight during the trial, but he was still a big guy. Martina grinned and shook her head.

Espinosa folded his hands on the table. A sleek gold Tag Heuer watch peeked from his cuff. "Blake, you understand you are here for moral support?"

"Yes, sir." His woodsy aftershave wafted by as he settled into his chair.

"You don't want me talking to him, do you?" Martina wanted to understand the ground rules for her first-ever FBI interrogation.

Espinosa's cool gaze reminded her of her high school principal's. "Blake has information about the investigation that you don't. We need to get your report on events. After we're done here, we may be able to share our information."

Martina nodded.

"If there comes a time when you'd like to speak without Blake in the room, you need to say so," Espinosa said.

"Yes, sir." She was relieved he had not recited the Miranda warning.

"Let's begin with the night at the club." Espinosa poised his pen over the clean pad of paper.

Slipping back into her time as Ruby, she recounted the days and nights from carefree dancing to captivity and on through to her escape. They paused for lunch and bathroom breaks and Blake handed her a clean, soft handkerchief when she became teary-eyed about being locked in the engine hold.

By the early afternoon, she'd told the whole story twice. On the second round, Espinosa asked questions.

"You said that on Wednesday night Green Mask had a gun. Where was it?"

"He had it in the front of his pants. No holster, just, you know, gangster style in his waistband."

"Go on."

"When I jumped overboard, I heard a shot go off. I swam close to the hull so he couldn't see me."

"How many shots did you hear?"

"One. I stayed underwater as long as I could hold my breath."

"Did you ever touch the gun?"

"No." She wanted to say that if she had the chance to shoot him she would have done so, but she let that go. It was a wish, not a fact. She didn't know if she could really pull the trigger to kill someone.

Later, apparently satisfied that she'd sufficiently gutted herself emotionally, he set down his pen. "I have enough information. Thank you. One last question, just to satisfy my curiosity. Why did you take this job?"

"It sounded like fun."

Blake burst into laughter.

She turned toward him. "Seriously?"

Blake shrugged. "That's the funniest thing I've heard in weeks."

Martina turned back toward Special Agent in Charge Espinosa and shook her head.

Espinosa stood and gathered up his papers. One corner of his mouth tugged upward, and he schooled his expression back into a relaxed state. "If you'd like to wait in another room, I'm sure Blake can answer your questions. Today is the ransom drop, so I need to get back to it."

Martina stood. "You didn't catch Black Mask?"

Espinosa opened the door. "Blake can answer your questions. Please follow me. There have been many people working long hours to find you. I'd like them to see you are alive and well."

Gooseflesh rose on Martina at the thought that Black Mask might get away. Blake and Martina followed Espinosa down the hallway to the large conference room. When they entered, all the people in the room stood. She assumed they were standing because their commanding officer had entered the room, but then they erupted in cheers. Their attention remained on her as Espinosa met in a huddle with uniformed officers by the whiteboard.

Men and women behind laptops applauded. People in various uniforms stood along the walls with their hats in their hands.

Martina clapped a hand over her mouth and her eyes welled as it dawned on her that so many strangers were working hard to find her, to rescue her, and to capture the kidnappers. "Thank you," she squeaked.

On the far wall, a giant photo of her face stared back amid navigation charts, notes, photos of *Seeker*, and mug shots of two dark-haired men.

A lovely woman with copper-colored hair crossed the room toward them. "Miss Ramos, Blake, come with me." She led them back into the corridor.

"This is my wife, Dr. Terri Pinehurst-Clayton," Blake said as if to remind Martina about missing his wedding.

Martina hugged her. "Thank you. Nefi told me so much about you I feel as if I know you." Nefi never mentioned Terri's beauty, only her kindness.

"It's so great to see you."

"It's good to be seen." Martina admired this accomplished

woman for all the things Nefi had said about her. A veterinarian, a pilot, and a saint for standing by Blake through his trial. With that red hair, she had Irish or Scottish heritage. Side by side, Terri and Blake looked like a perfect match. She wished for them to have many beautiful children and a long, happy marriage.

"Special Agent in Charge Espinosa offered us a room for privacy," Terri said.

Martina and Blake stared at her.

"Can't I stay in there?" Martina asked with a backward glance at the main conference room.

Terri glanced at Blake and bit her lower lip. "I don't know anything about that. Espinosa suggested you might want privacy. Ruby and Chad are on their way to see you."

At the Old Marco Lodge, Oscar's boss called for Oscar to return to Tampa to operate the second drone for aerial surveillance of the ransom drop. Oscar's anguish showed on his face and his whole body sagged.

Ruis loaded the last of Oscar's gear in the rental van's trailer. "Your choice is not between loyalty to your job or to your girlfriend."

Oscar secured the trailer. "Oh, really?"

"It might seem like a meaningful romantic gesture to rush off to Miami, but I can tell you neither Martina nor my parents are impressed by unemployment."

"Okay." Oscar pointed at Ruis's chest and apparently thought better of it and dropped his hand. He was head and shoulders taller than Ruis, but they both understood that height didn't offer Oscar much of an advantage if their discussion turned into a fight. "But if she's mad I chose work—"

"I'll vouch for you." Ruis strode to the front of Oscar's car. Knowing he intimidated people, Ruis decided to start treating

Oscar with the respect and familiarity he deserved as a potential future brother-in-law. He gave Oscar a back-slapping hug. "Thank you for volunteering before you knew it was Martina. That demonstrates the kind of moral character I'd like in a brother-in-law."

Oscar smiled and then his expression fell. "What about Nefi? Who's going to tell her?"

"Stand down. As far as I know, she doesn't know about any of this." Ruis raised his hands, palms out toward Oscar. "And I'm certainly not going to tell her."

"If Martina wants to tell her, she can."

Both men checked their watches, climbed into their vehicles, and sped off, one northward, one eastward.

On the drive to Miami, Ruis made national and international phone calls. He had to encourage Martina to resume her normal life as quickly and as fully as possible. Surviving the kidnapping put his sister ninety percent ahead of her ordeal. Overcoming the kidnapping emotionally would be the final challenge, the last ten percent of resuming her normal life. He also wanted to resume his life.

. 29 .

Oscar and his boss operated drones from a windowless room at MacDill Air Force Base. At noon, both drones rested on the roof of the hangar used by the National Oceanic and Atmospheric Administration (NOAA) for their hurricane hunter aircraft.

Mr. Yoshida, Oscar's boss, swiveled his chair away from his controls and removed his helmet. "I must thank your friend for this opportunity to demonstrate our drones under live surveillance conditions. I believe the committee is pleased."

"It's been my pleasure, sir."

Their side-by-side workstations allowed them to see both laptops. They had an air-conditioned room in a hangar all to themselves for the time being. They expected military observers to arrive by the one p.m. ransom delivery.

At forty, Mr. Yoshida was one of the wealthiest businessmen Oscar had ever met. "Thank you also for completing the paperwork in your name." And one of the humblest.

"You're welcome, sir."

The paperwork to operate the drones had to be submitted by a United States citizen, according to the recent Federal Aviation Administration policies. Like any governmental agency, the FAA had forms to fill and procedures to follow. Because domestic drones had been used carelessly close to commercial aircraft, the

FAA imposed strict controls over drones flying in Type B airspace, like the airspace around Tampa's International Airport.

For starters, to secure authorization to fly the drones over the ransom drop site and within a twenty-mile radius of it, Oscar had to complete a Part 107 airspace waiver. In the form, he had to name the specific statutes subject to the waiver. They included flying directly over people, flying beyond the pilot's visual line of sight, flying above 400 feet AGL, and flying near airports in controlled airspace. He added flying at night just because he couldn't ask for it later.

Next, he had to obtain permission from all the airports in the flight radius, including Tampa International Airport, MacDill Air Force Base, Peter O. Knight Airport, Albert Whitted Airport, and the St. Petersburg Clearwater International Airport.

Finally, he had to expedite the usual ninety-day waiting period for approval by submitting his paperwork through the Special Government Interest process. Thanks to the authorities at MacDill, the FBI, and the Tampa Police who wrote letters endorsing the urban test flights, the request was approved within hours.

MacDill Air Force Base, four miles south-southwest of downtown Tampa, was next to Gadsden Park.

At last, paperwork in order, Oscar and his boss waited for FBI Agent Cuervo to notify them to launch the drones. The plan was to get them airborne thirty minutes before the ransom drop-off time, which gave them an hour to idle.

Considering the number of people involved in the operation, it would be a miracle if the news media didn't find out. For Martina's sake and for Ruby's, he hoped for a quick, quiet resolution.

Mr. Yoshida left with his empty metal thermos. Oscar checked his phone. The tracker app Tapper had set up on Oscar's phone showed the location of the truck owned by Stas Petronin as a blinking orange dot on the map of Tampa. Since Tapper had asked him not to mention the tracker app to Tampa PD or FBI Agent Cuervo, it was probably not covered by a warrant.

In the half hour since he'd last checked, the dot had moved miles southwest of the Bell Channelside Apartments. The apartment complex, according to Tapper, sat between the Lee Roy Selmon Expressway and the Port of Tampa, where Stas Petronin worked. Oscar pressed the plus sign to zoom in on the dot.

Petronin's truck was close to MacDill. An hour early. He zoomed in farther, gasped, and called Tapper.

"Hello, Oscar."

"I found a certain truck parked northwest of Gadsden Park at Florida Rock and Tank Lines."

"Excellent. How many klicks?"

"What's a klick?"

"A kilometer."

Oscar checked the scale on the app's map. From the ransom drop site to the truck was less than a mile. A kilometer was .62 miles, so, "One klick."

"I can manage that."

"Where are you?" Oscar wanted to end the call before Mr. Yoshida returned.

"I'm walking Bailey. This is a dog-friendly park."

Oscar was momentarily relieved that Tapper was already in place when his train of thought derailed. "Wait. Where did you get a dog?"

"Bailey belongs to a friend who works at MacDill. An animal this size belongs outdoors."

"Okay. I'll see you later."

Oscar disconnected the call and set his phone facedown on the table beside his laptop and helmet. With a dog, a thirty-something-year-old man like Tapper would blend in better than other plainclothes officers.

Mr. Yoshida returned with a steaming thermos of tea and honey, his drink of choice, and a red can of Coca-Cola. He placed the soda beside Oscar's laptop, then he drew a paper-covered straw from his shirt pocket and laid it next to the can.

"Thank you for the drink, sir."

The boss took his place at his workstation. After a sip of tea, he capped the thermos. "Would it be appropriate for us to check the audio connection with the authorities?"

This was Yoshida's subtle suggestion to listen on the radio frequency of the investigators. Cuervo said he'd signal when to launch the drones with a phone call. "I believe it would be the proactive thing to do." Oscar propped his phone against his drink can and then donned his helmet.

Mr. Yoshida grinned like a gamer as he put on his helmet. For a multimillionaire CEO, he enjoyed operating the drones as much as any eight-year-old would.

Voices on the frequency sounded as if they were in the room.

"...eyes in the sky to record comings and goings," Tapper said.

"How long can they stay airborne?" Cuervo asked.

"I thought the operator said five hours. They can refuel at the Air Force base."

"Might as well then."

Oscar removed his helmet to take Cuervo's call. He answered on the second ring. "Oscar Gunnerson here."

"Could you launch the drones now under the FAA's approval?" Cuervo asked.

"Absolutely, sir. I filed for a time range from noon to six."

"Go ahead, then."

"Lift off in three minutes," Oscar said.

Mr. Yoshida looked thirty years younger in his helmet. Beneath the clear, curved faceplate, he was grinning.

"Stay on frequency and keep chatter to a minimum," Cuervo said.

"Yes, sir." Immediately after the call ended, Oscar began his preflight check.

Within three minutes, the drones had lifted off from the hangar roof and reached their flight positions, Yoshida's at five hundred feet above the pond on the west half of Gadsden Park and Oscar's over the baseball fields on the eastern half.

Oscar and Mr. Yoshida had agreed that Oscar would communicate with the police and FBI task force and Mr. Yoshida would communicate with the control tower at MacDill and the military representatives on the committee who were evaluating the drones.

Within five minutes, the military committee gathered in the room, some of them talking about seeing the drones rise from the hangar roof. They huddled around Oscar and his boss to see the view from the drones' cameras.

. 30 .

Martina, Blake, and Terri sat in a smaller conference room down the hall from the main room used by the team investigating the kidnapping. Martina was curious about the two eight-by-ten-inch photos of men on the whiteboard. One looked handsome and the other was blend-into-the-woodwork plain. "Those large photos on the whiteboard — are they the kidnappers?"

"The pasty-faced one is Gregorio Kuznetsov," Blake said. "He was living on a boat like the one you were on, but he mismanaged it and sunk it. He's the one you called Green Mask during your interview. The other guy is Stas Petronin, a repeat felon with a long, violent record."

Martina mentally added a beard to his image and shuddered. "He wore a black mask." Otherwise, they looked so normal. For some reason, the fact that they looked like normal people was creepier than if they looked evil.

Blake leaned his elbows on the table.

"They're both in custody now, right?" Martina wanted to be sure.

Blake and Terri exchanged a glance.

Terri picked up Martina's hands in her warm, manicured hands. By comparison, Martina's hands looked as though she'd been digging in gravel.

Terri said, "You're safe. They're dead."

Martina's mouth fell open. "How?"

Terri turned toward Blake, so Martina did, too.

"Petronin's body was found down current from a submerged dinghy," Blake said. "He didn't have a life vest on, and it looks like the thing swamped."

Martina's heart skipped a beat. Black Mask hadn't checked the craft before he launched it. In effect, she'd killed him. It disturbed her to learn her plan had worked. She hadn't mentioned to Espinosa about sabotaging the dinghy, because she thought he had escaped in it, so her sabotage didn't matter. Would they blame her for his death? Her breathing slowed, and her mouth dried up.

Blake planted his hand on top of Terri's and the weight of it rested on Martina's. "What's the matter?"

"I removed the dinghy's drain plug. It was under the gunwale at the bow."

Blake's eyebrows rose and fell. "Well, good for you. The criminal died of stupidity. It happens more often than you'd imagine." His tone of voice suggested they keep that information to themselves and never speak of it again.

Black Mask should have checked the dinghy. He'd overloaded it and didn't wear a vest. That was on him. Martina nodded. One less violent criminal in the world was a good thing. Wasn't it? "How did the other guy, Gregorio Whatsit, die?"

"According to Ruis," Blake said, "it looks like he shot himself while trying to pull a handgun from his pants. The bullet passed through his, uh, crotch, to his femoral artery." Blake lifted his hand.

Terri let go of Martina's hands. "They both died of self-inflicted stupidity."

If Martina hadn't jumped overboard, Green Mask probably wouldn't have shot himself. A wave of guilt over the two dead men threatened to crush her when Blake's hand landed on her shoulder.

"Don't even work up any Catholic guilt about this." Blake gave her shoulder a shake. "Do you hear me? They were going to kill you."

"Then why did they wear masks?"

"Probably to protect themselves from being identified if you got away."

"I guess we'll never know," Martina whispered.

Blake's green eyes bore down on her. "Petronin served time in Russia for multiple counts of kidnapping and murder. He apparently came here illegally, because there are no immigration records for him."

All threats of guilt fell away, freeing Martina. Considering the fate of the previous victims of Petronin, she set the matter in God's hands. It was meant to be. Her prayers and those of others had been answered with the kidnappers' deaths. They would have fared better with a jury of their peers than, in death, facing God.

"Did he kill the woman who owned the boat?" As soon as she asked it, she wished she hadn't. She didn't need to know, and she didn't want to know if the boat owner was a victim.

"The boat is owned by a retired couple. They're fine. The kidnappers stole the boat while the owners were away."

Martina exhaled loudly. She hadn't worn a dead person's clothes.

"Oh, I almost forgot." Blake pulled a glittery object from his back pocket. "I washed it real good. A homeless man found it in the trash at the marina."

Her phone! Her precious lifeline had a few new scratches. She held it over her heart. After a moment, she lowered it and pressed the power button. Nada. It probably had a thousand emails and text messages from the week. Her phone was dead, but she was alive. "Thank you."

The noise level rose in the corridor. Blake opened the door. Ruby and Chad had arrived, and Chad was signing baseballs for the agents. Martina caught glimpses of them through the doorway.

Terri left the room.

Martina planted her hand on Blake's forearm. "Wait a minute. If the kidnappers are dead, then who's left to collect the ransom?"

Blake leaned toward Martina. "That's the six-million-dollar question, isn't it?"

Moments later, Terri led Ruby into the room. "We'll give you two some privacy." Her glance at Blake prompted him to stand and follow.

Blake and Terri left the room and closed the door.

Ruby's hair was tucked up in a Texas Rangers baseball cap and she wore barely any makeup compared to her signature look. She was calmer than when they'd met to sign the contract. She stepped up to Martina and cringed. "I'm so sorry."

They hugged. When they let go of each other, both wiped tears, laughed nervously, and dropped into facing chairs.

"I'm alive. The kidnappers are dead."

"Thank God."

"I do." Martina reached up to her ear. "Do you want your earring back?"

Ruby snorted. "Not at all." She clasped her hands over her knees. "We brought your stuff in your suitcase."

"Good. Because my phone is dead. I can't believe I lived without it for six days."

Ruby's mouth fell open. "Wow. And I thought I was tough. You missed your phone?" She laughed. "You got kidnapped!"

Martina grinned. After surviving so much, she knew her perspective had radically altered. Far fewer situations that had once upset her really merited an emotional reaction. She was alive and longed to embrace her life with gusto. Did Ruby value her life again? "Tell me this was worth it. That your rehab worked."

Ruby drew in a deep breath and let it out slowly. "Rehab forced me to figure out who I am and what I really want to do with my life. Turns out I'm pretty tough, too."

"And?"

"I'm clean and sober and I'm not going to tour this year." Ruby rubbed her right hand over her heart, over the tattoo dedicated to her mother that was hidden under her shirt. "I need to eat, exercise, and take better care of myself."

"Me, too. I owe apologies to so many people I lied to. As soon as I charge my phone, that is. Everyone's number is in here." Martina sighed. She realized she was babbling because it felt so good to have someone listen, someone who cared about her life-altering experience. She decided to start apologizing to people. "I'm sorry your red sequined designer dress is ruined."

Ruby waved it off. "Mrs. Campbell bought that. That's not even my style." She clasped her hands together and set them in her lap. "In rehab I embraced a saying my psychologist quoted from a guy named Socrates. 'To find yourself, think for yourself.'"

How odd that Ruby's shrink quoted a man who had committed suicide, but the quote itself was inspiring. Martina warmed to this happy, casual authentic Ruby. Despite her public image, Ruby was still a teenager. Another inspirational quote rose in Martina's mind. This one from a child psychologist and author. "Be who you are and say what you feel, because those who mind don't matter, and those who matter don't mind."

"That's amazing. Who said that?"

"Dr. Theodor Geisel. I'm sure you've read his books."

Ruby punctuated her wan smile with a shrug. "I'm not much of a reader. I had to look up who Socrates was."

"Geisel wrote under the name Dr. Seuss."

Ruby laughed and grabbed Martina's wrist. "I loved his books!" With her inhibitions down, she behaved more like a teenager than a world-famous musician. Laughter uplifted the mood in the room.

Chad entered, strode straight to Martina, and hugged her. "It's so good to see you again."

"Thanks," Martina said into his chest. Every hug reminded her she was alive and loved.

Chad pulled up a chair. "How are you?"

"I'm alive and well."

Chad stared at her eye. The sore, bruised eye betrayed her glib statement. His eyebrows rose as if to challenge her.

"I'm well considering I was drugged, kidnapped, and zapped with a Taser. This happened when I was Tasered." Martina lightly touched her cheek. "I kneed myself while thrashing around on the floor."

"That must have been awful," Ruby said, grimacing.

"I wouldn't recommend it."

"So. What do you plan to do?" Chad asked in a gentle tone.

Martina turned toward Ruby. "Love you. Mean it. But I quit."

They shared a laugh.

"Okay, but then…?" Chad asked.

"Go back to school. Sit for exams." Realizing they didn't know much about her, Martina added, "I plan to earn a master's degree."

Chad reached over and took Ruby's hand. "What I mean is, do you plan to talk to the press?"

"Is it in the news?" Martina felt cold all over at the thought the kidnapping was broadcast where her parents might see it. And Nefi.

Chad and Ruby shook their heads in unison.

Relief fell away, and in its place rose traces of disappointment. *Huh. Nothing at all?* She had disappeared for almost a week without a moment's mention on the evening news, without a headline declaring "Youngest Daughter of Navy Admiral Ramos Disappears." Two anxious faces drew Martina back into the moment. "Nobody knows?"

"The press camped outside the St. Regis. They haven't seen me, well, they haven't seen pictures they think are me since Saturday, but that doesn't stop them from publishing guesses." Ruby fidgeted with her watch. "According to one rag, I'm on a bender, locked in my suite. Another one claims Chad is hiding me from a stalker. The truth is, I finished my rehab. Chad warned me about the media, so I've been staying in disguise at another hotel. We had to come here separately to see you."

"I'm glad you came," Martina said. They'd risked being seen by the press to come here. That was something. "I called the FBI as soon as I could."

Chad leaned forward. "After they learned you were alive, the FBI switched out the real bearer bonds for fake look-alikes."

"You were going to pay the ransom?"

Ruby nodded.

Martina pressed her hand over her mouth. How odd it felt to measure a life in money. How wondrous it felt to know that they valued her life. Six million was a lot of money. Did insurance cover that kind of loss?

"Are you planning to go public about the kidnapping?" Chad asked calmly.

"Certainly not. I want to get back to my life." Why did he keep asking about the media? "You don't want me to go to the press, do you?"

Chad and Ruby shook their heads in unison. Chad draped an arm around her shoulders. It was a casual, loving, protective gesture that made Martina think of Oscar. Ruby gazed at Chad in a way that suggested familiarity and passion.

Martina recognized that look. She suspected this was the true reason Ruby had entered rehab. The real reason she'd cancelled her tours for the rest of the year. Martina's sisters had had that look just before they announced a new addition to the family. "You should probably get married."

"Why do you say that?" Chad kissed Ruby's hand. The way he looked at her heated the room.

Martina spoke to Ruby, "I think you entered rehab to protect something other than your reputation."

"I told you she was smart." Ruby blushed and placed her hands over her belly. "We haven't told anyone yet, not even Chad's parents."

"I can keep a secret, but it will cost you."

Chad leaned back in his chair. His expression turned distant and neutral. "Name it."

"A signed baseball for my brother, Ruis. He loves baseball."

A slow smile spread across Chad's face. "Since you don't have a baseball…" He pulled a business card from his wallet and wrote on the back of it. "What's your brother's name?"

"Ruis Ramos."

"Give him this IOU. Have him call me."

Taking the card, she read his note—two VIP seats to the play-offs for Ruis Ramos. "Nice. He'll love it."

Chad jabbed his thumb toward the other conference room. "Do you think they'll let us stay to see what happens with the ransom?"

Martina automatically lifted her dead phone to check the time, then lowered it back to her lap. Her charger was in her suitcase by the door. "What time is it?"

Ruby checked her diamond-studded Tag Heuer gold and silver watch. "Noon thirty."

Martina shrugged. "I'll ask the boss." She left the room and found Special Agent in Charge Jorges Espinosa in the corridor talking to Maggie.

After a few moments, he turned. "Miss Ramos, what can I do for you?"

"Chad and Ruby and I would like to stay for the ransom drop if that's okay."

He flashed brilliant white teeth and placed a hand on her shoulder. "By all means. Let me get chairs." He then followed her back to the smaller conference room and rolled two chairs into the main room.

Chad followed him with another chair. Espinosa left to speak with an agent, then he returned. Behind him on the far wall, just in front of the giant whiteboard, a ten-by-twelve-foot screen lowered from the ceiling, blocking the information on the board. Agents closed window blinds throughout the room.

"You can watch the live feed as it comes in from Tampa. We expect feeds from two state-of-the-art drones"—he glanced at Martina—"which are overflying the drop site. The drones are experimental, so please don't discuss them with anyone outside this room."

Chad, Ruby, and Martina nodded. Martina longed to brag to Chad and Ruby that her boyfriend worked for the drone company, but the only thing bragging would serve was her vanity. She respected the value of keeping a secret.

Side-by-side aerial images of a park lit up on the screen.

. 31 .

Oscar operated his drone over the eastern half of Gadsden Park on this warm, sunny Friday. The park abutted the north barrier fence line of MacDill Air Force Base. The western half of the park was taken up by a square-shaped pond ringed with a paved trail and trees. At five hundred feet above the pond, Mr. Yoshida's drone hovered. West of the park was a no-man's land of scrub palms, pines, oaks, and wild grass that extended from the boundary of the military base outward as if runway 04/22 pointed to it.

No one wanted to build off the end of a runway, especially an Air Force base runway. The noise from landing a heavy transport aircraft, like the Boeing C-17 with a seventy-six-ton payload, could set off car alarms and rattle windows. And then there was the threat of an aircraft landing short of the runway, so the land remained undeveloped.

The eastern half of Gadsden Park contained a fenced dog run, a series of baseball diamonds, fitness stations for simple exercises, and a playground connected by trails and paved paths. Clusters of trees dotted the scrubby grass. Cars and trucks parked on the grass along the north, east, and west edges of the park.

Because of the park's proximity to MacDill Air Force Base, many of the joggers were in peak physical condition, which made it easier for the undercover officers to blend in. Tapper had brought along the biggest dog Oscar had ever seen. They played catch with a plastic yellow softball that Tapper tossed up. Even from five hundred feet above, Bailey resembled a wooly horse.

A group of women and children clustered in the shade of a copse of trees for a picnic. Nearby, more children climbed a colorful playset cushioned by a thick layer of mulch.

At quarter to one on a school day, the baseball fields were empty.

"I don't have a match yet on the preset," Oscar said. He couldn't tell his boss where to look for the kidnapper's truck, but he could remind him to use the preset search parameters. The drone would scan the area for trucks that fit the dimensions and color of the truck registered to Stas Petronin.

Mr. Yoshida nodded. He activated the preset search with two key strokes. The command released the smaller drone attached to the underside of the main drone. The smaller drone, by Yoshida's design, was shaped like a common pigeon and it emitted a sound that mimicked flapping wings. During testing, Oscar marveled at how the sound and shape had tricked him into dismissing the tiny aircraft as a bird while he was staring right at it in flight. It didn't need moving wings to fool people. Its camouflage was in appearing ordinary.

While the mini drone searched for the truck, the larger drone recorded images of the target drop site—a green bench made of curved metal slats. It was anchored to a cement slab on the north shore of the pond. Nearby, a cement platform with a railing on three sides jutted into the water from a paved walkway.

On a sunny day, the bench was likely to sear bare legs because none of the trees were close enough to cast shade on it. This bench was the only one on the north side of the pond. It was the one designated in the recording to leave a camouflage backpack filled with six million dollars' worth of bearer bonds and walk away.

A female Tampa Police detective carried the backpack under a light blue blanket in a stroller. She held a cell phone to her ear.

Oscar kept his drone camera aimed at the stroller as it rolled on the paved path toward the northeast corner of the pond.

"I have a match to the target vehicle," Mr. Yoshida said. "In the parking lot of Florida Rock and Tank Line, northwest of Gadsden Park."

The mini drone transmitted an image of the truck's license plate that matched Petronin's. The image, with a keystroke, was sent to Cuervo and the Tampa police chief. Two minutes later, an unmarked police car slipped into a parking spot near the entrance to the Florida Rock and Tank Line lot. Oscar was impressed with the speed of the police response.

With the officer watching the truck, Mr. Yoshida directed the mini to reconnect to the large drone. He nodded at Oscar, who had taught him how.

Meanwhile, Tapper eased along the south side of the pond with Bailey, stopping occasionally to pick up the yellow softball. If timed properly, the stroller would reach the bench at precisely one p.m. and continue counterclockwise around the pond. Tapper, traveling clockwise, would pass the stroller and be in a position to see who picked up the backpack.

Mr. Yoshida swung his mouthpiece away from his helmet. "The friendlies are designated by blue dots."

The committee members huddled around Mr. Yoshida.

Yoshida and Oscar had electronically tagged the law enforcement team members to easily follow their positions and movements. Nine blue dots moved on the screens.

"What about the hostiles?" asked a committee member.

Mr. Yoshida secured the mini drone. "When someone picks up the ransom, for example, the drone operator releases the mini to scan and track that person. Those images can be sent to other individuals or agencies at the operator's discretion. Once tagged, the hostile candidate will be tracked until the drone runs out of power, is recalled, or is destroyed."

Muted discussion ensued behind Oscar and his boss.

The stroller reached the target bench and stopped. The detective glanced at her watch and sat.

The discussion in the room stopped. A jogger, marked with a blue dot, passed the bench on his second lap of the pond.

"It's time," Cuervo's voice announced.

The detective at the bench glanced left and right, then she tugged off the blanket and lifted a camouflage-patterned backpack and tucked it under the bench seat. She set the blanket in the stroller as if tucking in a baby, then she stood and walked back the way she'd come, along the path heading east toward the baseball diamonds.

A man and woman jogged past the detective with the stroller. At a glance they looked like a pair of soldiers, muscular, agile, and wearing sweat-stained gray shorts and shirts. When they reached the bench, the woman slowed to a walk and circled back to the bench. There, she pressed two fingers to her neck while looking at her watch.

Mr. Yoshida released his mini drone but kept it circling over the woman at five-hundred feet, compiling three-dimensional images and measurements.

Oscar was tempted to measure his own heart rate. Was this woman just a jogger? She had long blonde hair pulled through the back of a baseball cap. An accomplice? Her head turned left, then right, then left again. In a smooth movement, she reached under the bench, snagged a shoulder strap on the backpack, and bolted west, toward acres of trees.

"Suspect running west with backpack. A woman in gray shorts and T-shirt," Cuervo said.

On the screen, blue dots flowed north and west and east. The officers on the far side of the park ran to their vehicles. The closest blue dot was Tapper running north. The next closest blue dot was outside the park, heading toward an opening in the park's fence that led to an east-west road. It looked like this person would cut off the runner as their paths converged.

Oscar directed his drone to descend, giving it speed on its way to tracking the fleeing woman.

The suspect didn't take the short path to the opening in the fence. Instead, she headed straight for the chain-link fence. With one arm in the strap, she slung the backpack to the middle of her back and leaped. One hand touched the top of the fence, providing a small push, and she landed, continuing her run.

Tapper stopped running and bent over. When he stood, he pointed with his whole arm. "Bailey, *jagen!*" The giant dog gave chase, bounding over the fence and disappearing in the trees. Tapper stuffed the leash in his pocket, then he and another blue dot scrambled over the fence and ran through high grass.

Oscar picked up the commentary. "The female with the backpack appears to be headed to her truck at Florida Rock." He dove his drone close to the treetops.

Four blue dots ran in parallel lines through the tall grass and wild trees.

The drone recognized the figure that Yoshida's mini had scanned. A human-shaped figure lit up the screen in red. The figure stepped out of the wild greenery into the parking lot. She twisted, looking back at the beast gaining on her, and then, moments after she turned away and lengthened her stride, she tripped and slid on the gravel parking lot.

The giant dog bounded over her and landed on the far side of the woman.

The police officer in the parking lot dashed toward the woman. Moments later, Cuervo and Tapper emerged from the woods, gasping for breath.

"Can you call off whatever that is?" He waved at Bailey.

Bailey's giant head hovered over the woman, who was on her

back, screaming and flailing her arms. The dog's giant head bobbed to avoid contact as if it were a game.

Tapper pulled the leash from his pants pocket.

Bailey pivoted toward Tapper and thumped his tail on Diamond's face.

Chuckling, Tapper clipped the leash and led the dog away from Diamond. A few feet away, Trapper doubled up the leash and held it out. Bailey took the leash in his mouth and sat. "Good boy, Bailey." Tapper scratched him behind the ears.

Diamond rolled over, revealing bloody scrapes on her chin and hands and forearms. She spotted the giant dog and pointed, "I'll sue. That beast attacked me. This is police brutality." She sat up.

The police officer plucked handcuffs from his belt. "Ma'am, first off, that's not a K-9 officer. Secondly, that dog didn't knock you down, you tripped. Now, place your hands behind your back."

"I'm injured, you idiot."

"Yes, Ma'am, and you'll get medical attention. Now, place your hands behind your back."

Panting, Agent Cuervo, gently tugged the backpack off Diamond.

"That's mine!" Diamond pointed a bleeding hand at the backpack.

Cuervo nodded. "Let's all make sure to note that in our reports."

The police officer nodded at him and handcuffed Diamond while she sat on the ground. He radioed for an ambulance and stood behind the suspect. "...Multiple scrapes and bruises and, uh, other injuries." His face turned red.

Tapper had heard that saline implants could break, but he'd never seen it happen before. Tapper and Cuervo exchanged a glance. Perhaps Diamond hadn't noticed, but the men certainly had. While waiting for the ambulance, the men and the dog stood in awkward silence.

The woman reached for the backpack at Cuervo's side. Her fingertips brushed the strap, close enough to touch but not to grasp.

Observing her struggle miles away on a screen gave Oscar closure. The committee applauded. The demonstration had worked flawlessly. Oscar watched the diminishing image of the woman, handcuffed and sitting on a gravel parking lot, as his drone flew back to the hangar. She'd ruined her life by her choices. She'd chosen a criminal boyfriend and she'd chosen to value money over the life of another person. How many smaller bad choices over the years had contributed to her self-destruction?

Oscar directed his drone to land inside the hangar. Moments later, Mr. Yoshida landed his drone gently beside Oscar's. The committee members discussed the success of the urban test flights.

Oscar heard the task-force team chattering on the radio. Tapper's voice carried through the other voices.

"Bravo, to the gentlemen with the drones."

. 32 .

Ruis owed his friends more than he could repay. He had invited them to meet at Daddy Diego's to celebrate Friday night. Tapper and Cuervo had flown back from Tampa to turn in their reports at the Miami FBI office. Ruis expected both of them at the club.

As they arrived, he greeted them and directed them to go in. They would soon receive gifts in the mail. For Blake and Terri, he bought a voucher for a seven-night cruise on Royal Caribbean Cruise Lines. Thanks to advice from Terri, Tapper would get a certificate for unusual attitude training in a P-51 Mustang by Lee Lauderback in Kissimmee, Florida. Oscar would receive a voucher for a first-class round-trip airfare from Tokyo to London. Cuervo would receive a case of Jose Cuervo Especial Gold Tequila. The only gift he couldn't deliver by mail, he planned to give to Maggie in the parking lot of Daddy Diego's.

Tapper waited with him. He had helped Ruis find it at a local store. "Are you sure Maggie's coming?"

Ruis grinned. "Yes. Agent Vega should be here soon."

Tapper eyed the large gift bag sitting in the driver's seat of Ruis's rented SUV. He waved at Maggie as she entered the parking lot. She parked beside Ruis's vehicle.

When Ruis placed the gift bag on the front of Maggie's SUV, she climbed out. "Whatever this is, even if it's chocolate, which I love," she said to Tapper, then turned to Ruis, "I can't accept it."

"I already cleared it with Espinosa. This is a gift from a friend." Ruis crossed his arms. "Tapper helped me find it."

She kissed Ruis on the ear then she kissed Tapper on the cheek. "*Muchas gracias, amigos.*" She plucked bright tissue paper from the top of the bag and lifted the box from it. "It's heavy."

It wasn't standard-issue FBI, but Ruis knew she'd appreciate it.

She opened the case and gasped at a new 9mm Sig Sauer P226. Caressing it like fine jewelry, she ran her fingers from the bright green tritium sights to the textured grip. "I read about this model. It has a more comfortable grip for smaller hands. It's beautiful."

Tapper grinned.

Maggie locked it in her glove box and the three of them entered the club together.

Diego himself greeted them and led them to a prime balcony table where Blake and Terri sat with Agent Cuervo. After handshakes and hugs, they settled at the table overlooking the Friday night crowd. A pitcher of beer sweated in the center of the table. A waitress set glasses in front of Tapper, Ruis, and Maggie.

Diego raised his voice over the sound of the band. "My lawyer told me that Ruby's agent called to apologize. She said the abduction"—he made the air quotes gesture when he said abduction—"was staged as part of a security practice drill. I assume she called your people as well, right?"

"We heard," Agent Cuervo said. He didn't go as far as apologizing, but his contrite expression apparently appeased Diego.

"And just so you know," Diego shouted, "I've upgraded my security cameras inside and outside."

That earned him a round of applause from the table. He bowed and returned to the bar downstairs.

Agent Cuervo leaned in. "I was telling Blake and Terri about Bailey's takedown. It was a thing of beauty."

"Where's Oscar?" Maggie asked.

"He's at MacDill with his boss," Ruis said.

"To Oscar and the drones," Cuervo said.

It sounded like the name of a grunge band. All raised their glasses. Starting with Cuervo, they tapped glasses to the left, going around the table, until Cuervo's glass was tapped, then they all took a swig.

Ruis raised his glass. "To good dogs and great friends."

All agreed and drank.

Maggie sat so close to Tapper their thighs touched. "Are you sure that's a dog?"

Tapper elbowed Terri. "Tell her, dear veterinarian."

Terri leaned in front of Tapper and raised her voice over the techno music. "It's a rare breed called a Leonberger. They can grow to one hundred and fifty pounds."

"He eats like a horse." Tapper grinned. "He belongs to a pal of mine at MacDill."

The fifth techno song sounded like the first four. If robots wrote music, it would sound like this. Monotonous. No wonder teens were so angry. Ruis was getting irritated after hearing just five samples of it. He leaned toward Terri. "How's Martina?"

Terri plunked her drink down. "You haven't seen her yet?"

Ruis shook his head.

Blake and Terri traded a glance. Tapper and Maggie gaped at him. Cuervo raised his eyebrows.

"Okay, listen," Ruis told the table. "She's flying back to England tomorrow to take exams. I'm flying to meet Sofia and the rest of the family in Southampton for a family reunion cruise. We'll have the entire transcontinental flight to catch up."

Blake eyed Ruis. "Does she know you're on the flight?"

Ruis gave them each a warning glare. "I want to surprise her."

"I knew it." Blake slapped his hand on the table.

"Yeah."

"Got it."

"What a good brother you are." Maggie saluted Ruis with her frosted beer glass.

The group relaxed and drank to celebrate the satisfying resolution of their case. The bad guys were dead, the bad girl was in jail, Martina was alive and unharmed. Unfortunately, though they'd solved the case, Ruis felt burdened by another secret. He wondered if Martina would be able to keep her kidnapping a secret from her best friend, Nefi. And how would Vincent keep this secret from his fiancée?

For that matter, how could anyone keep a secret from a natural-born lie detector like Nefi? Thankfully, Ruis would have less contact with her than Vincent and Martina, so he was less likely to trigger her curiosity.

Poor Martina. Poor Vincent. It was only a matter of time before Nefi discovered she'd been kept in the dark about her best friend's kidnapping.

. 33 .

Saturday evening, Martina boarded a British Airways flight from Miami to Heathrow. Holding the ticket Ruis had paid for in her name, she shouldered her large purse. When the line in the jetway stopped, she toyed with her MIA-LHR ticket. MIA. Missing in action. Almost.

She wished for a window seat to watch the night lights of Miami fade away. The wide aircraft had a seat configuration with two aisles. In economy class, the worst place to sit was in the middle of the center section, which meant climbing over people to get to the restroom. She had brought earplugs in case of snorers or unruly toddlers. It would be a long flight and she was exhausted.

She was headed into the economy class entrance when a steward checked her ticket and turned her around.

"You're back this way, miss," the steward said in a clipped British accent. "In first class."

"Oh, thanks." *Thank you, Ruis.*

The cost difference between economy and first-class reminded Martina of the vast difference between her student budget and Ruis's salary. That he had splurged on a first-class ticket for her made her eyes well. She had expected to see him at the FBI office and later at her hotel room, but all she got was a plane ticket delivered by the hotel bellman and a phone call.

He still loves me.

Entering first class, Martina counted four roomy seats or pods per row, one by each window and two central side-by-side pods separated by a privacy wall and a sliding accordion-style panel. She tucked her purse underfoot and buckled into her spacious, cushioned pod. Most of the first-class passengers had already turned off their lights and shuttered their windows for sleep.

While seemingly hundreds of people boarded the plane in pairs and family groups, she texted Ruis again to apologize. Hiding her bruised face from strangers, she hunched over her beloved cell phone to watch the local news. An evening recap of events in Miami began with the story of Ruby at the premiere of her new perfume line with her boyfriend, Chad, standing behind her. There, in front of the cameras and the world, Chad proposed, and Ruby accepted. Sure, it looked a bit staged, but the crowd cheered, and a second-tier reporter from the ABC affiliate WPLG Channel 10 sent to cover the event got the scoop. The engagement ring was impressive, but their kiss threatened to turn the newscast into adult entertainment. There was no mention of a kidnapping as if it never happened.

Martina sighed heavily. Her calls to Oscar went directly to voicemail. Her text messages and emails went unanswered. Maybe he was working, or on a flight back to Japan with his drones. Maybe he was too disappointed to bother with her anymore. She pulled her knit cap tighter over her scruffy hair. At least she had spoken to Ruis. Even if he was disappointed and angry, he apparently forgave her.

She checked her other text messages and read twelve from her best friend Nefi and one from Vincent. She read Vincent's first.

BLAKE ASSURES ME YOU ARE ALIVE AND WELL. PRAISE GOD. LET ME KNOW IF YOU PLAN TO TELL NEFI.

Next, she read Nefi's messages. The oldest texts reminded her to choose a maid-of-honor dress in red to go with the black and white and red color scheme for Vincent and Nefi's wedding. The twelfth and most recent text was brief.

DID YOU ELOPE WITH OSCAR?

Fearing Nefi could detect a lie from tone of voice alone, Martina sent Nefi a text.

LOST PHONE FOR DAYS. MUST CHARGE IT. WILL CALL YOU TOMORROW. STILL M RAMOS. MISS YOU.

Reluctantly, she turned her phone off and plugged it into the outlet to charge. Would there ever be a good time to tell Nefi about the kidnapping? Would she understand and forgive that her fiancé and trusted friends had kept it secret from her? Martina sighed heavily. She knew she would carry a grudge if their roles were reversed. Nefi was a more forgiving and generous soul.

Whatever messages Nefi or Oscar or Ruis might send would be received an ocean and eight hours away. To distract herself, she inspected the amenities of first class. On the eight-hour flight, she could order Herefordshire beef and three kinds of champagne, cheese, fruit, and snacks. Her comfy first-class pod had its own television screen, table, and a seat that reclined into a bed. She inspected the laminated information flyer about the aircraft and marveled that a plane large enough to carry so many people and their luggage could possibly fly. At long last, the crew closed the doors and readied the plane to taxi.

A flute of champagne appeared on her table. She sipped and stared at the narrow glass. As bubbles rose, tears fell.

When would she regain control of her emotions? She was an emotional wreck. Laughing one minute, angry the next, then weepy and exhausted. Was this post-traumatic stress disorder? This had to stop and the sooner the better.

She should celebrate her survival. She should celebrate Ruby's engagement. She should celebrate that her captors were dead, and their accomplice was in jail. Blake had explained that because Green Mask and Black Mask had died as a result of committing a felony, somehow the female accomplice could get the death penalty. He would know. Florida and North Carolina shared the Felony Murder Rule.

She should celebrate being able to return in time to sit exams at Oxford. Her life was hers again. She should be delirious with joy and triumph.

She sniffled and searched for a tissue. A tan hand bearing a white cloth handkerchief appeared over the divider between her seat and the next. Taking it, she noticed the handkerchief bore the initials EBC embroidered in white. She leaned close to the folding panel, which reminded her of the small separator in the confessional. "Thank you. I had a rough week." Her voice squeaked.

"So did I," the man whispered.

Oh, no. Was the offer of a handkerchief an invitation to a long conversation? She sighed and wiped her eyes. If they swapped stories, she believed she'd win the who-had-the-tougher-week contest. Everyone had problems. Maybe EBC needed someone to care about his for a few hours. Kindness, her mother always said, was never wasted. She took a deep breath and encouraged conversation with a question. "How bad was it?"

"The worst, but by the grace of God, I didn't have to kill anyone."

Martina recoiled from the panel. Had she heard him clearly? What kind of person had to kill? Then she recognized his voice and jerked the panel open.

He appeared as a silhouette, backlit by safety lights on the floor. "Hey, sis."

A whimper rose in Martina's throat, so she covered her mouth with the handkerchief to stifle it. She unbuckled her seat belt, dashed down the aisle, startled a steward, continued past the bathrooms, and rushed down the other aisle to Ruis, who was standing. Apologies and prayers and memories collided in her mind. She wanted to say so many things she couldn't prioritize them. She held him as tightly as she had the day he'd pulled her, terrified and coughing, from the deep end of the pool on her fourth birthday. Her shadow. Her guardian angel.

"Does Dad know?" she spoke into Ruis's chest.

"No."

Amen to that. "Where were you yesterday?"

"Paperwork." He hugged her tightly and whispered in her ear, "I'm so proud of you."

She had not expected him to say that. "Why?"

He held her at arm's length. "Would *she* have survived in your place?"

Ruby avoided conflict and confrontation. She'd sought numbness through drugs and alcohol and finally worked up the energy to fight for her life because she had another one growing inside her. Ruby wouldn't have sabotaged the boat and the dinghy. Her talents were more artistic than practical. Martina shook her head.

Ruis released her.

The steward strode down the aisle and stopped close enough to breathe on them. "Please take your seats."

The steward followed Martina and lingered nearby until she buckled in. Seated, Martina leaned toward the open panel between her pod and Ruis's pod.

"Will you be able to keep this..." he whispered, "event to yourself?"

"Absolutely. I want my life back." She picked up her champagne flute. "I am no longer pretending to be someone else."

Ruis chuckled. "Good. I would think being you is challenge enough."

She took a gulp of champagne. Bubbles popped in her nose. "I'm glad you're here, but you don't have to escort me back to school."

"I'm headed to the family reunion cruise, remember?"

Martina cringed. "Oh, right." This would have been the best reunion ever. Fourteen days on a Royal Caribbean ship in the

Mediterranean. And she had exams. "Where are you meeting the ship?"

"We set sail Sunday out of Southampton."

"Then you won't be late!"

He raised his glass. "Like it never happened."

"Ha. Ha. Ha." She gulped more champagne to celebrate Ruis and the reunion cruise.

The massive aircraft lumbered down the taxiway. The cabin lights dimmed.

After drying her eyes with the handkerchief, she read the initials again. "Who's EBC?"

"Blake."

She rolled her eyes so hard it gave her vertigo. Blake again. "What's the E stand for?"

"His ancestry is Irish, so I'd guess Eamon or Edmund?"

"Ernest Blake Clayton," Martina sounded out her guess and shook her head. It didn't really suit the big guy.

"Eugene?"

Martina laughed. "Why do you have his handkerchief?"

After a pause, he said, "He loaned it to me when I had something in my eye."

"What, like tears?" she blurted. She regretted her immediate reaction came from her inner spoiled child. Ruis loved her and feared for her. He wasn't superman or a robot. How could she be so dense to tease him for caring?

The steward refilled Ruis's flute.

Breaking the painful silence, she said, "I'm so sorry you have to keep rescuing me." She balled up the handkerchief.

"This time," he said, holding up his champagne flute, "you rescued yourself."

Her heart stirred, and she drew a deep breath. She picked up her drink, gently touched it to his glass, and then took a sip.

She had survived being kidnapped by armed men who had held her against her will in the middle of nowhere. True, she had escaped. After that, strangers smuggled her to civilization. Blake and Maggie then brought her to Miami. The kidnappers were dead. She was alive. But she also recalled her tearful, fearful prayers. The fact that so many people had managed to find her with so little information amazed her. She remembered Black Mask's lecherous behavior and the timeliness of his stomach flu. She couldn't dismiss his nausea as coincidence or luck. Sure, she had done all she could think of doing to survive, but there was another huge factor at work to acknowledge. This time Ruis hadn't rescued her. For all she had done to survive, she wasn't comfortable taking credit for rescuing herself. It felt like a lie.

Ruis faced dangerous situations in the military and then at work as a US Marshal, but he never bragged about them that Martina could recall. Others called him tough and dangerous and unstoppable, but he didn't talk about his work. He didn't bring up his service as a former Navy SEAL and when others brought it up, he changed the topic. His posture and bearing announced military training. Something beyond toughness, pride, and training carried him through deadly situations and kept him humble about them. Although some had been injured, he had never lost a teammate during a mission.

For the first time in her life, Martina recognized Ruis's powerful faith. While he depended on training and his weapons and his team, his faith didn't stand on them. He willingly risked his life for the sake of others as his life's mission. With this new insight, she knew it wasn't recklessness or bragging rights that motivated her brother. He wasn't a thrill seeker. Ruis, the shadow who had hovered around her in times of danger, placed his life in God's hands.

Being in danger had focused her faith in the same way. "I can't take credit."

Ruis leaned toward the partition.

"I did what I could, but really, my survival came through the grace of God and help from amazing people."

Like the Cheshire cat, only Ruis's white teeth glowed in the dim cabin. His silhouette disappeared as he leaned back in his seat. "Now, I'm even more proud of you."

THE END

Thank you for reading!

Your one- or two-sentence review on social media
and wherever you purchased this book is greatly appreciated!

ABOUT THE AUTHOR

After working decades in journalism, **Joni M. Fisher** turned to crime. Her Compass Crimes series has garnered attention in *Publisher's Weekly* and earned recognition in the 2017 National Indie Excellence Awards, the 2016 Royal Palm Literary Awards, the Indiana Golden Opportunity Contest, and the Sheila Contest. She serves on the Arts and Humanities Advisory Board for Southeastern University and is a member of the Florida Writers Association, the Kiss of Death Chapter of RWA, and the Women's Fiction Writers Association. She's also an instrument-rated private pilot.

Connect with Joni online:

Official website: www.jonimfisher.com
Goodreads Author Page: www.goodreads.com/jonimfisher

Thank you for reading!
Your brief review on social media is greatly appreciated!

CPSIA information can be obtained
at www.ICGtesting.com
Printed in the USA
LVHW041719200319
611280LV00004B/886/P